A TRIAL OF WITCHES

WITCHES

by Cameron Readman

A Trial of Witches
By Cameron Readman
1ˢᵗ Edition

First published in Great Britain by Cameron Readman

2019

Copyright © 2019 by Cameron Readman

Cameron Readman asserts the moral right to be identified as the author of this work

ISBN 978-1-91-619560-8

Cover Illustrations by Jasmine O'Hare

Acknowledgements

To Catherine, without whom this book would not be possible. Not only has she been my first line of editing and proofreading, helping me sort through my most idiotic of ideas, as well as being subjected to my enthusiastic wittering about minute historical details. She has supported me wholeheartedly throughout the entire process, becoming practically my carer at times. Feeding me when I forget, cleaning up around me as I work or simply cheering me on from the side lines. Her support has always been unwavering, even in the most difficult of times. I love you.

To my talented sister Georgia, who, without reward, toiled over this book, helping me edit it and craft it into something I can be proud of, simply because "that's what sisters do." Her little words of encouragement in the margins have spurred me on through this undertaking. I am eternally grateful, thank you.

To the Bothwell community. It's all your fault! When I said two years ago, "I reckon I could write a book on the history," they 'dared' me to do it. Little did they know they had created a monster. Not only did they spawn this idea, they then put their money where their mouth is and helped me fund it! Without them, the *real* story of Francis Stewart might've never come to light. Some of the most generous patrons are listed at the back of this book, however, even those who have little to give have done great things in support of this book. Thank you and I hope you enjoy this creation.

Historical Note

The witch hunting phenomena was one which spanned nearly three hundred years, over which time it is estimated over 40,000 were executed in Europe, most of them women. While this book is a fictional work, the horrifying realities should not be understated.

Many of the people, locations and dates in this book are real, and The Berwick Witch Trials were a truly shocking event that shook Scotland to its core. I encourage those reading to conduct their own research into the real events behind this story. Fact can sometimes be stranger than fiction! However, they have all been adapted for fiction and as such, should not be construed as an accurate representation of the persons mentioned. Timescales, particularly towards the end of the book, have been shortened and some individuals and events omitted in service of the story.

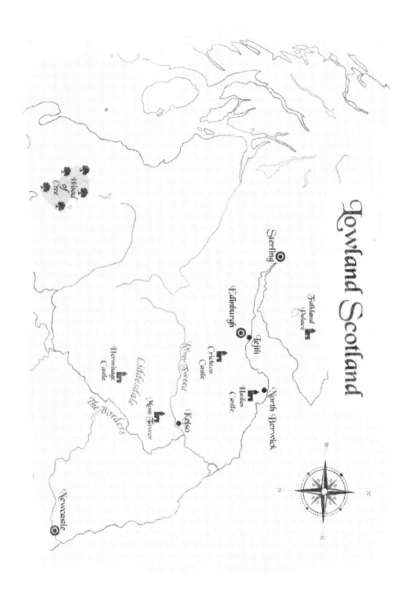

Lowland Scotland

Contents

Prologue

15ᵗʰ October 1589

"Where on God's green earth is Bothwell!?" exclaimed James, rushing his words before vomiting once more into the overflowing wooden pail by his feet. As the hardwood floor continued its perpetual motion the bile green mixture spattered across it. "He should be here!" James sputtered, as he steadied himself at his desk, using a laced handkerchief to dab his moustache.

"Bothwell, your grace?" said Maitland, "I hardly think the presence of that rascallion would improve our current situation, Sire."

"Now now Maitland, you do Bothwell a disservice. I merely meant I would be comforted by his presence."

"Pardon my ignorance Your Grace, but why Bothwell? He's encouraged rebellion against you, ignores your orders and causes you no end o' troubles."

"Oh, you're too serious Maitland," sniffed James. "Besides, while I must be seen to reprimand Bothwell on the borders, his raids do no harm. He simply wants what's best for the realm. He's proved his devotion many times."

James stopped to refill his cup of wine. The books on their shelf threatened to burst from their stoppers as the room creaked and heaved once more. "Although having said that, it *is* his bloody job to be here. Sickness? Bah!" James clasped his pewter cup with both hands and took a long drink.

"Never mind Your Grace, Bothwell isn't here is he. You are! Not since Arthur has a King endured such hardships to retrieve his princess!" Maitland stiffened as he finished his last words, a small gesture of his sincerity.

James stood shakily from his desk and strode with all the confidence he could muster to one of the windows. "Aye, 'tis a noble deed. Mayhaps the lords will show more respect for me when I return. A hero King no less! Although, I hold no great hopes for that squabbling rabble."

Maitland looked at the King as he grasped the window frame to stay upright. Despite the rough conditions he still wore all his finery; high white stockings, black breeches, a matching black silk doublet slashed with gold, a fur trimmed half-cape all topped off with a tall hat. He did look regal - albeit pale and dishevelled.

"Is it always like this Maitland?" asked the King, as he continued to look out of the rain streaked window.

"I'm nay a seafaring man myself, Your Grace, but from what I understand, no Sire. 'Tis a bad voyage."

Outside the cabin the sails slackened and snapped taut as the ship fought its way through the swirling winds. The vessel rocked over the vast waves at unnatural angles, as though at any moment it could capsize into the sea. Cannons rocked in their carriages as sailors nervously checked their life lines and clung to the railings. At port the ship had looked gargantuan. Now, amongst the ever-rising waves, it looked like a toy. Below deck the youngest of the crew looked wide eyed at each other as their hammocks swayed cruelly in the dark. Much like the King's pail, various containers spilled their contents creating a foul stench to accompany the heavier reek of fear.

After a long, quiet period of contemplation beholding the towering waves, James stepped away from the window. He stumbled back to his desk, nailed to the deck like all the furniture in the cabin. "Sit down man!" James barked at Maitland, who had been standing resolutely by his chair. "Maybe you're right," he sighed, "Noble as it is to voyage across oceans for my dearest Anne, what oh what would happen to Scotland if I were to perish here? I feel like a prize fool." At this he took another deep drink from his cup. "The lords fight for power, the Kirk does the same and all the while England looks on."

"Forgive me my..." began Maitland.

"Damn it man! Speak up! You need not ask my forgiveness for every utterance you make!"

"Speaking plainly Your Grace, that bunch needs a good flogging if you were to ask me.

James smiled, "Ha! The thought had occurred to me too Maitland. The problem is, if I flogged one of them, the rest would line up outside Holyrood to receive *their* flogging from the King!" His laugh was cut short by a flash of lightening that illuminated the cabin. It was quickly followed by the deafening roll of thunder. "We're close to the centre of the storm," said James, "hopefully this means we'll be out soon."

Lightning flashed again but before thunder could answer, the loud crash of the cabin's door being flung open greeted the King's ears instead.

"Forgive my intrusion your grace," the ship's captain poured water from the brim of his hat while continuing to speak. "I would like to request your presence on deck Sire."

"On Deck? In *This*!?" James jabbed a finger towards the window where the rain almost completely obscured its view. "You must be mad!"

"I wouldn't ask Your Grace, but the men...well...they're scared, you see."

"Isn't this all in a day's work for a sailor, Captain? Or are you to tell me these men aren't worth the wages I pay them?"

"Oh no Sire, this storm is much worse than anything we've encountered before, even in these waters." The King cocked an eyebrow, suggesting the Captain should make his request quickly, "I thought, perhaps, you could give the men a sermon or some other words of comfort. You could give it in the mess." He added quickly.

"And what, pray tell, has these men so scared? How will a sermon aid them?"

"There can be only one explanation for the ferocity of this storm, Sire," started the Captain.

"Witchcraft."

Chapter 1

10th March 1590
South of Liddesdale

"Are ye ready sire?"

"Hold on a minute!" barked Francis over his shoulder. He pulled his cloak tighter around him as he continued to trace an angular shape over his bare forearm. The old scar tissue that embellished his skin shone as it waited for the wand's caress. The small ritual had become a superstition of his and he refused to go willingly into any battle without conducting it. Once satisfied with his work, he tied a rag over the wound. He let his wand glitter in the morning sunlight for a moment, the folds from its forging creating a ripple of colour from its pointed tip to the large gem at its base. Then, he grasped his broadsword by the hilt and, with the tuneful scrape of metal on metal, concealed the wand by sliding it into a precisely cut hole in the ornate pommel until all that remained visible was the gemstone.

"How's it looking down there?" called Francis as he turned and stepped towards his manservant.

"Peaceful, my Lord, and they look to be ill-prepared. I suspect nobody's been through here in some time. Are ye sure we're not too far south?"

"Have I ever steered my men wrong?" said Francis as he heaved himself into the saddle of his prized charger. He kicked his heels into its flank and pulled on the reins, steering his horse away from the tree line and toward the rest of his assembled horsemen.

The score of men, to the untrained eye, looked like a ragtag bunch of ruffians. Their clothes were torn and dirty while their helmets were flecked with rust. The leather jack-of-plate armour formed a neat diamond pattern across their torsos, where the iron plates were sown in, only to be broken up by a missing plate and frayed leather. They all carried thin lances with long dirk knives at their belt. Despite their dishevelled look, these were some of the finest horsemen in all Northern Europe. Their slender, sinewy horses able to navigate the most treacherous marshes and their riders ruthless at the charge.

Francis, despite an attempt to 'dress down,' contrasted heavily with the horsemen in front of him. He wore a gleaming solid plate cuirass with a bright blue sash across the waist that held his two black powder pistols and at his side hung his broadsword. His charger too, taller and sturdier than others with a meticulously groomed brilliant white coat. He sat tall in the saddle, his narrow youthful features framed by a neatly trimmed beard, completed with heavily groomed pointed goatee and moustache.

"I do not need to tell you fine men of experience what to do, and I have only two rules. One! Nobody speaks my name or calls me Lord. You are to call me simply Captain and nothing else." He paused and let his first rule sink in. "Is that understood!?"

"Yes, Captain!"

Francis allowed himself to smile at their savvy response. "Rule the second, no rape! We are not common murderers and cut-purses."

The rider at the end of the line spat at this but said nothing. Francis rode closer to him. "Break these rules," he continued, "and you won't make it back to Scotland. You have my word of honour. Now, the village is only five hundred yards..."

"Beggin' yer pardon Lord, but what's your cut to be?" The spitter interjected.

"I take nothing, the plunder is all yours. I am here simply to perform my lordly duties and oversee justice on the borders," laughed Francis.

"Then, why are *ye* here? Why no just send us to reive ourselves? We dunnae raid just for some jumped-up young lord to cut down a few Englishmen. Men die that way and I won't be a part of it... Lord."

Before Francis could respond, the rider's neighbour slammed a gloved fist square into his nose, breaking it and sending a stream of blood through his moustache. "If yer don't like it, go home Duncan. Yer swine! This is Francis Stewart! He's been in the saddle and raiding the borders since he were a wee bairn and he haesne got time for the likes of you!"

"Thank you," Francis winked at his defender. "Now, if we're quite done with questions, there's some Englishmen down in that valley who would like us to relieve them of their cattle and silver!"

Francis led his men to the top of the ridge that overlooked the small hamlet. He looked down, even now the villagers hadn't spotted the immediate danger, despite the torches they were carrying acting as a menacing beacon of their arrival. It *was* peaceful, the bright reddish light of the dawn framing all with a tranquil glow. The farm village was half a dozen thatched cruck buildings in various sizes and states of repair.

The whole valley was covered in a blanket of white, snow glittered from the rooftops and the fields sparkled with the morning frost. One young boy split wood next to a crumbling cattle shed where, presumably his mother, was busy milking while the men herded the rest of the cattle from their fields with long canes.

Francis pulled a thick neck scarf up across his face. With a helmet covering his crown all that was left visible was his eyes. His warm breath fogged heavily in the air, as did that from the nostrils of his horse and the rest of his retinue. Coupled with the steam rising from the warm bodies of the riders, atop the ridge they looked somewhat ethereal; riders in the mist. He looked to his left and nodded at one of his company who unfurled a banner bearing the white on blue Saltire of Scotland. Francis drew the cold air deeply into his lungs before unsheathing his sword. He raised it high and shouted, "for Scotland!"

"And the King!" came the emphatic reply from the men. The horses and their riders raced down the ridge, their hooves thundering on the frozen ground. Francis pointed his sword towards the village and kicked his heels harder sending his horse into the full gallop. Finally, the villagers noticed the riders and raised the alarm. Francis rode straight at the centre of the village where a cart path marked the entrance, while the rest of his men, now much further behind, broke formation and rode wide to encircle it. Francis' eyes darted left and right, scanning the village for any sign of a resistance. For a moment, his heart sank as he realised there would be no fight.

There! Finally, the scoundrel, the hero, the troublemaker appeared to face the charge. A lone man with an old infantry pike sprinted to the middle of the path and readied himself in the brace position. *Perfect*, thought Francis as he grinned beneath his scarf. While collateral couldn't be prevented in a business such as reiving, there was never much sport in it. No, it's better if they put up a fight and much better they be so clearly a former soldier!

He sheathed his sword and drew a pistol from his sash. Even at 60 yards, Francis could see the defiance in the defender's eyes. As he got closer, he leaned forward in the saddle and aimed his pistol. As he came within 30 yards, he continued to hold his fire. The old soldier did not falter, he maintained his stare right back into the muzzle as it came ever closer. He readjusted his grip on the great 15ft polearm and levelled it at the breast of the oncoming horse. Francis waited for any sign of weakness before loosing his shot, but it never came.

A mere ten yards from the statuesque man, Francis tugged hard on the reigns, pulling his horses head sharply to one side and sending it into a skid. He stopped just paces from the tip of the stubborn pike.

"Impressive," said Francis, touching the brim of his helmet, "who did you serve with?"

"Who are you?" said the man, ignoring the question and squinting, as though to somehow peer through Francis' mask.

"A Scot," said Francis with a flippant wave of his hand. "Relax man, if I was going to shoot you, I'd have done it already." The soldier kept his pike pointed at Francis. "Have it your way. I simply wanted to offer you a sporting chance. I can see you have a soldier's heart."

A frown spread across the soldier's face but he remained silent. Francis sighed and dismounted. "I have two pistols in my sash, here." He pulled back the dog-head and placed one on the ground as close to the man as he dared and stepped away. "It's already loaded and wound, all you need do is pull the trigger. Even a simpleton could fire it." After pacing several yards, he placed his other pistol gently on the snow, and turned his back as he walked away from it. "All you have to do is pick it up and shoot me, if you kill me, you can have my horse and ride to freedom. Valentine is a fine beast, the finest product of my stud farm, a truly magnif... Ha!" Francis let out a bark of laughter as he heard the polearm thunk into the snow.

The old soldier had surprised him once more and was already sprinting for his pistol. Francis span and hurtled towards his own. The soldier reached his first, raised it, and pulled the trigger. The wheel spun against iron pyrite creating a shower of sparks. The black powder in the pan ignited with a fizz and a cloud of smoke, the weapon let out a great cough and more smoke shot from the muzzle propelling the round shot.

The soldier peered through the haze, waiting to see what he had hit. Against the white background of the snow, it was hard to see anything. As it cleared, he saw the masked Scot laying face up on the ground. His eyes were drawn to the tracks through the snow and saw that the man must've slid several feet before reaching his pistol. The pistol that was now pointed at his chest. Despite the scarf covering his mouth, he could see that the Scot was smiling.

"Very good, old man. Quick, just not quick enough."

Francis raised the weapon slightly and pulled the trigger letting fly his own shower of sparks. The shot snapped back the old soldier's head and his body was rigid even before he struck the snow. Francis, satisfied with his duel, gathered his weapons and remounted, leaving the body where it lay. He rode casually to the entrance of the village where he watched the ensuing chaos.

The reivers, now in full swing, weaved between the buildings hooting and yelling, tossing their torches through windows and open doors. One brave old farmer ran from his hovel armed with an antiquated bow but before he could even have it strung a rider thrust their lance through his back at pace. The point ripped through his stomach, spraying blood some ten feet and leaving him clutching his innards as a crimson pool melted the snow around him.

Another woman clutched a cleaver as two riders circled her. She swung at the lance points as their owners laughed and continued to prod, provoking her into swinging her make-shift weapon. After a nasty prick to the posterior, she finally gave up, collapsing to the ground, breaking out into loud, wailing sobs. Irked by the noise the riders dismounted and beat her until she fell silent.

Few others put up a fight and as quick as it had started, the fighting was over. The remaining villagers had already fled into the fields, running in all different directions. Some of the raiders rode over to the cattle to ensure they didn't escape their pen, while others dismounted and began plundering the assortment of small buildings.

It wasn't long before an ale keg was found. Two riders rolled the barrel out into the centre of the hamlet and split the top with the axe that, moments ago, the young boy was using to split logs. Francis, who had stayed at his post on the edge of the village, trotted towards them and dismounted, joining the others in dipping a cup into the foamy booze. He drank deeply, draining his cup before emitting a loud belch. The men laughed.

"So, we've found the booze," said Francis as he dipped his cup once more. "What else have we got?"

One rider upturned a sack and spilled its contents of eclectic metal objects. "Not much silver m'Lord but it should fetch a penny or two. We've stripped the windows of iron and some cheeses are already on Robert's horse. It's the heifers, though, what's going to fetch the most. We should leave with haste, it'll take some time to drive them back north."

"Aye," replied Francis, "well, as much as I enjoy your company, I shall be..."

His speech was cut off by a piercing scream. Francis dropped his cup and strode towards the building where a second scream cut through the air. He kicked open the heavy wooden door to find Duncan, the spitting rogue from earlier, holding his long dirk to a milkmaid's throat while he fumbled in her skirts. He turned in surprise to face Francis and was pleased to see a neutral expression on his face.

"Found 'er hiding under the bed, Lor..."

The milkmaid screamed as the pistol shot reverberated in the tiny room. Francis, arm outstretched with the smoking gun, watched Duncan's eyes widen as he stumbled backward clasping his chest. With his breeches still around his knees, he crashed into the wall behind him and slid down, his mouth opening and closing silently.

"Almighty God!" exclaimed Francis, "I only have two bloody rules!"

He turned on his heel without looking at the milkmaid and exited the building. The rest of the reivers didn't utter a word and moved out of his way as he returned to the ale barrel. Francis halted abruptly when he saw a jet-black raven perched on the rim.

The raven peered at him for a long while, as though examining him. Its beady obsidian eyes seemed to stare into his soul before it cawed three times and stretched its wings. It laboured its ascent and circled before flying north. Francis cursed under his breath and instead of resuming his drinking, mounted his horse.

"I trust you rogues will drive the cattle back to its rightful home safely, but I must apologise. I have an engagement and must away!"

To the bewildered frowns of his men, he turned his horse and rode back towards the treeline they had exited just hours ago.

* * * * *

12th March 1590
Copenhagen

As the sun began to set, the Danish sky formed a hazy vermillion backdrop against which the Blue Tower of Copenhagen Castle rose high above the other buildings of the town, joining the rest of the spires that stood like watchful guardians over land and sea. In the castle's small courtyard, James adjusted his pace to a shuffle in order to keep in step with the aging Niels Hemmingsen as they walked in the cool evening air.

"Why do you think us Lutherans don't pay much heedance to the Saints my good King?" Niels asked gently. "Most of these *miracles* were nothing but witchcraft! It is the hypocrisy of the Catholic faith."

"Witchcraft?" said James, his interest suddenly reaching loftier peaks. "Catholics have been burning witches since long before Luther's thesis?"

"They made a mistake. You see, a miracle, a *true* miracle cannot be called upon, we cannot channel the power of God at our own will. Sure, some miracles are genuine but God performs miracles through man, at his own whims, not the other way around. We know this from many verses, such as Hebrews 2:4. *That* power, Sire, comes only from the Devil himself!"

"With all due respect, you haven't answered my question. If Catholics would use witchcraft, why do they also burn them?" said James.

Niels sighed and gingerly lowered his frail rump onto a stone bench facing the castle's inner courtyard. "The answer is complex, my King, and spans much of history. I am afraid the sun is setting and we must end our discussion. I will ensure a copy of my works on the subject; '*Admonito de Superstitionibus Magicus Vitandis*' are sent with your baggage before you depart."

"Ahem, you there, boy!" James shouted towards a footman, dressed in the bright livery of the Danish Royal family. "Get this man a cup of ale and be quick about it!"

The boy simply looked at James and blinked in bafflement. Niels chuckled, "He doesn't speak English sire. Very well, I can see your appetite for academics is not easily sated. I will sit with you, but we must head inside and I will cede you only the short version! I am an old man, gone are my university days where I could debate late into the night." Niels repeated James' order to the footman in Danish, adding that a fire should be made in his chambers while he entertained the King.

They shuffled slowly back inside the castle and James waited as patiently as he could for Niels to resume; readjusting the stiff ruff at his neck and tapping his cane on the floor as he walked. Eventually, he could restrain himself no longer, "Forgive me Hemmingsen, for I know ye have devoted time to the subject, but I must say I have seen little evidence that witchcraft is more than a fisher wives' tale."

"Precisely because that is what the Papists would've had you believe!" said Niels, "With someone as educated as yourself, I will presume you know your histories. Why is it that before Europe was brought into Christ's embrace the world was so full of magick? The Greeks had oracles and demi-gods, the Norsemen of my own country had their sorcerers and even good King Arthur had Merlin. We know, of course, that before Christ heresy ran rampant through these lands and that does not preclude magic and witchcraft."

James opened the door to Niels' chamber and waited for him to enter while he framed his response. The fire was already roaring and two full tankards awaited the pair on a small table. "Throughout the Papist nations, Inquisitions to this day root out witches and heretics. I'm afraid I do not follow how this implicates them in witchcraft?"

"To your mind Sire, when did the true inquisitions begin?" said Niels.

"Why, sometime around the 11th century," replied James.

"Well then, this is the clue!" said Niels, beginning to match James' enthusiasm. "The Bible, of course, commands us to burn witches such as in Deuteronomy 18:10 and the Getica's verses describe ancient King Filimer doing precisely this with the witches among the Goths. Yet, sometime before the inquisitions, the strategy was to deny even the existence of witchcraft. Charlemagne himself ordered the death of self-proclaimed witch-hunters in the 8th century and Pope Gregory VII did the same in the 9th. By the 10th century it had become Canon Law in the form of *Canon Episcopi*. It denounces witchcraft as utter nonsense and anyone believing in it should be punished. Strange, no? The church we recognise today that maintains its inquisitions of witches once denied their very existence."

"In itself that is not too damning, nonetheless, if we are to mark this period on a timeline as well as the origin of sainthoods. Well, coincidentally this interval is when a veritable swarm of Saints come to light as they perform their *miracles* throughout the Christian Kingdoms."

James' eyes widened as he thought back to his own studies. He knew it was true, all the pieces had been there, he just hadn't connected the dots. "Then why the about-face?" Said James, suddenly all pretences of an intellectual debate lost, replaced instead by child-like fascination in the face of an encapsulating story.

"Like fools, they had hoped to keep magic for themselves. They denied its existence and practiced the black arts themselves. Did you know priests and monks used to perform ritualistic ceremonies to bring bountiful harvests? They did everything we now know to be witchcraft; burning herbs, casting incantations on the soil and the like. Monasteries became hives of improper worship and monks spread the disease of heresy. They had created a monster, soon magick had spread beyond the church, surgeons and wise-women everywhere were learned in advanced magicks, despite church denying it."

"Of course, even they began to realise something had to be done. Thus, the Dominicans began their holy crusade of burning witches and heretics and Innocent VIII later ratified it when he released his infamous papal bull. Alas, the effort has been to putting out a pyre with a thimble of water. The Catholics, as much as the Devil himself, are responsible for the plague of witches that live among us today." Niels took a long sip from his tankard while James appeared to have entirely forgotten his own. He thumbed the pearl knob of his cane as he thought.

"Then what of those who don't have a pact with the devil? I recall *Malleus Maleficarum* mentions specifically that witches are in league with the Devil. I suspect Scotland is not alone in possessing many simple maidens that perform healing with herbs and such of the like. I shouldn't imagine they would have performed such heinous acts."

"True, there are those some would consider harmless. All the same, I put it to you earlier, we pray that God may intervene and deliver us and our beloved from evil, but from there our involvement ends. We cannot channel his power like so many saints claim to have done. We must only hope and be faithful to the Lord. The devil comes in many forms and unfortunately, women, with their fragile disposition and simple minds, are likely to succumb to the dread incubus in the night or be tricked by the devil! They may not even know they have made any such pact! Still, ignorance is no defence. We must burn witches that their souls may be cleansed by the flames and reclaimed by the Lord. As God's children on this earth, that is all we can do. '*Thou shalt not suffer a witch to live,*' Exodus 22:18."

James stood and walked towards the fireplace. He placed one hand onto the mantle and stared into the fire for a long while. Sensing what the King was thinking, Niels continued, "Luther did great works on the subject my Liege, he burnt many a witch in Wittenberg. Remember still though, the Catholic is almost as dangerous as the witch. As a religious leader of Scotland, you must do your duty to remove it of both!"

14

James tossed a log into the flames before turning to Niels. "And what of the storms that so battered my ship and that of my Queen? Is it possible that that may be the work of witches?" James' eyes twinkled as he implored Niels, the flames of the fire dancing in them in the low light.

"Most certainly," replied Niels, "there is much testimony from witches themselves of the rituals required to turn the weather."

"It certainly can be of no coincidence that my new bride's ship, before mine own, were battered by most unnatural storms," said James to himself turning back towards the fireplace. "But if witches desire me drowned then what must I do?"

It had become apparent to Niels that by now all the intellectual spunk had vanished from the young King. Instead stood a boy, infantilised as he considered the sheer scale of the Devil's works and the magnitude of the Catholic conspiracy to hide it. Niels waited before giving his advice, allowing the King time to weigh and rationalise his thoughts.

"The only thing you can do, my Lord, is pray. I do not doubt you are alive today because of God's intervention. Keep your faith."

Chapter 2

13th March 1590
Hailes Castle

The great hall of the castle buzzed as the assembled throng waited for their meeting to start. The crowd was gathered in front of a raised dais upon which were five chairs, the middle being a great wooden throne. The seatback of the throne bore the engraving of an oak trunk. Its branches, which arced elegantly into the air, had ensnared various artefacts and looped to finish with a flourish of leaves to form the arms. The legs, in contrast, were twisted and knobbly, forming the roots and spread like tendrils across the dais.

Despite the thinness of the crowd in such a large space, its members moved about with an electric energy. Laughter and well wishes echoed through the rafters as they greeted one another. The noise rose with greetings as more entered the hall similarly cloaked. Most of them bore broomsticks which they stacked at the door.

The din descended as three people entered the great hall all dressed in silken mantles that covered them from head to toe. They slowly made their way to the dais, where, upon their approach, the roots of the wooden throne began to slither across the platform. They conjoined and twisted around one another to form a lectern facing the congregation. The lady at the head of the procession, clearly younger than the other two mantled figures, approached the lectern and spoke.

"We welcome ye all to this, the monthly gathering of the Great Order of the Kelpie, Lowland Coven, formerly Lothian Coven. Please be seated." Then quickly added in a hushed voice, "Torcull, ye broke yer stool last time, remember? Ye'll have to sit against the wall." She was talking to a hulking, crouched over figure near the back of the room, who was looking quizzically at the small chairs assembled for the other guests. The giant stood up straight, hitting his head on a roof beam as he did and moved to the edge of the room where he could sit, propped up by the wall. The rest of the crowd lowered their hoods and took their seats.

They were an eclectic gathering; young and old, man and woman, poor and wealthy. Most were dressed in clothes of the time while others wore an assortment of older garments. One gentleman had even gone so far as to wear the armour of a Roman centurion that must've been passed down for generations. The woman at the podium smiled as she looked around at them all. "Of course, we welcome and thank the Warlock Companion of the order, Sir Hercules Stewart, for generously allowing us to gather here again at his castle."

Hercules, who had been waiting patiently in a small nook behind the dais, stepped forward to take his seat to the immediate right of the great wooden throne. As he did, he gave a curt shake of his head at the woman conducting the meeting.

"In the absence of the Warlock Grand Commander, we shall continue with proceedings. We will begin as usual by..."

She was cut off by the scraping of a footman heaving open one of the huge wooden doors that led into the hall. Through the opening slinked a silver-haired fox that was entirely unperturbed by the gathered crowd who had all turned to stare. As the fox padded between the seats dust swirled about it and whipped the clothing of those nearest. Within a few paces, it grew larger and stood upright until where there had been a fox stood a man, who, without skipping a step, continued to walk towards the dais. He was clothed in all black with knee-high riding boots and a great cape that swept the floor as he walked.

"Not late, am I?" He said as he climbed the steps and took his seat on the throne, which groaned and shifted as though to embrace its new sitter. He kicked his legs up over the arm of the chair and the throne shifted once more to accept this new relaxed position. Nobody in the congregation answered his question as they continued to watch in silence. He twisted a gemstone in the hilt of his sword until it came free, it was followed by a thin metallic wand that shone like no earthly metal. With a flick towards his empty hand and a loud pop, a tankard appeared in his grasp.

"What ales have ye in yer cellar Hercules? Still got that strong Orkney stuff?" Hercules frowned but remained silent. "Ah! You do." He said with amusement as, with his wand still pointed at the tankard, it began to fill. As though only just noticing that the crowd were all looking at him, he continued; "well, don't stop on my count. Do continue Agnes."

Agnes turned back towards the lectern, closing her eyes and sighing before continuing. "Thank you for gracing us with your presence. May I announce to the coven Francis Stewart,

Lord Bothwell, and Warlock Grand Commander. As I had begun the..."

"Oh wait," Francis interrupted, "we're not going to start with all the ceremonial bother are we? Let's forego that shall we? Do we have any news? Let's start with that."

Agnes, now visibly irritated began again, "As you wish, m'Lord. As it happens, we do have some grave news. We have received word from our brethren in Zealand that King James has instigated a witch hunt over there for the storms he and his new bride experienced on their respective voyages." The crowd gasped and reanimated as whispers spread through them. She turned to face Francis, who, unperturbed, was enjoying a long sip of his ale. "Nothing to do with you I suppose?"

"I?" said Francis, not looking up from his drink, swilling its contents. "Nay, I had thought about it, naturally, but it's not my style. It must've been someone else or mayhaps, simply poor weather?"

"Damn it man!" shouted Hercules, now seemingly oblivious to the crowd. "What have ye done!?"

"Nothing." Francis sat up and let the flicker of smile cross his lips, he enjoyed getting a rise from his brother. "I swear it, on Merlin's grave."

"Not in recent history, has a witch been so elevated in the court. With the exception of course, of our dear Mary," Hercules scolded. Francis stiffened at the mention of Mary, even her name inspired a rage that ravaged his gut.

"And ye'd piss it all away for a swipe at James! Well!? What have ye to say?

19

"Calm yourself brother, I..."

"We've tolerated yer reiving and yer disregard for the rules, but ye always take it too far. 'Tis barely a year since ye were forgiven for treason no less! If ye hadn't noticed, we're the only two nobles left in the whole of the Lowlands to even take up council positions on this Coven!"

Hercules, realising he was now standing with his back wholly to the mass, sighed and unclenched. He walked back to the front of his chair and faced the crowd.

"Here gathered are simple folk. They're not like you or I. Most are simple healers and herbalists. They haven't the means to defend themselves. We've lost so many, this is all that remains through most of Scotland. We're dying Francis, we're scared. As a knight and warlock of this coven, more than ever we need men like you to protect us. Now I ask ye again, what have ye to say for yourself, Lord?" Spent, Hercules slumped back into his chair and looked expectantly at Francis.

Francis slowly and deliberately put down his tankard and stood, taking his place at the lectern.

"Witches of the Lowland coven. 'Tis true that in all of Scotland few possess my claim to the Scottish Crown." At this the crowd started up there murmuring again. Francis quieted them with a hand. "Yet, I harbour no desire for it. Surely, I could protect this and all of Scotland's covens from the royal throne, but as my bastard brother here asserts, 'tis a treacherous position, even for mine own godmother, Mary." More muttering rumbled through the rabble, though to Francis' ears they began to take the shape of agreement.

"Before his voyage, I hunted with the King. If I had wanted him dead, t'would be but a simple matter to arrange his misfortune. Nay, it is those *about* the King who trouble my dreams. Is it not the religious zeal of the Kirk that threatens our communities? Is it not the lawmakers in Parliament which so belittle us? Is it not the provosts and judges who condemn our kind to the bonfire!?"

"'Tis a fair question to wonder what is to be done about it. Yet who is the darling of the Kirk ministers?" Francis paused for effect while he let his words sink in, glancing around at the faces staring up at him.

"Who is sheriff of Edinburgh!? Lord High Admiral?" A small number let off soft cheers. "Who, I pray tell, is assistant Governor of the Realm in the king's absence!?" More cheers sounded out as the crowd got louder. "And who has a letter," he reached within his cloak to pull out a sealed letter and held it in the air for the crowd to see, "from none other than the Queen of England pledging her support for thine own political goals!?" Francis grinned as he revelled in the crowd's audible pronouncement of excitement. It was time to poke the bear, he thought.

"And yet, for all this, mine own brother has the cheek, nay the insolence, to ask what I have been doing!?" Jeers erupted directed at the scowling Hercules, Francis conducting them in their vocalisations like a choir.

"There, there, it is not his fault, 'tis true I am no saint. Nonetheless, I have fought, and for as long as I live will fight, for our coveted order of witches! I will do more for this coven than any Grand Warlock before me has done, though not as King. I shall usurp the lickspittle Maitland and become Chancellor!" At this, the crowd erupted in applause. They stood, stamping their feet and chanting *"Chancellor! Chancellor!"*

Satisfied, he beamed at the witches gathered before him, before turning on his heel and winking at Hercules as he took his seat. When the crowd finally quieted Francis picked up his tankard. "Apologies Agnes, for my dear brother's exceedingly rude interruption. Please, do continue with the meeting."

* * * * *

30th April 1590
The North Sea

"Would it help, my Liege, if I were to face away from you?" Said Anne, pulling the bed linen up to cover her breasts. "Only, my handmaidens tell me, well..." she looked away, unable to finish her sentence. She lay resplendent in all her beauty on the four-poster bed. Her hair, which was normally worn curled and up high, fell loosely about her snow-white shoulders. Her natural features, so sought after by other women of the court, looked all the more radiant in her nakedness.

"What?" said James who had already begun pulling up his breeches. "No no my dear, 'tis the wine is all. Never mind what foul rumours your maidens tell you, I am quite enamoured with you my beloved." James took her hand in his and kissed it softly. "And do away with titles, especially in the boudoir. I am James, your besotted."

She giggled at her new husband's charms and fell back onto the high pillows that adorned the provisional royal bed, dropping her coverings as she did. As the ship rocked, sunlight shone through the sterns stained windows, rippling and dancing in bright colours across her ivory body. James pulled a shirt over his head and paced to a table which bore his cup and a carafe of wine.

Once he'd poured a generous cupful he gazed out at the calm ocean. In the quiet, he could hear gulls and the sailors on deck, heaving on the ropes and busying themselves with their daily routine. Along with the smell of salt spray that assaulted his nostrils, it all acted as an unwavering reminder that he was at sea.

"What think ye of witches," James said after a long silence.

"I had one cast a spell on me!" said Anne. James turned astonished, "ye have?"

"Yes, when I was a girl. In the woods. She told our fortunes and cast a spell on my serving girl to cure her pox scars."

James hurried back towards her and sat on the bed. "Did it work? The magick I mean?"

"Mine did, she said I'd marry a prince!" Anne smiled, but James remained unmoved.

"Hmm, hardly a revelation for a princess such as yourself." James pulled himself up and returned to his position at the window. He remained still, in solitary silence, considering his thoughts for a long while.

"Maitland! Maitland are you there!?" James yelled suddenly.

Anne jumped and pulled the covers about her to cover herself as best she could just as the door to the cabin swung open and Maitland stepped in.

"Your grace," he said, then turned to the princess, "my Lady."

"What say ye about witches?" said James.

"Witches sire," said Maitland, his eyes lingering on the princess. "Why, the kirk says they are the Devil's own work, Lord."

"And ye agree?" replied James, "I've seen hags and healers but do ye really think they possess more sinister magicks?"

"Aye, I suppose I do sire. I've seen witches burned in mine own town. There needs be no faith involved lord. The accused did admit their foul deeds with their own tongues. They claimed to have spoken with the Devil himself and did consent to an unholy orgy with his earthly ghost."

"Indeed," said James, continuing to look pensively through the glass, his expression mired in the ethereal refractions. "Hemmingsen's arguments were also quite convincing. We shall see what becomes of the Danish inquiries, if it is so that my wife's and mine own vessels were bewitched."

"If it is so, your Grace, you can be sure my brother will burn them. My father never gave clemency to witches," Anne said, an innocent enthusiasm intoning her words.

"If it be the case," James continued, ignoring Anne's input, "it only begs more questions. I should not think many in Denmark would not endorse our union."

"You believe it to be Scottish witches sire?" interjected Maitland, suddenly cottoning on to the gist of James' thoughts.

"Aye, I do. I have many more enemies in Scotland and many who would benefit from my demise with no named successor."

"Bothwell, sire, he has the strongest claim," said Maitland.

Anger flashed across James' eyes, "Of course not Francis, you dull headed ninny! No, the Catholics. Is it not true that the Highlands are full of wise-women and apothecaries, well, there also be the Papists?"

"But Sire," Maitland said, a pleading edge to his voice, "I need not remind you of Bothwell's rebellion this last summer? In league with the papists no less!?"

"And need I remind *you*," James fired back, "that the Earl Bothwell was in constant contact with me throughout the affair. You just don't like the man as he covets your job."

"Aye, well, maybe I should give it to him, I did promise him advancement upon my return." James smirked, gratified with his precise warning shot across Maitland's bow.

"Are quite ye done with yer caterwauling?" he said, relaxing back into his usual cordial tone. He drank the remnants of his cup, poured another and seated himself at his writing desk.

"Bothwell is... lively... though he's never borne me any ill will, not truly. Nay, it makes much more sense for the Highland Lords to be behind this. We must form a strategy before we land."

"What would you have me do sire?" said Maitland.

James resumed his exasperating habit of thinking deeply before he answered. He looked thoughtfully at Maitland and then at his bride who shrank under his gaze. They both waited patiently for the King's response.

"We must set up an office for rooting out these witches. It needs be secret lest the witches try to bewitch its members as they did my ships."

"Very good sire, which lord would you have in mind?" Asked Maitland.

"No lords, none can be, or should be, trusted. Nay, it must be a commoner. Perhaps Bothwell's rogue, the pirate, you know... Hackerston? He could do with a more worthwhile pursuit. Nay, Bothwell will just use him for his own gains. No, never mind, someone else then," said James, speaking more to himself than anyone else in the room.

"And what of corruption? Might a commoner be easily bribed?" Suggested Maitland.

"Right you are. Yes, then they must be substantially well paid. Know you of anyone Maitland?"

"Some, your grace, there are certainly a lot of prickers about Edinburgh. I can have my agents search one out."

"Prickers?" said James.

"Yes sire, they are named for the long needles they carry to test the witches mark, by pricking them." Said Maitland.

"Ah, yes, of course. Of course," James leapt to his feet, suddenly impassioned, and paced about the cabin. "They'll need equipment too I suppose, they can use the royal smithy and bill me the expenses. Ah! And they'll need space in the vaults, have Colonel Stewart at Edinburgh make room. They'll need a uniform too, to identify one another. My tailor can see to that."

"All excellent sire," interjected Maitland, "although, the royal coffers are dwindling. Especially with the upcoming coronation preparations." He looked towards Anne who lay motionless, propped up on an elbow watching her husband.

"Yes, hmm, well, who's preparing them?" asked James.

"Er, 'tis Bothwell Sire."

"Ah, good, Francis won't mind extending me a line of credit for the time being, he's wealthy enough. This is important work we're doing! And I'm sure the ministers of the kirk may release some funds for the eradication of the Devil in Scotland."

"I worry they are more predisposed with the Catholics sire." said Maitland, wincing as he said it, all too aware at any moment he was at risk of derailing the King's enthusiasm. James though, appeared unperturbed.

"Aye, they are a prickly bunch. No issue, we'll find the money, see to it will ye? A King of Scotland must not suffer under the yoke of witches!" He finished these last words by raising his cup in the air as though it were a sword.

"You may excuse yourself now Maitland. Be sure to make preparations as soon as we land. I want a Witch Hunter General and a Bond of Secrecy signed within the fortnight." Continuing to imagine his cup as a rapier, he flourished it before draining its contents and made towards the bed and his princess.

"Get out, Maitland," James added sardonically when he didn't move. Remembering himself, he scuffled towards the door and closed it behind him. He stumbled down the narrow corridors of the ship to his own cabin where his manservant stood as he entered.

He sat down at his desk and began to scribble. "When we land, go directly to The Brass Claymore Inn in Edinburgh. Ye know it? Good." Maitland finished the letter and sealed it carefully with wax.

"There you should find a Welshman by the name of Oswyn Fletcher. Make him read this then tell him to burn it. Understand?"

Chapter 3

1st May 1590
Leith

Francis blinked in the bright morning sunlight that shone through the inadequate wispy curtain. He looked down at the woman lying on his chest, her long straight, mousy coloured hair spread like vines across his chest. She had simple features but still held an effortless beauty that few of the Ladies at court possessed. He slid as best he could from beneath her, to which she stirred and rolled over to the far side of the bed. She took the blankets with her as she did, revealing an ample buttock leading to a slender waist. Francis sat at the foot of the bed and admired her supple figure for a long time.

"Caught yer lookin'," she said, opening one eye and smiling at Francis.

Francis growled and spanked her arse, rising to his feet as he did. "Caught yer lookin', *Lord*." He corrected her, returning her wolfish grin. She watched him as he stretched and rubbed his eyes. *He looks better naked*, she thought, *than wearing the pompous, puffed out clothes of the gentry.*

Stripped, he looked like the old paintings of Greek wrestlers she'd admired at her mistress's house. His broad chest bore the weight of two robust arms and the considerable muscles of his thighs formed sharp edges, built and toned from years in the saddle. His whole frame exuded power and strength. Scars marked nearly every body part, most of them small nicks in his flesh, but some, like the one from navel to hip, protruded from his skin. Still, they did nothing to blemish his athletic figure. She threw the covers off the bed.

"Come back to bed, *Lord.*" She said, mocking his voice.

Francis beheld her for a fleeting moment. "Sorry Florie, I can't." He peered out of the only window in the cramped room. "The sun has been risen for some time. My ships will have already sailed out to meet the King. He'll be back in Scotland soon. Besides, no doubt Hercules has been at breakfast for some time."

Florie pouted but pulled the blankets back over herself in acceptance of his wishes.

"Damn it! There's no looking glass in here."

Francis walked to a small stool in the corner of the room where he'd hung his sword. He retrieved his wand from the hilt and turned towards Florie.

"You'll have to tell me how I look." He held his wand above his head, pointing it at himself and spun it, muttering an incantation to himself. As he did so, clothes materialised over his body. First white stockings wrapped themselves around his calves, then gold striped trunk hose adorned with gemstones bloated themselves out over his thighs. Next, a similarly bejewelled slashed jerkin over an embroidered doublet snaked its way up his abdomen and across his chest, concluding in a stiff short ruff about his neck. Finally, the whole piece was capped with a large velvet beret and white ostrich feather.

"Too much?" he said, looking at Florie.

"Not if ye were hoping to be the lighthouse?"

Francis grunted and flourished his wand again. This time conjuring a stiff silver jerkin which formed a v over his groin, out of which his black hose bulged. A short burgundy cape adorned his left shoulder while a low flat-topped hat covered his crown, with a narrow brim and a smaller plume extending from an ornate silver pin.

"Better," said Florie. Francis tugged at his jerkin and straightened his hat before walking back to his sword. He fastened it to his waist and made for the door.

"You'll wait for me?" he asked. "In Edinburgh, I mean?"

"Oohhh, how would a poor little maiden like me ever busy herself without her lord to serve?" said Florie, putting her hands on her hips and feigning an innocent look.

"Bah!" Francis replied, though he winked at her as he left the room. He stepped carefully down the warped staircase of the inn to the main eating hall. He ordered breakfast with the barmaid before examining the room. Most of the tables sat empty but behind a pillar he found Hercules reading a book. He closed it and looked up at Francis.

"A necessary companion when travelling with you." he said, brandishing the book. "Ye'd be late to yer own funeral. I take it Florie is in good fettle?"

"As ever!" Said Francis with a grin. "Brushing up on yer runes?"

"You know, it'd do ye some good to practice from time to time, besides conjuring your wardrobe."

"Hah! How could ye tell?" said Francis.

"For starters, yer didn't arrive with any baggage." said Hercules cocking an eyebrow. "And secondly, ye could never dress yourself that well. Shouldn't ye think it suspicious for a lord so well dressed as yerself to arrive without any baggage or footmen? And in an inn like this of all places."

Francis paused while the barmaid placed a wooden plate of bacon and eggs in front of him and waited for her to leave earshot.

"Lords are doing suspicious things all the time. Besides, I drink here with Hackerston all the time. They know me well."

"Perhaps too well, ye must be careful Francis. Not least with the rumours from Denmark." said Hercules. "You should not give them such a long list with which to indict you. You know if you fall from favour they'll use any charges they can. In the past few hours alone adultery and *witchcraft.*" He whispered the last word.

Francis speared an egg on the end of his fork and forced it whole into his mouth. "Hercules, brother, that's precisely the point. *If* I fall from favour. Worry not, the King is in my pocket."

Hercules sighed, "I do wish at times ye would slow down. Ye've proven yer abilities several times over as a soldier. You've reclaimed most of the titles your uncle lost, along with its wealth. You're a Hepburn *and* a Stewart, hell, ye even married a Douglas. What more can be gained from playing favourites at court? The coven needs you. I do the best I can with teaching but they need you, brother."

"Why I? You likely know more than me anyhow." said Francis between mouthfuls of bacon.

"Hah! I may read more books, but you were the one educated by sorcerers on the continent. You're ten years my junior and you've already done more than I can ever hope to imagine. Aye, they are simple herbalists most of them, but I see true potential in others. I see no reason why they couldn't, with time, be as accomplished in magick as you or I."

"Mayhaps that's because you need to live a little brother!" Francis retorted. He was about to continue his jibing when his ears pricked up. He held up a hand to silence Hercules. In the distance he heard bells tolling.

"Bugger! That's the King!" He leapt up and wiped the grease from his beard with a sleeve. "Sorry Hercules, you must continue your lecture another time." He kicked back his chair and bolted for the door.

"Your horse!?" Hercules shouted back at him.

"No time! Farewell! See you in Edinburgh!"

Francis sprinted out of the inn's door and bolted down a narrow alley. An elderly woman pushing a cart, already finished with her mornings business at market and likely heading to the docks herself, blocked the way. Francis called out as he ran, and she moved just in time for him to leap up into the cart and over it.

He stumbled out onto a cobbled street that ran alongside an estuary leading out to the waterfront. He held down his hat with one hand, kept his sword off the ground with the other and ran, as fast as one could in such a position, towards the sea. As he neared the docks the crowd was already thick.

"Make way! Make way!" Francis shouted to no avail. The throng only pushed even tighter together as to not cede their position, from which they hoped to glimpse the King and his new foreign princess. "I am the Earl Bothwell damn it! Let me through!" He tried to turn around, but the crowd had already pressed in behind him. He was stuck, and the bells kept up their relentless clangour, each toll a maddening reminder of his lateness.

"A plague on this!" he cursed. He shimmied his way towards the river where he spotted a low wall running along its edge, protecting the crowd from tumbling into its filthy waters. Seeing his opportunity, he sprang upon it and gambolled along its edge.

Mercifully, the welcome party came into view in the distance. The crowd, which had noticed the peculiar lord towering over them hopping along the wall, started to declare their shock.

"Tha' be Lord Bothwell," someone yelled out.

"For the love of Merlin, *now* they recognise me!" Francis muttered under his breath.

As more of the crowd turned to face him, they started to cheer on his agile gambit. He was just beginning to feel as though he'd make the arrival steps, when suddenly a stone gave way underfoot and he began to topple toward the polluted river.

In slow motion the river came up to meet him and a great gasp replaced the cheering. As though from nowhere a hand thrust out to grab him but only caught only his cape. Francis' fall was stopped abruptly, garrotting him on the fastenings of his cape. He kicked out, his feet splashing in the water. More hands reached over the wall and pulled him back over it.

Francis steadied himself and rubbed his neck. He stood back up on the wall, removed his hat and took a low bow.

"I thank ye, people of Leith! Ye have saved me from a drowning! You do me and the King a great service; I am told he prefers his council dry."

The crowd laughed and the cheers rose up again. Francis continued his journey along the wall at a more leisurely pace, prancing and skipping as he did so to the delight of the mass. Chants of "Bothwell! Bothwell!" began to erupt and with the throng spurring his jubilation, he reached the top of the steps where the waiting arrival party had all turned to see the source of the noise. Francis took a final bow towards the crowd and turned to meet their gaze.

"The King should've appointed you jester, Francis." said the man at the head of the group. He was young but stood tall for his age and was dressed in an ostentatious gold outfit that glinted in the sun, not unlike the first rig Francis had donned that morning.

"Well, if it isn't the scamp Ludovic! And where have you been hidden?" said Francis before meeting the man's hearty embrace.

"Well, ruling the Kingdom for one. I might've had more time for jollity had my appointed assistant been present." said Ludovic, straightening Francis' cape and tassels.

"A nonsense sire! A young duke such as yourself needs the experience! The King of Spain didn't invade and there's still peace with England, so you didn't trounce it up completely."

"I was surprised to see you didn't arrive with your wife." said Ludovic.

"Well, it's not easy to arrange all this," said Francis, waving a hand towards the assembly of people.

"Funny, I only ever saw your deputies."

Francis smiled and turned to his wife, who'd awaited his attentions gracefully. She was several years his senior though she retained much of her youthful elegance. She wore an extravagant indigo blue gown, laced and padded out at the hips. The bodice was tight and showed off her slender waist while the straight cut across the chest hinted at her ample bosom. Around her neck extended a large, open lace ruff and on her head she wore a small capotain hat.

"Lady Margaret," said Francis, kissing her on each cheek. "You're looking fine this day my beloved."

Margaret smiled, "No time for that now, look! The King arrives!"

Francis looked out over the sea and sure enough, there was the King's landing boat. He was sat with the princess of Denmark seemingly in good cheer, as liveried footmen in full regalia rowed the boat to shore. Maitland was with them, making himself unnoticeable in the King's shadow. Francis linked arms with Margaret and stepped to the fore of the steps with Ludovic, who did the same with his own wife.

After a pair of sailors secured the vessel, it was Maitland who stepped off the boat first. He held out a hand to bring James onto the rough-hewn steps, who in turn helped Anne onto the shore. As they did so, all the ships in the Forth let fly a volley of gun powder to welcome the King and a great roar erupted from the assembled crowd. They walked together, beaming at the raucous welcome, up to meet Francis and Ludovic.

"Bothwell!" he said, kissing him on both cheeks. "Lennox," he leant to kiss Ludovic. "I see you are alive and in good health. I've had no reports of a grand catastrophe, it seems you have kept my peace well." He smiled at the both of them.

"Might I present to you, my new wife, Princess Anne of Denmark, soon of course to be Queen consort of Scotland!" He held out a hand to bring Anne forward and presented her to the welcome party. Francis bent low and kissed her delicate hand. After more pleasantries and kisses were exchanged, James cut straight to business.

"I trust the coronation preparations are taken care of?" Said James, walking in stride with Francis towards the waiting Royal carriage.

"Aye, your grace," said Francis.

"And there's been no trouble on the borders?"

"Nay sire, the border lords are all quiet," he replied, barely able to keep his mouth from twitching.

"And Lennox, the northern Lords have given you no trouble?" said James, talking louder over his shoulder.

"No, your Grace, they've kept their word." replied Lennox.

"Most excellent. Well, I will wait for the full report from my agents before congratulating you both. Nonetheless, I see no cause presently to drop your advancements." said James, directing his grin at Francis.

Francis smiled back and helped James up into the carriage. Before he entered, James gave a wave to the crowd. They frantically shouted out their greetings and waved at their King, eager to take full advantage of their brief glimpse at the country's ruler.

When James was safely deposited, Francis turned to see Margaret already chirping away with the princess. They spoke in French, complimenting each other's dresses. Francis' smile remained fixed. It pleased him to see his wife fulfilling her courtly duties so well and with such grace.

* * * * *

20th May 1590
Edinburgh

Francis kicked out a chair for Hercules to sit down. The Cowgate tavern was full of Lords and other ministers fervently exchanging news with the return of the King. Many of them, like Francis, had been in the town for some time, waiting to be summoned.

"Nervous?" Asked Hercules.

"Nay, what cause have I to be? I've it on good authority Elizabeth was true to her word and sent commendations to the King. As far as everyone is concerned, I've been an obedient little lord." said Francis.

"The only trouble will be if that snake Maitland somehow manages to blame *all* the country's ills, past and present, on me."

"I suppose I should've never doubted your confidence," said Hercules, pouring himself an ale.

"Think what good will come to the coven if I get my advancement." said Francis, leaning forward in a whisper. "I bloody hope it's Maitland's job. How he's kept that position when there are better lords to be chancellor, I cannot answer."

"Better lords like you, you mean?" Hercules hurried on before Francis could riposte with one of his typically barbed responses. "To be frank with you Francis, I don't know how it will serve the coven. It's weak, it needs grow stronger. You elevating your position won't change that. Now, more than ever, it needs to become skilled. Not just in magicks but in concealment and warding too. The reports from Denmark have left me with a bitter taste."

Francis sighed and put down his cup. "Look, as sheriff I can, and have, stepped into trials to save those dear to me. Think what is achievable as chancellor? All I've heard you speak of is dangers since those reports and I grow weary of it! The King will, *at most*, set up an inquiry and have a few unfortunate maidens hanged. And if not, well, we can cross that ford when we arrive upon it. It does no good to keep tearing your wits to shreds. It makes you look more suspicious. Drink! And be merry!"

Hercules looked around the teeming tavern and suspected he wasn't the only one nervous at the King's return. Francis was right, he supposed, and popular enough with the other Lords, even common folk, to be so easily unseated. "Very well," he said and took a long swig from his drink. "You're still a rogue, a pirate, and an ass though!"

"That's the spirit!" exclaimed Francis, chortling at seeing his stiff counterpart adopt his version of easing off.

Hours passed while they awaited summons. No one else appeared to receive instruction either. The King, evidently, was taking his time over business.

They were several ales down before a small boy, dressed as a steward of Edinburgh castle entered and asked for Lord Bothwell. Francis stood and thrust his tankard in the boy's hands as they left the tavern and escorted each other towards Castle Rock, leaving Hercules with his drink and threadbare nerves.

Two more liveried stewards opened the doors to the Great Hall of the Crown Palace. The wood panels surrounding the room bore intricate carvings, many displaying the thistle of Scotland and on others the rampant lion. The roof beams arced high above the flagstone floor, resonating Francis' footsteps as he walked towards the King. He sat in a relaxed fashion at the very end of the hall, along with Maitland and several ministers, some with writing boards to take notes. Not a soul gave any acknowledgment of Francis' arrival.

Ludovic was already present, Francis looked to him for a sign, but the Lord simply shrugged his shoulders. Francis reached the end of the room and stood while the King remained distracted by other business. Francis' attention was drawn to Maitland, who had stopped concerning himself with the King's matters and was considering him with a wicked grin.

"Lord Bothwell," said the King eventually, shooing away a scribe. "Your arrangement of my arrival was creditable, as was the coronation. Similarly, both Queen Elizabeth and Lennox here," he waved a hand towards Ludovic, "have given me their commendations of your behaviour these past months." Francis smiled, unable to contain his excitement, anticipating the form his advancement would take.

"Nonetheless, I have heard reports of a captured Spanish ship? Tell me of it."

"Well, your grace," replied Bothwell, not expecting the question, "we captured the Spanish barque off the Whithorn in January. There was some dispute over the ownership of the vessel and the crew, but that matter was resolved and, as High Admiral, the ship was placed in my care. After that, there's not much else to tell sire."

"And no doubt that had nothing to do with the lucrative cargo." said James with a hint of derision. "Then what of the letters from the Marquis de Ceralbo offering ye..." he consulted his papers, "20,000 ducats to join with the Papist faction?"

"Fakes sire," said Bothwell, panic beginning to edge his voice. "The Ambassador Bowes and Elizabeth will testify so."

"Indeed," James continued, "And the Englishman, Thomas Fowler, conveniently for you a longstanding enemy, died and you seized his assets in my name? A diplomatic crisis I must now resolve no doubt."

"Sire, he left no will, the estates are within yer..." started Francis.

"And perhaps worst of all," continued James, now brandishing several sheets of paper, "letters from the English border lords claiming recompense for raids conducted by you and the men of Liddesdale up and down the marches."

"The English wardens have never liked me, I..." Francis tried to defend himself.

"Enough!" barked James. "While on the one hand I must thank ye for keeping the peace these past months, on the other I must reprimand ye! I forgave yer old transgressions afore I left. Can ye not see ye cause me no end of trouble?"

Francis, whose head had been awhirl during his swift marshalling back to earth, tried urgently to recover his senses. He realised there was no use arguing with the King, not unless he wanted to worsen his situation. "I do see how these predicaments besmirch your good name, sire. I never intended it so."

"Then what am I to do with yer, ward you in Linlithgow again?" said James, retreating into a more resigned tone.

"I should hope you do not feel that necessary, no sire."

"Lucky for you, I am married, back in Scotland and feeling generous. Ye will face nay punishment, though I cannot give you the advancements I promised ye."

Francis unwittingly allowed his face to express his stunned despair. It was quickly remedied though, by Maitland's predatory grin over James' shoulder. A blinding anger shot through Francis' veins like a bolt of lightning. His heart pounded in his chest as he stared at the old man.

"And on whose council do you take these actions, sire?" said Francis through gritted teeth. "His!?" He pointed at Maitland, his hand barely able to keep steady.

"'Tis none of your concern from whom I take my council, 'twas my decision. Lord Maitland..."

"*Lord* Maitland!? That weasel has..."

James stood suddenly and thrust the tip of his cane at Francis. "Ye will address yer King appropriately!" he shouted in an uncharacteristically booming voice that echoed through the cavernous hall. Ludovic marched quickly to Francis and put a hand on his shoulder.

"Don't do anything you'll regret Bothwell," he whispered.

"I have no other business for you today Lord Bothwell. Remove yourself at once from my presence afore I change my mind," James returned to his seat and straightened his jerkin, attempting to restore his regality.

Francis, fists clenched, took a deep bow. "Your grace," he managed to utter before turning on his heel and striding towards the door, keen to extricate himself from the volatile hall.

"Wait!" said James, having just been handed another paper from an aide. "There is one other small matter."

Francis turned back. "Your grace?"

"Just a small matter. A number of persons have been apprehended in your sheriffdom of Haddingtonshire. They have been placed in my custody."

"On what charge, sire?" said Francis.

"Witchcraft and treason," said James. The colour drained from Francis' face as he searched the King's eyes for a jest or a knowing glint.

"If they are in my jurisdiction, I will set up courts of inquiry right away sire." said Francis.

"No need Bothwell, as it pertains to treason they are in my charge. You are dismissed. Oh, and don't leave Edinburgh. There's more yet to be done."

Francis opened and closed his mouth silently before giving his bow and making for the door once more. Bile rose up his throat where it burned his gullet and his legs struggled to bare his weight to the exit. He tried to quicken his pace but found his body was no longer listening to his commands. Each step echoed, reverberating through his skull and obscuring his thoughts. Finally, he made it out into the Crown Square where he gulped in the crisp evening air and slumped against a wall to let his mind race.

What on earth had just happened?

With a grudging resolve, Francis picked up his legs and made his way through the spiralled courtyards to leave the castle. Despite the late hour, other courtiers were still buzzing about, waiting for gossip and gawking at the people entering and leaving the King's presence. To Francis, they were all a blur, until at last the gatehouse of the complex came into view. As he got closer a shadowy figure materialised from under the portcullis, heading in his direction.

"Hercules, I was just coming to find you."

Hercules ignored Francis' greeting. "They have Agnes!" he hissed.

"I had guessed," said Francis. "It's Maitland, he's up to something. What about Florie, is she safe? Does she know?"

"She's safe, right where you left her. What are we going to do!?" said Hercules, rubbing his hands.

"Nothing, yet. But we must get out of Edinburgh. Tonight."

Chapter 4

29th July 1590
Edinburgh Castle

Maitland steadied his hand against the coarse stone wall as he made his way down the narrow staircase to the vaults. He kept a hand out in front, the only light being from a nearly extinguished brazier at the bottom, half-obscured by the archway guarding the entrance.

He reached the bottom and stepped through the arch to a stifling blast of hot, stale air. The hallway was lined with iron sconces between each vault entrance, though only a few had candles burning in them. Their flicker cast long shadows across the floors and walls of the underground chamber. Every so often a sputter would shoot ghostly apparitions across the stone surfaces.

Maitland continued his journey, making his way past the heavy wood doors. Each was numbered with chalk. At vault 6 he stopped and rapped on the door. When he heard no answer, he pushed it open and stepped through into pitch black.

"Who goes there!" Came a cry from inside the gloom.

"It's me Oswyn." replied Maitland.

"Ah, my Lord, forgive me, I were just restin' my eyes," said Oswyn, his welsh twang ranging tunefully off the arched ceiling. He rustled for some time before stepping out into the lit hallway. He wore a baggy, dirty uniform of all grey. His hose, lacking the padding of the nobility, simply drooped about his knees, while his jacket remained unfastened to reveal a heavily stained shirt. He lit a small rushlight from one of the hallway candles and made his way back into his vault where he lit more and placed them in holders around the room.

Slowly the dank living quarters came into view. There were several ramshackle bed frames scattered around the edges of the room and in other places, simply piles of blankets on the floor. A modest table with chewed legs formed the dining area where a lump of bread and square of hard cheese sat atop moulded scraps. The stink, however, was overpowered by a waste pale in the corner. Oswyn brushed some dirt from the top of one of the stools around the table.

"Please, sire, take a seat," said Oswyn, motioning to the stool.

"I'd rather stand thank ye," said Maitland, keen to remain as close to the door as possible.

Oswyn let out a wheeze of laughter that sounded more like a dog being strangled than any human sound. "Hah, if youse don't like it here lord, you isn't gonna like what's next door."

Maitland remained standing.

"Suit yourself, sire, you bring news from outside do you?"

"Aye," said Maitland. "The Danish witch, Anna Koldings, has finally confessed to witchcraft and has been sentenced by a court."

"Oh, wonderful news...isn't it?" asked Oswyn

"Yes and no," said Maitland. "The King's enthusiasm for justice against witches has been greatly emboldened by the reports. Nonetheless, I grow concerned that if we show no progress soon, he'll soon grow tired of this witchcraft phenomenon."

"Ah, you doubt their authenticity lord?" said Oswyn.

"I care not either way," said Maitland.

"Tut-tut sire, I have seen their magick with mine own eyes. You must not underestimate the witch, even the *nice* ones. Their sorcery comes right from the devil!"

"So, I've been told," said Maitland. "Where are the rest of your men?"

"Ah, it only takes one to interrogate lord, 'tis a lot of waiting mostly. They're out investigating the area we found this one. Around, uh, North Berwick I believe the place is called."

"And still no confession from this one I take it?"

"None at all I'm afraid. She's a tough nut to crack, this one. We'll have her though, we'll have her. Would you like to see the prisoner? Mayhaps she'll take one look at you lord and that admission will pop right out!"

"Very well," said Maitland. "I suppose I should see the wretch."

"Oohh, very good lord, very good," Oswyn clapped his hands as he rose and gathered his things. He picked up one of the rushlights as well as the night bucket and made his way to the door. Maitland stepped out of the way quickly as to avoid a splash from the pale. Oswyn fumbled his keys and made his way to the vault next door, vault number 7.

"Prepare yourself Lord, the smell is not pleasant," he said before pushing the iron key in the lock and opening the door.

Oswyn was right, the new, more powerful stench hit Maitland like a blast from a cannon. It was a wonder the door kept in the violent fumes. He choked as he stepped into the room after Oswyn. Oswyn repeated his ritual of igniting the small rushlights around the room.

"Wakey wakey Miss Sampson. Don't be rude now. I've brought a visitor for you," said Oswyn as he shuffled about the room.

Steadily the thin outline of a skeletal woman came into view. She was stripped to the waist and hung from heavy iron shackles. The sturdy chains that held her extended only halfway to the ground so she was scarcely able to sit. Maitland inspected her from a distance. Her legs were covered in deep welts and bruises, presumably from the boot, and were fouled with her own excrement. Her torso and arms bore more black and purple bruises, as well as several shallow nicks from which she still bled. Her hair fell to cover her face while she hovered motionless. For a second Maitland thought she might be dead until Oswyn sloshed his waste bucket onto the woman.

"Come Agnes, now haven't I been nice to bathe you for our esteemed guest," said Oswyn.

The wraithlike figure raised its head to reveal a face that looked somehow even more gaunt than its malnourished body. Over it, she wore an iron contraption with straps around the head and a mouthpiece that seemed to extend in through her lips. Her skin seemed almost paper-thin, as though at any moment her cheekbones would slice through it. She blinked and opened her eyes which bulged out from the hollow recesses of her skull. Oswyn slapped her, hard, with the back of his hand.

"Awake!" He shouted. "Come closer lord, she won't bite. Well, not with the bridle on she won't." he let out his wheezy laugh again.

Maitland drew a handkerchief to his mouth and shot a horrified look at the jovial Oswyn as he stepped closer. The vacuous eyes of the prisoner stared back at him. Even though her face lacked the strength for expression, in their void he saw only hate.

"What's with the headgear?" Asked Maitland, pointing at the woman's skull.

"Ah see, she's been trying to inflict curses on me and my men sire. This stops her." he added, proudly patting the wretched woman's bound head. Unexpectedly, the prisoner squirmed and fought against her restraints, emitting stifled shouts from beneath the bridle. Maitland leapt back and tripped over a coil of chains, falling to the ground with a clatter. Oswyn slapped the woman again before rushing to help Maitland to his feet.

"What did I say Lord, despite all this hardship you must still beware the witch!" said Oswyn as he turned back to her. "It seems you're feeling talkative this fine morn...eve...day. Care to sing for our dear lord?"

Oswyn yanked at the chains and kicked a bolt holding them in place. Agnes fell and hit the floor with a sickening slap as the chains loosened. Oswyn undid her shackles and pulled her by the hair to a chair in the centre of the room. The seat and arms were studded with iron and he clapped her ungainly limbs into the chair's irons. Then he undid the buckles strapping the bridle to Agnes' head and removed the spiked protrusion from her mouth. As he did a frothy mixture of blood and spittle ran down her chin.

"Play nice," he said and struck her once more.

"Enough, Oswyn," Maitland sighed. "Fetch two cups of wine and a hunk of bread will you? Head upstairs, I want none of that crud you've been eating."

"Right you are lord," said Osywn as he scurried from the room.

Maitland pulled up a chair from the corner of the room and sat opposite the woman. He considered her for some time and watched her as she studied him back.

"I am Lord Maitland, chancellor of Scotland. Do you know of me?" he asked, tentatively.

Agnes nodded.

"Good, and you are a witch?"

Agnes looked up at him with a blend of incredulity and bitterness.

"No," he said, "I shouldn't have thought it'd be that easy. No matter. I am led to believe you are a midwife and you use magicks, herbs, potions... whatever, to relieve the pain of your patients. Is that true?"

Agnes remained silent. Maitland was preparing to continue, when Oswyn's uneven gait became audible through the door. He shuffled in and placed a tray with two goblets of wine with some bread on a stool and carried it to Maitland. Oswyn picked up one of the wine cups and made to drink it.

"Ah!" said Maitland, raising a hand, "feed it to her."

Oswyn's mouth dropped open. "*Her!?* She's nought but a witch!"

Maitland sighed, "just do it. Gently."

Oswyn obeyed and tilted the cup up towards Agnes' mouth. When the wine touched her lips she instantly spat it at Maitland. Patiently, he used the handkerchief to wipe the spittle from his face.

"Urgh," he grunted, "give her the boot Osywn."

Oswyn clapped his hands and retrieved four wooden slats hanging from the wall. The slats were connected by leather cord to make three slots between them. He untied Agnes' legs one at a time, despite some weak struggling, and placed them into the outermost gaps. He then pulled the cords taught so that there was a board on either side of each lower leg and in the middle two boards pressed against one another. He then retrieved a mallet and some wedges from a table of more ominous looking implements.

Agnes screamed in pain as Oswyn hammered the wedge in between the two boards in the centre, forcing the cords tighter, increasing the pressure on the planks and crushing her shins. Oswyn hammed away, seemingly unphased by the screams of protest, until the wedge was fully seated in the gap.

"Now, drink," Maitland said.

Oswyn once again poured the wine into Agnes' mouth, which this time she obediently swallowed. Maitland then motioned for Oswyn to give her some bread and she chewed it sluggishly, fearing what form this newest torture would take.

Once satisfied, Maitland continued, "Hark my words miss, for if you listen it'll save you a great deal of pain. I couldn't give a fig about your predicament here all I want is your confession."

Agnes winced under the pressure of the boot still constricting her legs.

"I have chosen Oswyn for this job because he is a sick depraved man whose imagination does not limit his cruelty. This can all be over if you give me the confession he asks you for. Or, it can go on for weeks, months even. Clearly nobody cares for you or they'd have petitioned for your release already."

Agnes stayed silent, though he saw the burning hatred melt and Maitland could see he was talking some sense into the girl.

"Very well, I will return in a fortnight. If you've said nothing by then, I'll give Oswyn permission to use some of his more...creative devices," he said standing and waving a hand over the assortment of torture devices.

"Oohh, the breast ripper's a good one lord, never had to use it twice," said Oswyn.

Maitland left the room and waited for Oswyn to follow him out and lock the door.

"Feed her up man," he scolded, "she must look healthy when she gives her confession before the King and so help me if she dies, I'll have worse tortures done unto you! She must burn."

"Er, of course Lord," said Oswyn, seemingly confused at the prospect of feeding a prisoner.

"And get the food from the kitchens will ye, yerself included. I'd hate to have to find another such as yourself if ye die of dysentery." With that, Maitland turned and walked briskly to the exit and the clean air that waited outside the hellish vaults.

* * * * *

2nd September 1590
Edinburgh

Francis paid his toll and the huge Netherbow gate was heaved open for him to pass through. He stuck out as he rode through into the main street, finely dressed and astride his dazzling and well-groomed white charger; Valentine. He veered left, off the main street and down a steep sloping path, heading towards his lodgings along the Cowgate stretch of the town.

It was here most of the nobility kept their townhouses and the streets were considerably cleaner than elsewhere. Servants busied themselves beating out rugs or heading out on errands for the day, while the finer folk called for their horses or made for their places of work. A few noticed Francis, tipping their hats and he returned the gesture.

Francis carried on westward, past his residence under the shadow of Castle Rock and the great looming towers of the castle. Despite the townhouses getting taller and wider, their heavy beams and wattled faces jutting out over the street, the presence of the King was never far from the townsfolk of Edinburgh. All one had to do was look up to see the might of the Scottish crown. Stretches of the walls were lined with cannon, primed to deter those who would threaten it, and the stillness from within gave onlookers a notion of omnipotence rather than of absence.

Francis stopped when he reached the Grassmarket and jumped down from the saddle of his horse. He walked him to one of the stables, considerably less plush than the ones he'd passed on Cowgate and pushed the reigns into the hands of a young boy.

"He's a stud, you hear me! Take good care of him!" he said, flipping him a groat.

He stepped through one of the narrow closes off the street. The thin walkway was caked in filth and Francis' boots slid in the slime that coated the lane as he walked. At the end of it, he arrived at the rear entrance to a tavern and waited for a second, checking nobody else emerged from the close behind him, before pushing open the door and stepping inside.

The loose boards creaked underfoot as he climbed the rickety staircase leading up to a series of private rooms. He found the chamber he was looking for and pushed the door open, striding through to find Hercules and Florie.

"About bloody time man! Where have yer been?" Hercules challenged.

"Oh, a fine welcome, no how do you do brother?" Francis chimed back. To which Florie leapt to her feet and charged Francis, pushing him against the door.

"That's my bloody sister," she snarled, forearm pressed against Francis' throat, "what's been captured and ye come strolling in here like it's time fer tea and cake!"

Hercules rose and put a hand on her shoulder, "Calm down Florie, let's hear what he has to say. And, let's keep the noise down eh?"

Florie relinquished her grip and sat down folding her arms, "Well!?"

Francis rubbed his neck.

"I've been at Kelso, as to not raise suspicions. Margaret has the new bairn and I've been there playing at family and keeping the borders quiet," he hurried on when he saw the furrows of Florie's scowl deepen. "My agents, instead, have been keeping tabs on Maitland trying to find out where Agnes is."

"*That's* your plan? Play father to yer new bairn and do nothing?" Florie spat back.

Hercules put out a hand, "No Florie, 'tis a good plan. We cannae raise suspicion, not with Maitland's, the King's and even the English Ambassador's men watching Francis. Though, don't keep the borders too quiet eh? That'll raise suspicion unto itself."

"Agnes has been... *somewhere*... for months, tortured and maybe even dead and yer two lumps have nae to say aboot it!?" said Florie, ignoring Hercules' appeals for calm.

Francis stepped further into the room and sat down. "Florie, Hercules and I are both lords and the only warlocks of the coven. We can't just go charging into the palace to rescue her, we'll indict ourselves and there's nowhere to hide. Not to mention it'll leave the coven defenceless. I assure you dearest," he tried to put her hands in his, but she snatched them away, "my agents are good, they can go places I never could and are trying their damndest to get Agnes back."

"That's nae stopped yer from charging the king before," she said, pouting and returning her arms to their folded state.

Francis sighed, "Florie, the simple fact that no trial date has been set nor have we heard anything means she's still holding strong."

"So, what news have ye from yer agents," said Hercules, keen to resume business.

"Agnes is either here in Edinburgh or at Sterling Castle," said Francis. "I believe Maitland to be behind these new witch hunters and have had my men tailing him."

Florie tutted in disapproval but let Hercules ask the question, "why Maitland Francis? Surely with poor Anna's fate in Denmark and other murmurs, the King himself has more cause to seek out witches?"

"The King is far too logical a man to believe in witches, at least in the way we are portrayed to mundanes. He has a keen interest in the sciences and puts his faith in evidence. I do not credit that he would himself put out a witch hunt, not without first witnessing an act of magick," said Francis. "Nonetheless, I had my men tail him and they found nothing."

"Nay, Maitland has been spending coin, but no-one knows on what. My guess is he's funding the witch hunt. I figure that stoat of a man is wanting to extract a confession and further his goals by *saving* the King." Francis said, waiting for the others to consider his words.

Hercules paused, carefully framing his next words. "Convenient for you, don't ye think? That yer biggest political rival should be in yer way? What cause does Maitland have, more so than the King, to persecute witches?"

"I think not that Maitland entirely believes in our existence either," said Francis. "I think it possible any confession would do. Agnes just happened to be too infamous as a talented midwife and healer for her own good."

Florie's nostrils flared at the mention of her sister's name. "And he'll get that confession too if yer spend any more time dallying! Who knows what she'll say, poor Agnes, she must be beaten half to death by now! She could name you and the rest of the coven!"

"She's right Francis," said Hercules. "At any moment she could break and give all of our names. We'll be rounded up and burnt."

Francis bowed his head, "I know, I know. 'Tis difficult. My agents are working day and night, there's little more I can do. Hopefully, we can get to Agnes first. What of the coven Hercules? How goes it?" said Francis, changing the subject.

"We're still keeping meetings suspended and communication to a minimum. The new witch hunter band is still sniffing around but they've found nothing yet. Though, we did have to keep a stupid woman quiet when she tried to inform on her neighbour for the reward," said Hercules.

"Her neighbour was a witch?" asked Francis.

"No, but the reward, it would appear, is enough for neighbours to turn on one another," said Hercules.

"Damn it! We need to put an end to this. We need to remove Maitland, the head of the snake," said Francis.

"Provided Maitland is indeed the head, then I agree," said Hercules, resigning, but not before shooting a nervous sideways glance at Florie.

Francis cursed again before rising to his feet, "I have other business to attend to in the town. You two are welcome to lodge in my town house if you wish. I shouldn't think it would arouse any suspicions."

"We have more meetings here with coven members. Checking in and to see if we can't find more about these witch hunters," said Hercules.

"Very well," said Francis, "Though I insist we have breakfast on the morn. Florie, we'll get Maitland, I swear it."

"Just get Agnes, I dunnae care aboot the swine you share the King's trough with!" Florie spat.

Spurned, Francis nodded and left the room, glancing back at the pair in the tumbledown room before closing the door and heading back down the stairs.

He retrieved his horse from the stables and decided to walk his way back. The day's business was well underway by now. Francis absentmindedly watched boys scurry about on errands and the gentlemen making their calls for the day. He continued to tip his hat to the folk who paid him heed. Along with the growth in activity came the fumes of sewage, compost and smoke.

It was the sight of a hat and feather that woke Francis from his daze. He knew that hat. He quickened his pace to get a glimpse of the owner, and there he was. *Maitland the weasel.* For a moment, Francis halted, taken aback by the sudden appearance of his rival. Then, teeth gritted, he strode towards him.

Maitland hadn't seen him yet, he quickened his pace into a jog and was running full tilt by the time he collided with his prey. He used the force of the impact and a strong arm to shove Maitland into a nearby close. Francis entered after him, drawing his sword. Maitland recovered his balance and turned to face Francis, only to find a gloved fist in his chest. Francis shoved him hard against the wall and drew his sword up to his neck.

"Yer swine Maitland, what in God's name are ye up to, eh?"

Maitland swallowed, "I'm afraid ye'll have to be more specific?"

"All this witchcraft talk, sucking up to the King like the wee arse kisser ye are. What's next for ye? A dukedom for yer miserable toiling's, eh?" Francis growled.

"If ye be t-t-talking about the prisoners, I'm not privy to what the King does with those who've been a-accused of treason," stammered Maitland, watching the blade of the sword that was pressed against his Adam's apple.

"Yer pernicious, toad-faced, sluggard!" growled Francis, drawing Maitland back and slamming him into the wall again. "Hark my words, yer bootlicking won't save ye. Remember when ye wet yer britches last spring and offered me yer office?

Next time ye won't get the chance to make an offer. Yer days as chancellor are numbered, I suggest ye make use of them."

Francis sheathed his sword and threw Maitland back towards the entrance of the close by the scruff of his collar. He laughed at Maitland's stumble before leaving through the other end of the narrow alley.

Maitland rubbed his throat with a shaky hand and gulped in the air. He leant against the wall and recovered his senses. He looked around the covered alley and the neighbouring street, nobody seemed to have noticed the brief scuffle at all, or cared, he thought. He brushed himself off and prepared to resume his journey, when a fiendish smile spread across his face. He remembered where he was heading and realised there was an easy solution to two of his problems.

Chapter 5

10th April 1591
Edinburgh Castle

Oswyn slurped the last of his broth then stood to adjust his outfit. His grey uniform had been cleaned and he'd fastened it carefully ensuring all the buttons were aligned with the right holes. He pulled a full-length cape of a similar grey about his shoulders with a simple iron fastening. He then picked up a silver pin from his table. It showed a simple horned devil figure and the inscription beneath read, *Deorum Agens Contra Malum*. He fixed it proudly to his chest and left his room. Waiting outside were two other similarly dressed and pinned accomplices.

"You've bathed her?" he said.

"Aye, general, she's ready," replied the tallest of the two. A hulking man, whose muscles were evident even through his padded clothing.

Oswyn placed his key in the lock of vault seven and swung open the door. The room was already well lit, and Agnes drooped in her familiar position, chained to the rearmost wall of the vault. She wore a faded full-length black woollen dress, laced up at the front over a white smock and her head was covered by a simple white head wrap.

"Today's the day Miss Sampson," chimed Oswyn, "What's the matter? Aren't you excited to meet the King?"

Agnes simply lolled her head in the direction of Oswyn.

"Now, now Agnes, that simply won't do." Oswyn picked up a small cauldron that had been kept warm over embers. He poured the warm water in a cup and sprinkled in a grey-green powder from a mortar. He brought it over to Agnes and held it up to her lips. She drank slowly as tears formed in her eyes. Once Agnes had drained the whole cup, Oswyn clapped as he set it down on the table.

"Well, don't you look pretty," he said as he kicked the bolts out of the chains. Agnes remained still while Oswyn threaded them through the iron hoops on the wall. "Come now Agnes, let us go."

Before they left, Oswyn clapped an unspiked scold's bridle over her head. He held the chains behind her like long heavy reins and she led the way out of the chamber. They climbed the stairs out of the rank darkness towards the surface while two of Oswyn's men led the way. Agnes swayed gently from side to side while they climbed, until the bright sun twinkled in the cracks of the door above.

Evidently, word had gotten out that something exciting was to happen this day, as when the three men entered Crown Square there was already a crowd of courtiers outside. They gasped at the sight of the chained and bridled Agnes.

Whispers of "a witch," rang out and they pointed at the dishevelled woman. Oswyn puffed out his chest and baited the crowd by whipping the chains and making Agnes stumble. After showing off his prize, they arrived upon the doors to the Great Hall where a steward of the castle fussed and hurried inside the room.

* * *

Francis waited with Ludovic and the rest of the 'Stewart' faction at court while the King bothered himself with other business. The courtiers were stood in lines either side of a red carpet that ran up the centre of the room towards the throne, raised up on a dais. Francis wasn't quite sure why they had all been gathered, though he had a sinking feeling in his stomach. Francis looked towards Maitland who wore his cocksure half-smile, yet, that could mean any number of things.

The crowd all straightened and then relaxed every time the door to the Great Hall opened and closed, as though the door were somehow emitting a shockwave through the crowd. On this occasion though, no one relaxed. A steward came hurrying up the red carpet towards the king. He bowed then whispered in his ear and James nodded. The steward scurried back and all of the eyes in the room followed him as he beckoned in his partner to pull both doors open all the way.

It took all within Francis' power not to audibly gasp when they opened to reveal three uniformed men and a woman with her head bowed. She looked thin but he knew her instantly. Agnes.

He suddenly realised he'd stopped breathing and exhaled slowly. He looked at Maitland who confirmed all his suspicions by stepping forward next to the King. Francis ground his teeth as he saw the half-smile turn into a wanton grin. He saw Maitland's gaze turn from Agnes to him and he snapped his head to look back towards the strange procession of the prisoner. As he watched them bring Agnes towards the King, he allowed his mind to race.

All is not lost, he thought, *they've just got her confession. There's no way they could know of a connection.* He exhaled again and tried to calm himself. He'd be in irons if they knew he was somehow involved. He was safe.

The procession reached the King and there was a pause while he took measure of the woman. He then nodded to Maitland who stepped down from the throne platform.

"Behold!" He shouted, breaking the awed silence. "A Witch!" Maitland turned on the spot to address every man in the room and revelled in their gasps and hushed wittering's.

"As the gentlemen of this chamber will be aware, in Denmark one Anna Koldings was sentenced and burnt for bringing the storms that threatened our brave King and his bride!"

The crowd rumbled, Maitland left a long pause, allowing them to indulge themselves with rumour and speculation.

"Upon arriving back in our great country, the King charged me with conducting an inquest into witchcraft in our own lands, and those who wouldst use it to do harm to his person. *This* is the result of those inquiries." He pointed at Agnes with a quivering finger.

Curiosity got the better of one member of the crowd who shouted out, "Forgive me chancellor, but how do you know she is a witch?"

This was the cue Maitland had been waiting for. He smiled, clearly enjoying his amateur dramatics.

"Because, sire, she freely confesses so!"

The gentlemen outdid themselves, gasping louder than before. Francis' heart picked up speed as it anticipated what would come next.

Maitland motioned for Oswyn to remove Agnes' headgear but James finally spoke.

"Stop! Is that not a contraption for stopping the witch from cursing us all!?"

"Worry not, my King. The witch has been sedated with a remedy. She is lucid, though she is in a complementary state. Nonetheless, I would ask the King permit my sword so I might run the hag through before she can utter any curse." Maitland turned back towards James.

James consented and a steward brought Maitland his rapier. He stood in an exaggerated stance between Agnes and James and unsheathed it. He held the tip just below Agnes' sternum, then he nodded again for Oswyn to remove the bridle.

"I reckon that's the first-time old squirrel-face has drawn that sword," Ludovic whispered to Francis. "Are you alright," he added, noting his expression, "yer've gone pale."

"Aye, fine, it's just...a witch," Francis managed to utter through his dried throat.

"Don't worry," whispered Ludovic, "it's all a nonsense if yer ask me. Poor woman." Ludovic straightened back up again to watch the rest of Maitland's contrived mummery.

"Name yourself before the gentlemen of Scotland," rang out Maitland's voice.

"A-Agnes Sampson," said Agnes.

"And your profession?"

"I am a midwife and healer," she said.

Francis noticed something was wrong with her. She had definitely been doped but it was something more. The fire that burned through both her and her sister had been extinguished. She was a ghost of the woman he knew. He shifted in his boots as Maitland continued.

"Is it not true that you used witchcrafts to excel in your profession!?"

"It is true."

A great roar erupted at the answer and the mass had to be quieted. Tears ran down Agnes' cheeks as Maitland continued his questioning.

"And these witchcrafts, these magicks, they come from a pact with the Devil himself do they not?"

"They do."

"And these pacts, they are generally not taken alone are they?" said Maitland as Francis' heart abruptly halted its rapid pace and sank to his boots.

"N-no," said Agnes.

"Please, Miss Sampson, describe one of these... meetings," said Maitland. The crowd hushed each other to hear the witch's account.

"W-we would gather in the k-kirkyard where we would have our sabbat. Our dark priest," a few of the devout protestants in the assembly hissed at the mention of a priest, "wouldst summon Satan and w-we would partake in his orgy and give ourselves to him."

Francis couldn't help from scoffing cynically at the ludicrous imagery while the rest of the gentlemanly mob had become positively boisterous. The noise created such an unbearable pressure in the room. It seemed as though any louder and the roof would explode from the structure. Maitland flapped his free arm, in what turned out to be a fruitless attempt to still the crowd, so he resigned himself to waiting.

"And!" He shouted, "And! Would you be able to recognise anyone else at these sabbats?"

Francis froze, glued to the spot. Agnes nodded.

"If such a person were to be in this room, would you be able to point them out?"

Agnes nodded again and began to sob openly. Oswyn jerked the chains and paraded Agnes along the rows of gentlemen. She looked at the faces of the men one by one as she made her way down the lines. Then she stopped and, whimpering, raised a hand to point directly at Francis.

Francis didn't know what to do. He wanted to bolt for the door but his legs remained motionless. He thought about what his reaction should be, indignant outrage, surprise? Then he realised he'd been silent for too long, what *had* his reaction been? He searched around the room for answers. He looked at Agnes who was weeping into her hands, then at the King who looked on shocked from his throne, then finally his eyes rested on Maitland. He was working hard to retain a mask of indifference, Francis could almost see the muscles behind his face working to keep the rouse alive.

"Lord Bothwell Miss Sampson? Are ye sure?" said Maitland.

Agnes raised her head and confirmed, then said, "he is the black priest."

The tumult rose again, louder than before, yet it sounded muted in Francis' ears. He could still hear the jeers of "heretic!" and "witch!" directed at him but he did not feel connected to the insults. Others defended him with shouts of "hearsay!"

He was bumped forward as those around him jostled to better leer at him while others, including Ludovic, pushed back. Francis stopped the noise by walking coolly out into the middle of the hall. He ignored Maitland, turned to face James and waited.

James thumbed the pearl tip of his cane while he thought. "Know ye this woman?"

"Nay, I've ne'er met her in my life, Your Grace," said Francis, to a fresh chorus of outrage.

"You deny the accusations of this woman?"

"I do sire, with all mine heart I do."

"This is a rather unusual case for the Crown. Lord Bothwell, do you agree to be warded, here, in Edinburgh castle while I gather council on the matter?" said James.

"If that is what you wish Sire, then I will do so," said Francis, deciding at this stage his best course was acquiescence. He just needed time to clear his head and think.

"Very well, then go, leave this chamber. I will have the stewards make up a room for ye. Ye may send servants to collect one trunk of belongings," said James. He nodded to signify that Francis should go.

The rambunctious chorus of jeers rose up again as he turned to leave the room. He kept his head low, not daring to look at anyone else. He did manage to get a last look at Agnes as he passed her, she was on her knees now, crying into her hands. She looked utterly broken. He wished now he'd listened to Florie and made more of an effort to find her. For the first time in his life, Francis didn't know what to do.

* * * * *

5th May 1591
Edinburgh Castle

James followed Maitland through the entrance to the vaults. This time Maitland carried a candle lantern to light the way down into the heart of Castle Rock.

"Be careful Your Grace, 'tis narrow and steep," said Maitland.

They made their way down into the long, broad hallway of vault doors. All of the sconces had candles burning in them for the King's visit, brightly illuminating the curved ceiling. Waiting for the party was Oswyn with two soldiers of his retinue. A table and chairs had been set in the centre of the hallway with wine ready at its centre. James took his seat, followed by everybody else.

"So, Maitland, tell me everything that has happened here and what you plan to do with the witch's testimony," said James.

"Very well, Your Grace," started Maitland, "As you know we apprehended the witch..."

"I know that much! Speed it up man, you recruited this... Oswyn is it?" said James, looking at the hapless gentleman who had obviously tried and failed to spruce himself up for his visit.

"Yes, Oswyn was a pricker I knew of. His men found Agnes and brought her here. She was defiant but we eventually got her confession," said Maitland subtly puffing out his chest.

"And she confessed this under torture I presume?" said James.

"Well, sire, we needed to break her spirit. She would hardly sign her own death warrant willingly. As you saw in your hall, she was under no duress when she confessed then" said Maitland.

"That is true," said James. He paused while he considered Maitland's point. "Have you seen her actually *do* any magick?"

"Well, no sire, we haven't but we do have accounts from Keith *and* North Berwick of her sorceries," said Maitland.

"And she bares the witch's mark Sire!" chimed in Oswyn.

"Interesting," said James, "may I see it?"

"Of course, Your Grace!" said Oswyn. He excitedly jangled his keys and opened up the vault containing Agnes then beckoned James to step inside.

James stepped into the vault which had been further repurposed for Oswyn's depravities. The floor was still damp after being scrubbed for his visit, nonetheless, the place still reeked of sickness. In the middle of the room there was a studded chair. It looked somehow small, isolated from everything else that had been pushed against the walls. Above a heavy wooden table hung various cruel-looking implements. Against the other, iron rungs had been driven into the stone, clearly meant for some prisoners that did not yet occupy the dungeon. Then, shackled to the far wall, was the witch.

They had dressed her up in the same clothes as she had worn to give her confession. She seemed to be looking healthier than a fortnight ago and she even bowed her head to acknowledge the presence of the King.

"She wears no bridle?" asked James.

"Nay sire, she is quite compliant since confessing her sins against God," replied Maitland. "Oswyn show the King the mark."

Oswyn pulled a long needle off the wall and scurried over to Agnes. He begged her pardon then turned her and lifted her skirts to reveal her rump.

"I hope this is necessary," protested James.

"Oh yes Sire. The book says the devil's mark is from his lick and that he does so in hard to find places. So's us men of the lord won't find 'em, see?"

James inclined his head and Oswyn continued with his business. He pricked Agnes' right buttock with the needle and it began to bleed.

"You see sire, when the skin is pricked it bleeds. However," he stopped and pointed at a small birthmark just below her left buttock where he pricked it. "Hah! You see, the witches mark doesn't!"

James leaned closer in the dim light to inspect the hindquarters on show. Sure enough, the small incision wasn't bleeding.

"I see," said James. "Put her back to her usual state will you."

Oswyn obliged and smoothed out Agnes' skirts and turned her back to face the King.

"Miss Sampson," he said, "If I were to ask Oswyn to unshackle you, would you be able to perform some magick for me?"

Agnes shook her head, "No Your Grace, I have forsworn the devil and cleansed myself of his presence."

"Pity," said James, "thank ye Miss Sampson."

James turned and left the room indicating he was done with the prisoner. Maitland and Oswyn followed in silence as he resumed his seat at the table in the hall.

"Set her trial as soon as possible," said James.

"About that, Sire, I had thought of delaying it on two counts. The first being she must be witness at Lord Bothwell's trial. Second, I had promised her life in exchange for names. She would have to be imprisoned, to be sure, but alive." said Maitland.

"I care not," said James, "treason is treason and she engaged in a ritual to bring harm to me and my dear wife. Would ye have me seem weak to mine own subjects?"

"No, of course, Your Grace," said Maitland.

"Then she burns. And what makes you think Bothwell will stand trial?" said James.

"Well, witchcraft! Treason!" said Maitland, indignantly.

"I have not yet decided how to proceed with my cousin. Rebellious? A thousand times yes. An enemy of the crown and a witch to boot? I think not."

James watched as Maitland screwed up his face but he held his tongue. He'd made his argument against Francis near on a thousand times, further protestations would only serve to incite the King's wrath.

"Fortuitous for you, is it not? Your greatest rival accused of witchcraft. My memory serves me better than you might think Lord Thirlstane. Was it not you, who, before any investigation, mentioned that Bothwell might be a witch on our journey back here? No, the witch will burn Maitland!"

"As for my cousin, I will go now to visit the Earl and hear what he has to say." James stood. "Thank ye Oswyn, for your hospitality."

"Why, thank you Your Grace, visit any time!" said Oswyn cheerily.

"And thank ye Maitland, for this time. It has been most enlightening. Our business is concluded for the day."

James turned and he could almost sense Maitland's incredulity behind him. He climbed the stairs alone back up to the castle. A guard, who had been waiting at the surface, stood to attention as the King stepped into the sunlight and followed him back to Crown Square.

James reached Francis' room in the Royal Palace and motioned for the guard to open the door. The windows of the room faced east and sunlight burst through them, spotlighting the dust in the air. Francis' four-poster bed was already made up and he sat at a writing desk in the corner of the room with an empty plate of breakfast in front of him. He stood and beamed at James when he entered.

"Your Grace! I have been awaiting your visit, please sit down." Francis motioned to his chair while he pulled another to face James. James sat and inspected Francis carefully.

"Ye are in good spirits I see," he said.

"As good I can be Sire, given the circumstances," said Francis.

"I have just come from Maitland and the witch," said James, with just a hint of disfavour in his voice. He let out a deep sigh, "I must say, I do not credit the accusations, they seem fanciful at best."

Francis sat up straight and almost visibly lit up in the morning sunlight. "Thank ye, Sire! Yer see Maitland for his fraudulence?"

"Hold on Francis," said James, "I am not here to settle old feuds. I have forgiven but not forgotten yer deeds against him, and me. Though it is true he may harbour a vengeance, I also think it beyond poor Maitland's imagination to concoct such a scheme."

"Still, the matter remains that a woman did accuse ye of witchcraft *and* in doing so, also accused you of treason. In front of nearly my entire court no less." James took in breath and sighed again. He stood up and walked to the window. Outside he could see the batteries of the eastern defences and beyond it, the smoke rising from a bustling Edinburgh. He turned back around to look at Francis who was studying him with a quizzical look.

"I fear, cousin," he said, sitting close to Francis, "this time I cannot help ye. Ye must stand trial for the charges."

"But witch trials are always a farce, they're naught but a show!" said Francis.

"Aye, but your history does you no credit. Thrice, at a minimum, ye have been involved in a rebellion against my person. It looks bad Francis," said James.

"Your Grace, ye have to help me!" said Francis, his morning jollity evaporated, replaced with angst.

"I am helping ye cousin, yet there is no alternative to a trial. I will delay and harry it as long as possible nonetheless, eventually, ye must face it. I tell you now only so that you may begin organising your defence," said James. He sat back in his chair and placed both hands on top of his cane regarding Francis as he handled his words.

Francis looked at the floor as he thought, though James did catch a sideways glance he made towards his sword. Several minutes passed before Francis spoke again.

"Very well, Your Grace, I will organise my defence," said Francis, seemingly resigned to his fate.

"Good man Bothwell, chin up lad. I will allow you visitors so you might organise, and I will continue to keep you here in Edinburgh," James stood and made to leave the room.

"Good luck, Francis," he said at the door and left Francis to plan.

Chapter 6

22nd June 1591
Edinburgh Castle

Francis looked out of his window at Edinburgh town. Smoke billowed from the chimneys creating a greyish haze that made the lights of the houses twinkle, like hundreds of earthly stars. The spire of St. Giles Kirk penetrated the skyline, yet from the height of Castle Rock, Francis still looked down upon it. Beyond it, the main street extended to the towers of the Netherbow Port. Beyond that was completely obscured, but Francis knew there stood Holyrood Palace.

Francis turned back to his quarters. He would have to leave a lot of his belongings behind, though mostly, it was things that could be replaced. All he needed was money, his sword, and his horse. He tapped impatiently on the desk. *The boy should be here by now,* he thought. He recounted the plan in his head while he waited but it wasn't long before his thoughts drifted to Hercules and Florie. He had tried his hardest to get communications out to them, but, either they hadn't responded or they did not care to.

The only person who responded was Margaret, she had been in constant communication. There had been a convention set to protest Francis' innocence, she had worked hard to get the Stewarts, Hepburn's and Douglas' to his side but in the end, the convention was cancelled due to poor attendance. Francis had surmised that, while he was imprisoned, no-one dare move against the King. Francis continued to let his thoughts wander to Margaret.

He hadn't been kind to her. He had married her young, while she was an older widow. Even in their honeymoon, Francis hadn't been permitted to be alone with her for '*reasons of his youngness*'. She had served her purpose as a wife well though. Already she had borne him many children, extended his influence through lands and rents and was almost as well-liked as himself at court. She certainly held influence with the new Queen Anne.

A soft tapping at the door awoke Francis from his thoughts. He hurried to open it and ushered the young steward boy inside.

"Ye have done as I asked?" asked Francis.

"Aye Lord," the boy replied, "Your horse is waiting at the Canongate stables and I have sprinkled the sleeping herbs into the guard's broth this eve."

"And?" said Francis.

"And I've unlocked the gatehouse doors," said the boy.

"Very good," said Francis, flipping the boy a coin. "Now I want ye to come over here and take a look at this on my desk for me. Can ye read? Good. Read this letter to me."

"Dearest Francis," the boy began.

Francis drew his wand, that ever since the Kings visit he'd been keeping in a sleeve, and stood behind the boy. He pointed it at the back of his head, closed his eyes and began muttering an incantation under his breath.

"Young John," the boy read, "grows to be strong like his father and... Henry is... young... John... butterfly... rainbow... cannon..."

Francis turned him around and spoke to him.

"Ye saw nothing this night and remember naught of my stay, isn't that correct?" said Francis, gripping the boy by the shoulders.

The boy nodded, so Francis led him towards the door and gave him a gentle push out of the room. Then he strode to the window and thrust it open. He climbed onto the ledge and looked down. Luckily the upper rooms of the palace were reserved for the King so his drop wasn't too great. Still, it was some distance and there was only a narrow jut of rock to land on.

He looked briefly back into the room and dropped. As he did so, his body contorted into inhuman positions and the night air swirled around him. When he hit the rock below, it was a set of paws that broke his fall on the stone.

He panted in the humid night air as he made his way along the narrow rock edge to the square. He looked around and sure enough, two guards lay resting against one another, sleeping soundly. Francis sprinted past them and up a set of stairs onto the castle walls. He padded past cannons, hiding in the shadow of the embrasure.

He took a turn down a steep section of wall when a light appeared up ahead. Francis ducked behind a cannon wheel and did his best to hold his breath, waiting for the sentry to pass. He was holding a candle lantern, walking slowly and kicking at the ground as he walked. When he came level with the cannon, Francis tried to turn with him and avoid his sight. The sentry must've seen him, for he stopped and looked bewildered at the spot Francis had just been. Francis averted his eyes from the candlelight so they wouldn't reflect its beams and remained as still as he could. He was directly underneath the cannon now and he hoped that its shadow would hide him.

The soldier coughed up a globule of phlegm which he spat onto the hard stone then carried on his journey along the wall. Francis sighed and continued in the opposite direction. To his dismay, he saw another lantern off in the distance further along the stretch of wall. He got as close as he dared then waited again under his canon.

They've doubled the guard, thought Francis as he waited in the darkness, *did someone know of my escape?* He had to wait one more time before he eventually reached the portcullis gate. There was a small wooden door leading from the wall walk to the inside of the gatehouse where Francis would be able to leave the castle.

Damn it! Francis cursed internally. The door wasn't open. Either the boy lied or he'd had to wait so long for the sentry's someone had closed it. He rose up on his hind legs and tried shifting the iron handle. Nothing. It was locked. It was then he noticed that in his efforts the door had become illuminated and he could see his own shadow. He turned his head and saw a soldier looking at him curiously.

Panicked, Francis tried to recover with his best fox impression. He began whining and scratching at the door.

"By my eyes, I don't believe it," said the soldier aloud. "How'd you get in?"

The man put down his lantern and his pike and moved to come closer to Francis. Francis growled, baring his teeth and backing into the corner.

"Come now boy, can't have ye inside the castle now can we," he said, stretching out a hand to try and pet the silver fox. Francis couldn't believe his luck. He stopped his growling and let the soldier pat his head.

"There now, yer just a scared wee fella aren't ye," he said as he picked Francis up. Francis whined and let the solder carry him. The soldier knocked on the door, it took a few moments before someone answered.

"It's ye Davie, why ye knockin' an makin' me climb all these stairs?" said the guard from inside the gatehouse.

"It's this fox," said Davie, "I found him stuck. I need to get down to let 'im out."

"Lord almighty! Come on then, leave the door open though, I ain't coming back up to let ye out again," said the soldier. Together they walked down the spiral staircase to the base of the gate where a second door led out into the square.

"I swear 'pon my soul that I saw this fox trying to use the door," said Davie as he placed Francis on the ground near the exit. He threw his arms out wide discouraging him from going back towards the castle.

"Aye, and did he play the pipes for ye too?" laughed the other.

A third guard leaning on his pike at the other side of the gatehouse suddenly stood up straight. "Hold on just a minute! There's witches up there, ye don't think that be a familiar?"

"A familiar?" Said Davie, "what's one of them?"

"It's a little animal witches have to help 'em."

Francis didn't wait to hear their conclusion, slipping through a square gap in the iron portcullis, and scurrying away into Edinburgh town.

As he reached the high street, the bells of the kirks in the town chimed to signify curfew. Lights were extinguished in all the houses and those still out late stumbled their way home. Francis kept to the edges of the street, padding along in the darkest corners until he arrived at the staggering Netherbow Port.

He had expected this to be another obstacle too, however, the gate was raised just six inches from the floor and he was able to glide through into the Canongate. He ambled down the street to the stables where, and as instructed, Valentine was saddled and in the foremost stall. *At least the boy got that part right.*

Francis joined his horse in the stall and morphed back into his human form. He pulled himself up into the saddle and was checking his riding gear when he heard the sound of a horn.

He cautiously rode out into the street where he saw several riders making their way through the gate. He tried to turn his horse around and squeeze through an alley instead, but it was too late. He heard the shouts from over his shoulder.

There was nothing for it. He abandoned his turn and kicked his heels into Valentine. He cursed for having not loaded his pistols. Fortunately, his wand was still in his sleeve and he retrieved it while keeping low to his horse. He extended his wand arm out over his shoulder and kept his eyes on the trail.

"*Gasdh!*" he let out as quietly as he could. His wand fizzed, sparked then cracked, just like a pistol shot. The discharged projectile made its way toward the oncoming cavalry but the lack of a reply meant he'd missed his mark. Francis looked over his shoulder to see there were at least five horsemen pressing hard on his trail.

Up ahead Francis could see the outline of Holyrood Palace. He knew if it could make it there and out onto the main road east, he would have more cover to mask his escape. The horn blast sounded again and as if in answer to its call, another group of horsemen emerged from the palace gatehouse onto the Canongate street.

For what seemed like the hundredth time that night, Francis swore again. He fired off a shot from his wand in their direction to slow their pursuit and made a hard right, jumping a fence into a thin strip of field. He raced Valentine through it, though his turn had cost him valuable seconds.

He was in range of the horsemen's carbines and they sounded off a report in his direction. The loud cracks echoed through the darkness.

"*Skeito!*" he yelled, with his wand over his shoulder. The spell formed an indiscernible boundary behind him that vibrated the air around him when the lead shot struck it.

He reached a path at the end of the strip running parallel to the Canongate and took a right, assuming the horsemen from Holyrood would've already cut off the path east. *Good,* he thought, *that's less to deal with.* Though it did mean he was heading right back towards the city walls.

Only three of the horsemen had followed Francis through the field. Two others had wisely turned their horses and found a path. They came bearing down on Francis' right. He fired off another shot, this time striking the front rider and sending him flying over the rump of his horse. His flailing body hit the second horse which reared and threw its master.

Francis whooped but his victory was cut short as another crack sounded and a shot whizzed past his ear. The men behind had holstered their spent carbines and drawn pistols. Francis was coming up on the walls again. He could see the path veered left sharply, right at the base of the wall behind a small kirk. He took the sharp bend as fast as he dared, to complaints from Valentine, as another shot thudded into the stone that would've surely hit him had he been any slower.

He slowed slightly, looking over his shoulder with his wand primed, waiting for a horseman to appear around the corner of the building. It was his best chance to catch them as they slowed for the turn.

A bright light caught the corner of Francis' eye and then the sharp report of the pistol followed. The third horseman had cut the corner and come out on the other side of the kirk. The shot thudded into his shoulder like a titanic punch. It threw him back, snapping his head, the shape of the saddle the only thing keeping him in place. Valentine halted and whinnied. Francis used his remaining strength to pull the horse around and face the shooter.

He smiled, "you've no shot left do you boy... *Gasdh!"* His wand let off its black powder mimic and the shot hit the soldier square in the chest. The man slumped forward in his saddle and fell into the dirt.

Francis reared Valentine, firing one last shot in the air before wheeling him around and taking the southern road.

He stopped at a safe distance to cast a charm that would help his shoulder until he could get better care. He looked towards Edinburgh, which was beginning to light up at the sound of the alarm. The adrenaline drained from his body and suddenly he felt shaky as his emotions caught up with him. He let a tear roll down his cheek as he looked upon the great city, dominated by its castle. He realised he wouldn't be back for some time. He turned his horse to face away from the town and begin his life as an outlaw.

* * * * *

23rd June 1591
Holyrood Palace

James thundered down the stairs of the palace to the assembled men in the hall.

"Maitland!" he shouted halfway down them, "ye'd better have a damn good report!"

Maitland winced at the yell and braced himself for the King's interrogation. "We have found all we can Your Grace, the investigation is still ongoing."

James took in a deep breath and tried to calm his anger, he knew it would not be conducive. "Start with his escape from the castle, what do ye know of that?"

"Very good sire. We know that Lord Bothwell didn't leave via his door which was guarded all night."

"That doesn't mean he wasn't bribed or duped," interjected James.

"No, sire, that is true," said Maitland hurriedly, "but nobody else saw him in the palace last night. His window was left open and we have surmised there he did drop down to the ledge."

James rubbed his eyes, "that's what, a ten-foot drop?"

"Twelve we count sire," said Maitland

"And you have discovered this because there was a rope of some kind?" said James.

"No sire."

"So yer telling me ye believe the man dropped 12 feet from the window onto a crag no wider than a horse's back, is that it?"

"Er, well yes sire, if he hung from the window he'd only have to drop around seven foot," said Maitland.

"Bothwell is a fine figure but even I doubt he could make such a feat. Let's assume this to be true," said James, his anger rising, "what next?"

"We do believe he made his way along the walls and out through the castle gate. A soldier there by the name of Davie Broune admitted he left open a door. He is being flogged as we speak sire,"

"The whoreson, beetle-headed dogfish!!" screamed James, "be sure for me to arrange a muster of the castle guard. Then what?"

"We do not know how he made it out of Edinburgh, though Bothwell's guard checked on the lord and found him not to be present. He raised the alarm and sent our cavalry. There they did catch Bothwell mounting his horse on the Canongate."

"And there they did pursue him out of the town," said James summarising for Maitland.

"Pardon Your Grace, but there is more," said Maitland. "Firstly, he did kill two of our cavalry and wounded another. A grievous crime that should be added to his charges. Secondly, there is an account you may wish to hear from Captain Logane."

Maitland pointed towards one of the cavalrymen who had clearly not yet been to bed. At the King's assent he beckoned the man forward and encouraged him to speak. He took a bow before starting, to which James tutted.

"Your Grace, I did pursue Bothwell from the burgh and, well, he fired five shots from his pistol sire, in quick succession."

James was taken aback, "He reloaded, surely?"

"Forgive me sire, but nay, 'tis not possible. He was riding his horse at the full gallop, even a seasoned man cannot reload like that. Certainly not that quickly."

Maitland stepped in front of the captain. "You see sire! Witchcraft! He has bewitched his pistols!"

James staggered back slightly and took a seat on the stairs.

"You are sure Captain?"

"It seems unlikely, I know Your Grace," said Logane, shifting slightly, "but my men will confirm the story. Not one of us saw him reload."

"There must be some likely explanation," said James, "some new German design perhaps."

The others watched on as James retreated into his thoughts tapping his cane. Abruptly, he rose and in a bout of unbridled fury began kicking a chair at the edge of the room.

"That! Mull-headed! Fool-born! Distempered! Fustilarian!" he bellowed, kicking between each word.

James stood over his chair panting, its legs now detached and strewn about like dismembered limbs. He rounded on Maitland.

"Where did the rudesby go?"

"He was last seen heading south so we assume his castle at Crichton, or further south perhaps to Liddesdale to raise the borders. We have sent scouts."

"The villainous boar! *This* is how he repays my kindness!? He can mean only to rebel, surely. He knows full well what this means!" James booted one of the chair legs and it skidded across the palace rugs.

"Your orders sire?" said Maitland, more confident now that the King's temper was focused on Francis and not the inept guardsmen.

James had to think for a moment, pacing. "He must be put to the horn. Immediately. I must see it done myself. Thereafter I shall petition the kirk and raise an army. That churlish sot will learn what it means to challenge a King! You! A quill and ink!"

James waited while a steward brought him his writing equipment and he scribbled furiously before handing the document to Maitland.

"Maitland see to it the documents are prepared! You! Ready my horse and guard, we will ride to the cross."

His orders given, James retired back up the stairs to prepare himself for the business of the day.

James' horse was already waiting for him when he returned. He had donned a gleaming cuirass that he wore over a pastel yellow doublet. Over the top of his metal plate, he had tied a sash across his midriff and a long cape flowed from his shoulders. He heaved himself up into the saddle and without a word set his horse into a trot towards the Great Cross.

All the city gates were swung open or hoisted swiftly for the King as he rode. He paid no heed to anyone acknowledging his presence, instead content to continue brooding about Bothwell. When he and his entourage arrived at the Mercat Cross a crowd had already gathered. News travelled fast in Edinburgh and the primped trumpeter was waiting patiently for the days business to be read. James stayed towards the rear of the crowd, using his height atop his horse to watch proceedings.

The crier stepped out to an incensed wittering amongst the crowd. Rumours spread like wildfire between the townsfolk, each more ludicrous than the last. Then, a deathly silence as the trumpeter made three blasts on his horn.

"Francis, sometimes known as the Earl Bothwell, having that honour to be the same tender blood to the King's Majestie and, in that consideration, did advance himself during the King's infancy to the earldom of Bothwell and other lands, lordships, great offices, honours and preferments that extend beyond his succession at birth. And in respect thereof, Francis should have rendered himself and all his actions to the advancement, honour, and standing of his Majestie, his crown, and his estate."

"Yet, so malicious and ungodly is his nature, that after he committed sundry slaughters amongst other odious crimes, overseen and left unpunished by His Majestie, did Francis treasonably and unnaturally take up arms against his Highness, for the purpose of furthering the crimes of others within and without this country by subverting the true religion and the periling of His Majestie's person, crown, government and estate."

"Yet! His Majestie did give him clemency and superseded before the pronouncement of judgement upon him in the hope of his conversion, penitence and amendment. Nonetheless, His Highness now perceives that he has given himself over, all together, to the hands of Satan!"

The gathered townsfolk gasped and the nattering rose up again so that the herald had to shout louder to be heard over them.

"And that his spirit, he says, prevails so mightily into him that he yet still insists, without fear of God or respect to honesty and shame of this world, to continue in all kinds of filthiness, heaping treason upon treason against God, His Majesty and this, his native country."

James smiled as the crowd was at uproar with righteous anger. Men shook their fists and women covered their children's ears.

"He, who also, for the better execution of his wicked intentions and treasonable conspiracy against His Majestie had consultation with necromancers, witches and others wicked and ungodly. Confessed, by some of the same kind already executed and some others yet to be executed for the same crime! Being warded in Edinburgh Castle for said crimes, he has escaped and taken with him his offences"

Upon hearing of Francis' escape, the crowd's anger turned to exclamations of fear. James' grin got wider to see his letter was having the desired effect upon his subjects. Each reaction the one intended while writing.

"Therefore, His Majestie is caused to pronounce the sentence of forfeiture against him. Removing said earldom, lands and lordships, great offices and preferments as well as those obtained by marriage. So that presently he remains a declared rebel, traitor and enemy to God, His Majestie and his native country."

"His Highness also declares that no man should reset, supply, show favour, intercommunicate nor have intelligence with said Francis, privately or publicly, nor furnish him with meat, drink or lodgings under whatsoever colour or pretence under pain to be reputed, held and charged with partaking in treasonable crimes. Likewise, all men betwixt the age of sixteen and sixty should present themselves to His Majestie on the first day of July with fifteen days victuals and provision so that His Highness may repress the treasonable practices of the said Francis so to better settle the quiet estate of this country."

James, satisfied with the reading of his letter began to turn his horse when shouts from the crowd diverted his attention. James turned back to see that some had taken to scuffling with one another. He listened to what they were saying and deduced that some were defending Francis. *After that!?* His good mood vanished and he kicked his horse a little too hard, sending himself galloping down the high street back towards Holyrood.

Chapter 7

30th July 1591
Hailes Castle

"You've sent your ravens?" Asked Francis, straightening his half cape.

"Aye, Francis, but I can't guarantee they'll answer the call. Your horning is posted from Sterling to Berwick. Folk can be killed just for consorting with ye," said Hercules, "even me."

"Aye, tad much didn't ye think?" said Francis. The two were sat across a small table in a reception room of Hercules' castle, illuminated only by a single candle. Most of the castle lights had been extinguished so onlookers might think it empty.

"If I'm honest, brother, I think it long overdue," said Hercules, looking at his feet, "It mentions yer role at the Brig O'Dee and yer murders, not to mention everything else. It seems as though James will persecute ye for all of it. I've been telling ye for a long time man, ye've been playing a dangerous game and yer chickens have come home to roost."

Francis looked forlornly into his cup, "I suppose. James is right, I have nay conducted myself all that well, but consider

Huntly, Angus and those of that ilk. They are far more treacherous than I."

"That may be true but it doesn't change yer situation. Though, perhaps it does offer hope of reconciliation one day," said Hercules. "The best thing ye can do is go quietly into exile and hope the King forgives ye."

"I can only go to exile if the King grants Margaret back my land and rents. Otherwise I'll be some penniless vagabond wandering the likes of Madrid for the rest of my days, and I bloody hate Dagoes."

"Aye, well, we'll see what the coven has to say. I cannot gather the mood, I have nay clue as to whether they'll take pity on ye as a wounded bird or a failure."

Francis looked up when he heard someone approaching. Light spread into the room as Florie entered holding a candlestick.

"How's yer shoulder?" she said coldly, taking a seat between Francis and Hercules and extinguishing her candle.

"I anticipate it'll be good as new before the fortnight," said Francis, smiling.

"Agnes, of course, would do a better job," said Florie.

Francis stayed silent, fearful of invoking Florie's anger. She had been civil these past few days. She had tended to his wounds with potions and poultices, even burning some herbs to numb the pain while he slept. Yet, she remained cold. Francis had tried to end the rift between them but all of his mild advances had been unsuccessful.

"I suppose we should prepare the hall," said Hercules getting to his feet.

The three of them left the reception room and made for the Great Hall. Hercules drew his wand from a holster he kept hidden under his hose. Together, he and Francis cast charms, levitating the seats and placing them gently upon the ground for the guests.

"It all looks easier with a wand. Why shouldn't I have one?" said Florie, lifting and straightening the chairs by hand.

"I don't know," said Hercules, "it's just always been that way, only Warlocks carry wands. Something to do with education, I guess. Though it does seem half-witted now there's only two of us."

Their conversation was stopped by the sound of a soft thudding on the roof.

"They're here," said Francis, straightening his half-cape again. He strode to the dais and cast his last spell at the ground. From in between the footboards, tree roots sprouted up and snaked their way across them. The wood continued to twist, grow and writhe until they took the shape of the coven throne. Francis took his seat to more thuds on the roof. Hercules made his way to the great wooden doors and thrust them open so people could enter.

One by one the witches entered, depositing their brooms against the wall and taking their seats. Francis watched them arrive. They all wore dark cloaks with heavy cowls to cover their approach in the night sky. For several years past there were an increasing number of members who refrained from ever lowering their hood, choosing to keep their identity hidden. Francis noted that many more had chosen to keep their hoods up for this meeting.

He tried to gauge the feeling in the room by looking upon those who did show their face. Some looked back up at him with curiosity, some with awe, but there were those who displayed only a rank indignation. Even worse, he saw, was a small number who showed fear.

Once everyone had arrived, Hercules walked between the rows of seats and took Agnes' usual place on the dais, where the lectern formed itself from the roots of the throne. The remaining two mantled councilmen followed and took the furthest seats either side of Francis.

"In place of Agnes, who is not currently with us, I will conduct today's proceedings. We welcome ye all to this gathering of the Great Order of the Kelpie, Lowland Coven, formerly Lothian Coven. Please be seated," said Hercules, motioning for everyone to sit.

"My apologies for the lack of meetings these past months, but we live in turbulent times." Some of the congregation glanced at Francis. "As such, we will keep proceedings brief. As ye know, Agnes was captured by witch hunters and, under torture, did accuse our Grand Warlock, Francis Stewart, formerly Earl Bothwell, of witchcraft and thus causing him to be outlawed."

Hercules paused as the crowd shifted uneasily. "There are some decisions for the council to make," he continued, "so we needs must elect another person to the council, at least in a temporary capacity until Agnes is back with us, so we are able to vote. Since there are no other Warlocks in this coven, it needs be a yeoman member. Is there anyone who would like to put themselves forward for the nominations?"

Hercules looked over the hall and for a while nobody stood, until Florie, from the front row, rose from her chair. Francis' heart shot into his throat. She stood while Hercules continued to wait for other nominations. Nobody else put themselves forward.

"Then no vote is required," said Hercules, "Please welcome the newest council member, Miss Florie Sampson."

Florie made her way to the seat on Francis' left and Hercules paused for the round of applause that typically accompanied new council members. When there was none, he carried on.

"Before the council raises its own motions, I cede the floor to the members of this coven. Please though, do keep the topic to our current plight." Hercules looked around the room waiting for somebody to talk when he cut across himself. "Hold on, where is Torcull?" suddenly noticing the absence of the enormous figure.

A man near the back of the room stood. "Brother John of Galloway," he introduced himself. "We received news that the giants have moved further north to the Highlands ever since the witch hunters began their scouring of the landscape. I anticipate Torcull will not be joining us."

"Ah," said Hercules, blushing, "well, is there any business ye wish to bring before this council?" He said, addressing the room.

Eventually, one woman stood up, "Sister Mary of Kelso. I address the Grand Warlock directly when I ask how he proposes to keep us safe!?" she said in a squeaky yet stern voice. The hall echoed with sparse and staggered cries of "Hear, hear!"

Francis stood and made his way to the lectern. "It is true, Sister Mary, I have failed Sister Agnes in my duty as a Warlock. I and my network were unable to locate her. Yet I believe it evident to all here, I have suffered in my failure."

"I have borne all the peril in the face of this great tragedy, *not* this coven. I will continue to suffer that burden for you all. Nonetheless, in the meantime, I think it prudent to follow Brother Hercules' policy of suspending all coven meetings, excepting emergency, until such time as we deem it safe."

"And what of the peril Agnes *still* yet faces, rotting in the King's dungeon! She faces burning!" challenged Florie from her seat. The crowd repeated its nervous shuffle at this direct confrontation. Before Francis could answer, Hercules stepped in front of him at the podium.

"Sister Florie, we will address the manner of Agnes' rescue, but 'tis a separate matter. I think it sage we address first Sister Mary's concern regarding coven safety since she has raised it." He kept a sympathetic eye on Florie as he turned back towards the throng.

"Expanding on the Grand Warlock's words, I think it necessary that magical activity should cease. Bury yer equipment and be wary of neighbours. My ravens are following the movements of the witch hunters and come direct to me in any danger. Does that satisfy you Sister Mary?"

"So we're to stop being witches altogether?" she said.

"My apologies, no, 'tis a temporary arrangement until we can figure a better solution to keep you all safe."

Another member stood rapidly, "Brother Bruce of Fife, and how long is this *temporary* arrangement to last? My wife's healing puts bread on the table!"

"Er, until we can be safe," said Hercules, eyes darting about the room.

"We'll ne'er be safe!" Shouted a harsh voice from the back. "The witch hunters have been through my town thrice already, 'tis but a matter of time!"

"We should go north like the giants!" Another shouted and suddenly the whole room erupted into fractious yelling and jostling.

Francis withdrew his wand and shot a bright green ball of light, high into the centre of the hall which exploded with a loud bang. Some of the crowd screamed, then they all fell silent. He stepped back to the lectern again.

"Brother Bruce is right. We'll never be safe until the witch hunters are eradicated. This is a war now. We must remove the head of the beast, Maitland Lord Thirlstane," he turned to Florie to address her directly, "for we know now that he is indeed the head." He turned back to the coven, "We must remove his person from about the King in order to restore normality to the realm."

Florie stood, "That has been yer plan these past months and look where ye are now!" The mass became restless again and a few more cheers of "hear, hear!" cut the air.

Francis held up a hand, "I have admitted my failures and suffered for them have I not? Before, I did not know where to look, now I can strike Maitland down as soon as he is unguarded and his lean-witted lap dog Osywn too for that matter. For 'tis Maitland, too, who does defame me so. He speaks poison in the King's ear. Given an audience with his Majestie, I will restore his faith in me."

The assembly seemed to become aswirl as some nodded in agreement and others demonstrated their frustrations. Florie remained standing.

"And where does Agnes come into all this? Her sentencing is to be carried out next year. A whole *year* Francis!" Her indignation had turned to pleading.

The two, though keeping their voices raised for the benefit of the crowd, spoke directly to each other.

"I will have Agnes out before even her trial. I just need time to raise the borders, gather men and supplies. I saw Agnes, her image haunts my every waking moment. I will *not* allow her to suffer any longer than is within my earthly power."

Florie looked back into Francis' sombre gaze. Her vice grip on the arms of her chair softened when she saw a sadness and a resolve in them. Then, her defiant facade broke with a muffled whimper and she sat back down. Francis turned back to the crowd.

"I agree with Sister Florie!" said Bruce. "A pox on this primped up Maitland. We should put all our efforts to rescuing Agnes and go! To the Highlands or England or France even!"

Hercules, who had been stood considering his own stance on the matter, signalled to Francis that he should field this latest outburst.

"I think Warlock Francis is right on this one Brother Bruce. If the witch hunters are allowed to flourish, they will infect not only the whole of Scotland but elsewhere. If they are proven effectual, even France will set up its own orders until we are hunted from the face of this earth like vermin. *Nevertheless,* I do take the points of others. It is true we have tried this policy before and failed, worse, we are likely in more danger. To move this along I would like to put a motion to this council that we at least *try* to fight back. *If* we do not succeed by a month before Agnes' sentencing, we will make an attempt to rescue her and proceed to somewhere safe, together."

Hercules looked out over the coven and could see that there was general agreement amongst the mass. Certainly, nobody moved to block the motion. He slowly to face the four other council members.

"Nays, raise yer hands," he said. Nobody moved.

"Ayes?" he said. Francis, Hercules and one of the flanking council members raised their hand. The other and Florie kept there's down.

"The Ayes have it. Lord Francis shall raise troops for the removal of Lord Maitland and the witch hunters. Until then, all non-urgent magick activity and coven meetings are to be suspended. I believe that concludes the matter."

Slowly the councilman who hadn't cast his vote raised his frail hand. He lowered his hood to reveal a shock of long white hair and an inexorably wrinkled face. "I would like to propose a motion."

"Brother Conall, of course," said Hercules.

"I propose before this campaign is undertaken that the Warlocks of this coven do seek out the wise Elf of the Wood of Cree for guidance and bestowments of favour."

"Brother Conall, do we even know if the elf still lives? It's been some time since anyone last saw them," said Hercules.

"I know not, I request only the Warlocks seek out his counsel and magick. He has aided us in times past."

"Of course, straight to the vote shall we? The ayes?" Both Conall and the other councilman raised their hands, as well as Hercules, keen to keep favour with the coven.

"Well, the ayes have it. Francis, you will seek out the Cree Elf," said Hercules. Francis raised an eyebrow at Hercules, who shrugged.

"With an action proposed I suggest we conclude matters there. Besides, it gets late. Please all return safely to your homes. Fly high and don't get seen!"

There was a great scraping as everyone heaved themselves out of their seats and made for the exits. They nattered as they left, grabbing their broomsticks and making for the roof.

Once most of the congregation had left, Florie jumped up out of her chair and ran to Francis. She wrapped him up in a tight hug. Francis, his arms aloft, looked at Hercules for some kind of an explanation. He smiled and shrugged again.

"Oh! I'm sorry Francis. I'm so sorry," she said. "I've been so cruel to ye and yer've got yer wound and yer an outlaw now." Tears dropped onto Francis' chest. "Yer deserve it, mind, yer great codpiece. I've just been so... so angry and... lost without Agnes. But yer'll get her now won't ye? What did she look like? Ye never told me."

Francis softened and pulled Florie tighter to him. "She looked well Florie, she's a strong woman. She could teach that wagtail Maitland a thing or two about toughness."

Francis felt Florie smile, "I'm comin' with ye ye know. I'm comin' ter fight."

"I don't suppose I really have a choice in the matter."

* * * * *

1st July 1591
Holyrood Palace

James looked out over the fields. Lords had been arriving with their men for several days. Tents of different sizes and colours had been assembled on the first plot of land the soldiers had come upon. They formed a haphazard maze of poles and guy lines. Smoke rose from fires hidden somewhere between the structures as the men enjoyed their breakfast and ale.

James was already armoured and upright in front of his command tent. The flaps were tied wide open to reveal a large table with simple cloth chairs around it. Some of the seats were occupied by lords in various states of dress. On top of the table, held in place with tankards, was a great hand-drawn map of southern Scotland. Upon it castles and towers had been drawn marking Francis' strongholds.

"'Tis already long enough past sunup," said James. "I want these tents cast down and the army ready to march before noon. Hopefully by then others will have joined us."

"And where is it exactly we march to Your Grace? Your scouts have not found Lord Bothwell," said one of the Lords.

"We march to Kelso. That's where his wife is and it's where he'll raise the borders."

"Pardon, Your Grace, but if we march to Kelso, certainly we do cut off his advance to Edinburgh from the East March, but if he comes from the south, from Crichton or Hermitage he may be able to take the city or come upon our rear."

"If he does, our scouts will notify us. Whichever route we choose we damn ourselves, so 'tis better we march to his wife and ward his children."

"Sire, if that be the case, do we need this many men? We could split our force. Some one thousand five hundred have turned up between us and you anticipate more lords will arrive with their armies before noon?" said another of the men around the table.

"'Tis better to be safe. Francis has raised more than that number before and if the northern Catholics come to support him, we'll be outnumbered. In all honesty, I fear we have not raised enough. Hence the artillery."

When nobody replied, James turned around and placed both hands on the table. "I assume your silence means there are no further questions. Go then, ready your men. Be sure they are well mustered. I want them to look impressive as we march through the country. This should be a show of the crown's might, any philandering I will treat as a personal insult. Go!"

The lords stood, performed short bows and made haste towards their areas of the camp. James ordered his stewards to cast down his own tent and sat in the morning sun, considering those who had not shown yet.

It had taken until just after noon to organise the camp and sort the new arrivals into the marching order. The estimate James had received was at 3,000 men. James sat on his horse and watched the procession pass him along the south-eastern road. Most were infantry. The pikemen carried huge 15ft polearms that towered above them and swayed as they marched and the musketeers, nestled between them, carried their pieces over one shoulder while containers of powder oscillated from bandoliers across their chests. To the fore and aft of the infantry were the hackbutters, mounted musketeers, and lancers. Lastly, the wagon train brought up the rear, heavy oxen heaving the carts loaded with tents and supplies, as well as the heavy artillery.

James anticipated they could perhaps only move 15 miles a day, making the march to Kelso a three-day affair. Furthermore, Francis would likely know of their coming already and he'd spent huge sums of gold fortifying his residences at Kelso. James sighed as he began to doubt his own actions. He wanted to suppress Bothwell's pride and arrogance, but some wild skirmish up and down the country was not something he could afford. *Damn that man!*

* * *

The vanguard had already formed up in the fields as James gazed down on the town of Kelso. The tower of the abbey rose high above any of the other buildings. A lone, towering reminder of the grace of God. The river Tweed snaked in a great arc on the southern side of the town, embracing it with a natural moat against would-be English aggressors. It was late afternoon and the evenings preparations should be well underway, yet the village folk had all come to the edge of the cluster of buildings to see the King's armies.

On the outskirts was Francis' residence. The windows of the tower house were built up high so no soldiers could enter through them, and the roof was surrounded with extended castellated walls for musketeers to rain down fire. The corners of the house were where Francis had improved the construction. Circular towers of differing heights adorned them, in some places jutting out, away from the main structure of the house, allowing more walkways and to act as bastions.

There were lights glinting from inside the windows but James saw no signs of soldiers or cavalry. His attention was drawn away from the house when an officer from the vanguard came riding up to him.

"Your Grace," he said, with a little bow from his saddle, "we've sent riders into the town. They say they've seen neither hide nor hair of the Lord Bothwell."

"Then who's in his house?" asked James.

"The Lady Margaret and the children sire," said the officer.

"Furnish me more cavalry for my guard and march your men behind me. I think we should pay the countess a little visit."

The officer rode off, shouting at his aides to get his men moving. James cantered down the slope at a more leisurely pace. By the time he reached the formation some twenty cavalry had already lined up to be joined to James' personal guard. James motioned for them to ride ahead towards the house.

He decided to err on the side of caution and halted his horse a hundred yards away and gave the forward riders the order to continue without him. As they approached, he watched the windows and battlements, fearing some volley of gunfire at any second. None came and his horsemen had already dismounted by the time James felt safe enough to kick his horse forward.

Someone knocked on the door as he approached and a steward opened it. He dismounted smartly and walked up the stone steps to cross the threshold. Inside Margaret was already waiting in the hallway. She wore a simple dress and a sober expression.

"Your Grace, I had not anticipated your visit," she said. "Please excuse my lack of preparation, I do perhaps have some wine that you may find to your liking?"

James looked over his shoulder to his captain, "Search the place, check for priest holes... *Don't* break anything," he added quickly. "We are guests in Lady Margaret's home."

"Please, don't mind the children," she said genially to the soldiers, "they are currently conducting their lessons quietly upstairs. Please, Your Grace, come into our dining hall here and we will drink and talk."

They both stepped through into a lavish dining room. Paintings hung from the green painted walls and a great chandelier shadowed a highly polished table. The wine Margaret had spoken of was already waiting on the table with two silver goblets. James removed his riding gloves slowly and placed them on the table, looking about the room.

"Mm, this wine is quite to my liking, thank you Margaret. So, I think it safe to say Francis is not here? If he were, I'd have expected more of a resistance."

"No, I am afraid not, Your Grace. I haven't seen him at all since your proclamation."

"Ah, so it reached you? You've read it?" asked James.

"Yes sire, I've read it. Everyone south of Inverness has read it, Your Majestie," she said, watching the King.

"Yet, you have nothing at all to say about it?" said James.

"I would petition you my King, for leniency and clemency. You know Francis has never born you any ill will. Even at the Brig O'Dee 'twas Maitland he sought. Though, from the harshness of your horning, I fear your mind is made up on the matter."

"'Tis Margaret. He's pushed the boat out too far. There is only so much I can forgive before he must face my retribution. No other lord in Scotland, nay, the known world, has gotten away with as much! My leniency for Francis is all but used up."

"Have you heard reports of his whereabouts, Your Grace? Is he raising the borders?"

"Nay," James sighed, "I've heard nothing. If he had a force, I'd have heard about it by now."

"You know if you pursue this he'll fight. By any means necessary he'll fight you, be it with Catholics or Spaniards. He wouldst not want to, Your Highness, but he would. He knows no other way."

"Precisely why he needs a thrashing!" said James. "He should live in fear of his King, not making a constant mockery of me."

"Then give him a way out," said Margaret, reaching out to hold James' hand. "Restore to him his lands and rents and ask for him to resume his wardship. You hope to extinguish his pride, so be it, but if you corner a beast it will fight tooth and nail to get out. Whereas if you offer him a route to his cage, he will take it. Besides, if he does not take your offer then you have shown mercy on your enemy and will win others to your cause."

James considered her words for a moment then barked with laughter. "Margaret! You give better counsel than my own court! It should be you as chancellor, not Maitland or Francis. Alas, I have already shown myself to be too kind and merciful a King. There comes a time when one must be strong and hard-hearted."

"I will grant you though, that I have not the energy nor the patience to chase Francis up and down the country. Nay. There is some wisdom in your words and I shall consider them."

"Most excellent Your Grace," said Margaret, bowing her head.

"I had thought to take you all into my wardship, however, now I think it not necessary. I shall take just your eldest, what's the scamp's name? Francis, after his father isn't it? Of course, he will be given the best care and tutors." said James waving a hand. "As hard as it may be for a wife, keep yourself out of this and no ill shall befall you."

"Now, have you any food? I am starved."

Chapter 8

1st August 1591
Wood of Cree

"There's just one more road to cross," said Francis.

The trio couched and walked steadily through the undergrowth. The summer had been unnaturally warm and the thickets had grown dense and tall. They pushed their way through until they could see the causeway. Francis ventured out just beyond the bushes and looked left and right. *Damn it!* he thought.

They had come out on a wide curve. He couldn't see more than fifty yards in either direction. He hushed the other two and put his ear to the ground. He was about to give the order to cross when he heard what he was listening for, the barely audible rumble of hooves. Francis dove back into the cover of the bushes.

"Just two riders I think, close," he said.

"Two?" said Florie, "Then we can just do away with them?"

"No," said Hercules, "when they don't return to whoever sent them this area will be swarming with hundreds more."

Francis nodded silently. He withdrew his wand and pointed it at the bracken around them.

"*Qwatso,*" he whispered. Slowly the stems of the scrub rose up and moved under the influence of his wand. Francis pulled and shaped them, directing their fluctuations like a conductor, forming a leafy cocoon around the group. Hercules let out a hiss when one of the riders became visible through the gaps in the leaves. Francis tried to hurry his work as best he could but was forced to stop when the other rider became into view. He pulled Florie and Hercules down on top of him into a cramped prone position as the riders came within earshot.

"It'll be harvest soon, cannae be doin' wi this ridin' aroond," said the front rider.

"Aye," said the second.

"Me wife'll chop me balls oof if we have another low yield."

"Aye."

"There's nay reward to be had wi' this work. Nay pillaging, nay food. I'm tellin' ye, if they dunnae find tha' Earl by next week, he's already in France and I'm leavin' fer home."

"Aye."

"Let's stop Davie, I need to relieve meself."

"Inn soon, wait."

"Ach, I dunnae think a can."

"I buy ale, wait."

"Well, I cannae argue wi' that. Good man Davie. I've always seid ye were a good man."

The two continued their one-sided conversation all the way down the path until, mercifully, thought Francis, they left earshot.

"Davie is a talkative man is he not?" Florie giggled, standing and pushing back the bracken swaddle. Francis stepped out of their hiding place and walked to the middle of the path. He checked both ways then ushered the other two across the road.

"They're right though, I suppose. It's a waste of time being oot here. Couldn't we just say we tried to visit this elf?" said Florie.

"If we don't the coven and our duty doesn't mean much," said Hercules sadly, "besides, it seems to be working to our favour. The soldiers have farms to attend to. They'll all be going home soon."

"Only because it's taken us weeks walkin' on foot! I know, I know, *we cannae use the roads!*" She said imitating Hercules' voice.

"Florie is right, unless this elf soars to Holyrood and murders Maitland himself, I can't imagine this trip being much use," said Francis, kicking a stone as he walked.

"I don't know," said Hercules, "maybe Conall knows something we don't. He has to have a reason for imposing this journey upon us."

"The only thing Conall knows is how to dribble," laughed Francis. Florie added her guffawing to his as they walked through the forest.

"Ye know, for a man outlawed by the King, yer in good spirits Francis," said Hercules.

"I suppose things can't get any worse from here. I truly believe the King will soften eventually. He has before, and I look forward to the prospect of killing that fool-born Maitland. It'll be Ludovic and I running the country," said Francis, kicking his stone again.

"Wait!" said Hercules, stopping in his tracks. He chased after the stone Francis had just kicked and picked it up. "This is elf-shot! We must be close."

They all stood close and peered through the forest, neither of them entirely sure what exactly it was they were looking for. Hercules crouched and tried to look for any signs of tracks while Francis pricked his ears.

"Shh, do you hear that?" said Francis. In the silence all they could hear was the rustling of the light breeze through the treetops, then the noise came again. It sounded like sticks rattling in a pot, though it only lasted for a brief moment. His eyes scanned his surroundings, trying to identify the source. Slowly, he cast them upwards into the branches of the trees. He was about to tell Hercules to carry on looking for tracks when he saw a shimmer, the bark of a trunk appeared to be shifting ever so slightly, like a thousand minuscule insects were crawling over it. Then, as he narrowed his eyes the shimmer jolted. It jumped from one branch to the next. Then another.

"*Sedag!*" shouted Francis. The shimmer stopped in mid-air and he used his wand to manipulate it down to the ground. He approached it and gave it a kick with his boot.

"Ow!"

Francis looked around at his two companions who nervously kept their distance. He reached out a hand and felt fine silken cloth between his fingers. He pulled at it and the cloth came away to reveal a tall figure, at least a head taller than Francis. He kept his wand on his target and moved to face them.

The figure looked feminine, though it was hard to tell, all of their features were somehow both soft and pointed like no person he'd ever seen. Their hair was long and white, reaching to the posterior and kept back with a silver headpiece. They wore a long robe of green and silver that looked finer even than silk. Yet, the more Francis looked at it the more the colours seems to blend together, dancing in and out of one another, glimmering. The robe clung tight to the stranger's body which was lean and supple. On their hip they wore a short quiver with arrows, which must have been the source of the noise.

"Are you going to let me go?" said the stranger, in an airy voice.

"Are ye going to hurt us? Are you the Cree Elf?" said Francis, adjusting his footing into more of a fighter's stance.

"No and yes. Why, what were you expecting?" replied the elf.

"I'm not sure," said Francis, "A little man with a beard and a pointy hat I suppose." He winced, even he knew how juvenile that sounded. He flicked his wand to the side, releasing the elf from his spell but he kept it trained on them. "Why were you hiding from us?"

"I have to be careful," they said, "I'm the last elf of these woods. I've been following you for days."

"We were sent to come find you by a member of our coven. Do you have somewhere we can go? A home perhaps?"

The elf laughed airily, their voice seeming to carry tunefully on the breeze, "This is my home, all around you. Do sit, you are quite safe, and please eat, I've barely seen any of you have food."

The elf raised their dainty hands over the ground, spreading their fingers out wide. Francis rechecked his stance as the earth began to move beneath his feet.

The natural world shifted, moving together as one to form earthen stools and a small table, made up of a mixture of wood, plants and grass. Squirrels, birds and mice revealed themselves from all different directions, bringing fresh wild berries and fruits. They assembled them on the table in a fanciful arrangement to rival any banquet and scurried away, back to wherever they had come from.

"*She* doesn't need a wand," said Florie, taking her seat first. "Pardon, are ye a boy elf or a girl elf?"

The elf repeated it's enchanting laugh, "I am cheered to see humans have not changed. Obsessed with genera so they might know whether they should hump something or kill it."

Florie blushed, "I did nay wanna take yer to bed," she muttered under her breath.

"I did not expect as much child," said the elf to Florie's horror. Her face turned a deeper shade of scarlet. "Merely, that humans must needs classify the world about them so simply."

Florie resorted to stuffing her face with berries to avoid speaking any further and Hercules tucked into the food himself. Francis, instead, sat studying the elf. Every time he looked at their face, their features shifted. He could see that their right eye was milky white, with a forked scar running from their forehead to their cheek. It wasn't red and lumpy like his own scars but recessed and silver, elegant. They had not a single wrinkle but he could tell they were old. He got the sense that they were most likely older than anything earthly he'd ever seen. Yet, quite simply, they were beautiful. He jolted when he realised the elf was staring back at him.

"Er... Well... I... Well. I'm not quite sure what I am to say. We were sent without instruction." said Francis.

"Why is it you *think* you've been sent here," said the elf.

"Truly, I do not know. For guidance and favour?"

"Ah, I see. And what is it you seek guidance for?"

"Well, er, I got myself into a predicament ye see. I was a bad lad and was outlawed by the King. I have never meant him any harm, but my actions have been, well, poorly thought out. We're planning to destroy one of his advisors whom we believe to be behind his actions," said Francis. "They also have captured one of our own and by destroying him we hope to release them."

The elf reached out and touched Francis' hand, closing their eyes. "Yes, I can sense you have caused a great deal of pain for many people Francis."

"How did you know my name?" said Francis pulling back his hand.

The elf opened their good eye. "I listen to the travellers as they pass through my woods. I know who you are. I am an elf, not a hermit." They smiled and closed their eye again, pulling Francis' hand back.

"You do, however, face a perilous path ahead. Ill deeds, such as the murder you propose, *can* undo others, though good ones are better. Particularly as you seek to repair broken relationships. You are no longer an adolescent, yet you still behave with all the impetuousness of one."

Francis looked at Hercules and Florie who, as he suspected, wore sickeningly knowing expressions. He quickly looked back down at his hand entwined with the elf's.

"You must consider each action with the care and attention you would give each step when traversing a narrow ledge. Take one false move and you will plummet far into the depths of loneliness, dejection and sadness." The elf opened their eyes. "I fear, young Lord, I have no great prophecy or prediction for you. I know not what you were told our meeting would bring. Your actions are purely your own and your fate is determined by your choices. Yet, I beseech you to realise the precipice you stand on."

Francis nodded.

"I am the last elf of these woods or any other within a five-day march. Do not lose sight of what is important in this world and pursue it with all the veracity that exists within you."

Francis nodded again, his plans whipping past his mind's eye.

"Now, while I do so enjoy company, it would be selfish of me to consume more of your time. All of you have great work to do and share heavy burdens, you shouldn't dally. Please, stay, eat, fill your bellies but then begone from this place. Francis, my cloak if you don't mind."

Francis looked at his companions and saw they were as bewildered and disappointed as he was. He reached out his hand to give the elf their cloak when the elf grasped it tightly. The world seemed to stop. It was blurry, like he was passing everything at speed, yet everything was fixed in its place. He looked up at the elf and their white eye was now a pulsating beacon of purplish light.

"Do not be frightened," they said, in a much deeper, echoing voice than before and without moving their lips. "I speak directly to you alone. You have a grand role to play in the betterment of witches and their relationship with this world. Do your duty and you will find your path simple. But beware, Francis, of those in whom you place your trust. They care not for you but only seek to further themselves. You will be betrayed and it will derail everything you are destined to build."

The world seemed to come back round to a halt, despite the fact he'd never left his stool. The elf took their cloak and fastened it around their neck. The cloak shifted and refracted the light, hiding their body.

"Good morrow, travellers, and fair journeys," said the elf before pulling up their hood and returning to its concealed state. Up close, it was obvious there was something present. A silhouette was still visible, changing the light, but when the elf leapt into the treetops Francis lost sight of them.

"That's it?" said Florie, "Pull yer britches up and mind how yer go? Me maw could've given the same advice. Oh, so sorry we're late Agnes, we had to go see an elf and eat berries." She mocked. "Damned jack-a-nape."

Hercules frowned when he realised he had no rebuke for Florie's assertions.

"It's nay bother, would've had to wait some anyhow." said Francis. "My plan is already underway. I'd sent messengers to Ludovic and to the borders before we left. By time we're back we should have replies and we can get to work!"

* * * * *

3rd September 1591
Holyrood Gardens

"The men are ready for your inspection, Lord," said Oswyn, bowing as he entered an antechamber at the rear of the palace.

"Splendid," said Maitland, rising from his chair and donning his cloth hat. Together they stepped out of Holyrood into the palatial gardens.

Oswyn had mustered the men to the very rear of the palace's gardens in an open field. It was already proving to be a hot day and Maitland was perspiring heavily by the time he reached the formation. Equipment had been laid out for his inspection and for demonstration.

There were fifty men or so in the retinue, organised into a square. They were all dressed in the same grey uniform as Oswyn, though, for the muster they had been cleaned and pressed. On their chests they wore their pins of the horned devil and the inscription, '*Deorum Agens Contra Malum*'.

Maitland inspected each and every one of the men. He checked their clothes, their teeth and questioned their devotion to God. All of them were volunteers, their recruitment had been simple after Francis' denunciation as a witch at the Mercat Cross. Many had seen or heard of witches accused, but it was the first time in the memory of most that a member of the nobility had been dubbed a witch. It had created a fear that ran through all echelons of society. These men were hardly the finest in all of Scotland, thought Maitland, but he didn't need soldiers, he needed ruthless killers.

"Are we ready for the demonstrations, lord?" said Osywn, wringing his hands with excitement.

"Carry on, Osywn," said Maitland, unsure as to how he'd react to his investments.

"Very good, lord," said Oswyn, almost jumping for joy. "As you are aware, we have consulted a minister of the kirk for their advice in combating witchcraft. The key, we have found, is cold iron. Step forward Duncan," said Osywn to one of the witch hunters in the front rank. Duncan stepped dutifully forward and Oswyn pulled up his shirts. "See here, sire, a ward against spellcraft. We have had smelted thin iron sheets, sewn into their shirts. Now, as I am sure you would point out, these would not stop lead shot, but we work here against the agents of the devil! Thus, we must adjust our means of defence."

Maitland tapped at the thin iron plate, "you could make one of these shirts for me Osywn?"

"Already done sire, in a finer cloth than this," said Osywn. "Now, to weaponry. The harquebus is noisy, slow to reload and does not fit the demands of our outfit. Instead, we have chosen to repurpose some old crossbows."

"The tips of the bolts have been fitted with also with iron and the shafts are of hazel. If you would step this way with me, Lord, the men will show you what they have learned."

Oswyn pulled Maitland to the edge of the formation. The front rank all had crossbows by their feet and five bolts each.

"Front rank! Draw!" Shouted Oswyn. The front rank picked up their weaponry and with their foot in the cocking stirrup heaved back the strings of their bows into the latching mechanisms with goats-foot levers.

"Knock!" They picked up their bolts, placed them in the flight grove and held up their crossbows, ready to fire.

"Loose at will!" Came Oswyn's order. They squeezed their triggers, and the strings twanged forward, loosing the bolts as one. They thudded into their straw targets with loud thwacks and already they were winching back their strings for the second shot. They continued their volley until every man had expended their bolts and the targets resembled human-sized pin cushions.

Osywn grinned proudly. "We do have some firearms sire, and for those we have had iron shot cast. Just in case we are needing them, though I take it you are satisfied with the bows?"

"Very, Oswyn, you work fast. These recruits appear well drilled. I'll see to it you are rewarded," said Maitland.

"Thank you, lord. Naturally they are versed in prayer also, to protect them and their families from curses and the like. We have more demonstrations if you would see them Lord. All their weaponry is iron, down to their dirks," said Oswyn hopefully.

"I'm contented with what I've seen, thank you Oswyn. Step up these men's rations and continue to drill them. When and wherever Bothwell rears his fat head I want them ready," said Maitland.

"But sire, they've worked hard on their manoeuvres."

"And it will serve them well, I'm sure, in the conflicts to come." said Maitland, already beginning to walk towards the palace.

"Might I walk with you sire?" said Osywn. Maitland nodded and Oswyn jogged to catch up to the chancellor.

"Forgive me sire, but what is the plan for these men?" said Oswyn.

"Acquiring them was the first step my dear Oswyn. Though, I do not yet know if their training will be effective against the witch. What Francis has done, if it be true, I had not thought possible."

"Of course it be true, sire. Why, the witch did confess so," said Oswyn, with indignancy.

"Aye, you will forgive me Osywn, but I remained a sceptic. I still do, but the manner of his escape bears no earthly explanation. Unless Bothwell has equipment and weaponry beyond which my knowledge extends, he must be a witch" he said. "I fear greatly for the state of the realm if he is allowed to return to court."

"Surely not lord, the King would not allow it," said Oswyn.

"The *King*," said Maitland, a sudden venom in his voice "marched three thousand men to Kelso and came back with only a boy. Already the armies have naught but dispersed and we remain exposed once more, at the hands of a witch no less. I fear that we have not yet seen the extent of his devilish powers." Maitland shivered. "I fear, perhaps selfishly for my own skin, it's me he seeks to remove."

"He has both tried and failed already lord. The devil is powerful, there can be no doubt, but those who take solace in God's grace cannot be harmed," said Oswyn.

"I hope you are correct. Though without knowledge our weapons are useless, you cannot read can you Oswyn?" asked Maitland.

"No lord," said Oswyn.

"Then recruit someone who can, a minister or a clerk. Have them read every book available on the subject to the recruits and you," he said, stopping and turning to Oswyn, "are to study with him. Learn the ways of the witch, find accounts, determine their strengths, their weaknesses. Beyond cursed iron. Where a usual guard might fall for trickery our soldiers must be ever vigilant. Wherever Francis and Agnes come from, there must be more. You, Oswyn, are to be mine and the realm's sword and shield against this threat."

Oswyn grinned at the import stressed on his new role. "And the plan lord, you mentioned a plan?"

"My agents amongst him have informed me that Bothwell readies himself to attack my person and prostrate himself before His Majestie. We cannot let the King repeat his mistakes, we must perform our duty to the realm and ensure the Lord Francis is not permitted even the slightest opportunity of an audience with King."

"So, we are to murder him lord?" said Oswyn. Maitland rolled his eyes.

"Yes, Oswyn, we are to murder him. What's more, we are to entrap him. Where he can wholly disgrace himself, and his death can be in the cause of protecting the King. His memory will be reduced to an abhorrent stain and his lands distributed to those who have shown faith to the King and God. So, Oswyn, be sure your men are up to task."

Chapter 9

27th December 1591
Outside of Edinburgh

Francis sat atop his horse in all of his war gear. His polished steel cuirass reflected the moonlight, as did the white coat of his horse. It created, to the rest of the assembled horsemen, the image of a man sent directly from the heavens to rescue the realm from the clutches of its evil ministers. He looked down on Edinburgh. Castle Rock and the spires of St. Giles and other churches lay to the left, while on the right lay Holyrood Palace. There were no signs anyone knew of their coming, nor tolling of bells. Francis turned his horse away from the brow of the hill and to his captains.

"You all know the plan? Captain Colville, recount to me the start," said Francis.

"Aye sire, those with lances, under the command of Spott will cover the exits and protect our retreat. Yourself, Hercules, Niddrie and I will enter through the Duke of Lennox's stable entrance. There the entryway to the palace has been left guarded and unlocked. We will obtain the keys from the guardhouse, unlock the fore-gate and there we will let in the pistoleers and musketeers," said Colville.

"Most excellent," said Francis, beaming. "We must ride in silence to Holyrood. We will go around the eastern side of this hill and approach with haste from the eastern road. That gives us the most cover. Lancers will ride ahead and dispatch any resistance we do see. No powder! Ye hear me, I do not wish noise until we're inside the palace."

Francis looked around at the Captains, "Ludovic has assured me that both Maitland and the King are present at Holyrood and my other agents about the town did see them both going about their stately business. There is much sympathy for our cause. Tonight, we undo the failures of Brig O'Dee and remove Maitland once and for all! Go! Have your weapons loaded. Brief your men. We ride as soon as we are ready!"

The captains rode off to instruct their men one last time and prepare themselves for the raid. Francis dismounted and, under the pretence of leaving to pray, found a tree under which he could perform his private ritual. He withdrew his wand and re-burnt the protective rune into his skin. His wand gave off a light blue-ish glow as the heat seared his skin.

Once he was done, he sat, looking at the wound, his mind truly blank. He'd debated his plan for months, to the point of exhaustion. The elf's words had played on his mind, yet there seemed no other way. If he did not kill Maitland, he would be forced to leave Scotland. He exhaled and stood, covering his wrist with cloth.

He walked slowly back to his horse, ramming powder, wadding and shot into his pistols and depositing them in his sash. His waist was crowded with powder horns, leather pouches of shot, his dirk and not least his sword.

He mounted and his Captains were already waving to show they were ready. Bothwell motioned for Spott to ride ahead with his Lancers and followed quickly behind. He looked to his rear and already a cloud of dust hazed the sky as three hundred borderers made for Edinburgh.

As soon as they made it around the hill, they cantered their horses. Speed and precision were the name of the game. Already Francis could see the lights of Holyrood approaching.

The night air filled with the sound of a thousand hooves colliding with the soil. It was comforting to Francis, like the crackle of a good hearth is to some. He relaxed in the saddle and smiled to himself. The noise was defending in the midst of the cavalry, but Francis knew to even those on guard, it'd be but a low, barely audible rumble.

When they finally reached the edge of the palace, Spott rode on with some fifty horse, clearing the streets. Francis motioned for the musketeers to make their way slowly and quietly to the front gate, while he and his company of five rode straight into the stables. To his surprise, he found them completely clear. Ludovic had done well. The infiltrators dismounted, leaving their horses untied, and made for the entrance. The door had been left ajar so that a slither of light shone through the crack.

"The grouse season is over," he whispered through the gap.

"Though the partridges are good for another few months," came the reply.

Francis pushed open the door to find a steward in the livery of Lennox. *Ludovic had done very well indeed.* He winked at the guard and the five men entered the palace, remaining crouched as to stay below the window line. They made slow progress through the hallways, having to keep their swords and regalia from scraping along the floor. The keys were kept in a steward's room which was the other side of the kitchens.

By the time they reached the adjoining hallway their legs were stiff with cramp and they'd been halted by the patrolling of guards more than once. Outside the kitchen door, they could hear the noise of servants preparing late meals and cleaning the dishes of those already consumed. Francis nodded at Coleville, who removed his weapons and handed them to Hercules. He stood and waited outside the kitchen doors until the other four had concealed themselves, then huffed and strode into the kitchens.

"Where is Lennox's supper, it was ordered more than an hour ago!" He demanded.

"But Lennox..." began one of the cooks before Coleville slapped him hard across the face.

"But what boy!? I haven't time for yer insolence. Where is the steward who was sent, is he in here?" He said, moving towards the steward's room.

Nobody answered, instead opting to busy themselves with their work. Coleville stepped through into the steward's quarters. Two young boys playing cards looked up at him startled while others slept in improvised bunks. Coleville spotted the keys, they were exactly where they were supposed to be, hung on the wall barely a foot from the door. He positioned himself in front of them.

"None of you are the boy I gave orders to, are there others in the castle?" He said, as he slowly hooked his fingers around the key hoop.

"Yes sire, but they attend the upper floors. Is there anyone yer'd like me to fetch?" said one of the boys, trying to be helpful, while the other scowled at him for ratting on another.

"Nay lad, I didn't catch the scamps name. I'll go look myself."

With that Coleville lifted the keys and turned with one motion to hide any noise. Once turned he gripped the keys to stop them jangling. He put his head down and strode from the room, not stopping to acknowledge the cook he'd slapped. He made his way back into the lobby and closed the kitchen door, sighing with relief.

He nearly gasped aloud when he spotted a body in front of him, gushing blood from the neck. Francis was pulling the man into a corner and raised a finger for Coleville to keep quiet. He wiped the blade of his dirk on the man's clothes and stood, motioning for the others to do the same.

"May as well walk now," he whispered, "best be quick afore someone finds *that,*" he motioned at the body.

They all stood and made quickly for the front gate. The palace was arranged in a square with a courtyard in the middle. The front doors opened up on the western side and they had entered the stables from the southern. The kitchens were, as typical, located close to the front gates. They didn't have far to go before they came upon the grandiose entrance to the palace. Four of them positioned themselves, facing the inner courtyard, while Coleville went to the doors and fumbled with the keys.

"Hurry up Coleville," hissed Hercules, "someone's coming."

Coleville was hurriedly trying keys in the lock, none of them fit.

"Any moment now would be nice," said Francis, his vision trained on two shadows that were making their way across the courtyard. A few more steps and they'd be spotted and the alarm raised, with the backup locked outside the palace.

Coleville pushed another key into the lock, then, mercifully, it clicked and he turned the bolt. He began pushing the doors open, when others from outside grabbed them and helped force them open wide.

Francis turned to see fifty borderers waiting on the steps, their eyes glinting in the light of the burning chords on their muskets and he whooped for joy.

Coleville drew his sword and raised it up high in front of the cut-throat company.

"Justice!!" he yelled, "Justice fer Bothwell!!"

The men let out a blood-curdling roar before storming through the gates and into Holyrood. Francis' grin spread from ear to ear, their cry stirred a fire that welled up within him. It is the kind of fire only a warrior knows, when the battle is begun and all else is forgotten. He raised his own sword and joined his voice to theirs as he watched them charge past him.

They filled the entrance and spread into the corridors and courtyard.

"Fer Bothell!" and "Justice!" they repeated as they tore through the lobby.

The clamour was instantly drowned out by musket fire. The men pulled their triggers and the lit chords of the muskets swung down into the firing pans, igniting the powder with a great fizz. Fire, sparks and thick black smoke were blasted from muzzles and shot pounded into walls, doors and the soft flesh of the resistance that faced the bordermen.

The corridors and courtyard billowed with smoke and a number had already stopped behind walls and columns to reload. Thrusting the powder and shot down their barrels with ramrods.

Finally, the guards of the house had roused themselves and were fighting back. They fired from the upper windows, peppering the courtyard and any unlucky enough to have not found cover. Francis knew that they only had a short amount of time now to get to Maitland and the King. Spott could only keep the Edinburgh guard out for so long and their retreat would be cut off.

"This way!" shouted Francis over the clamour. He ran to a service staircase that opened up on the higher floors. The five of them raced up the spiral stairs. Francis tested to see if the door at the top was open and when it was, he nodded at the rest of his retinue before bursting through it.

A soldier was firing down into the courtyard and hadn't noticed his entrance. Francis charged, sword pointed at the small of his back. He ran him through entirely, jolting his arm when his sword struck the stone of the wall on the other side.

He used his foot to kick the body off his blade and looked around. Coleville and the others had already engaged with more defenders further down the hallway on their right.

He looked instead to Hercules and they took the left-hand route. They were still on the western side of the palace and they would need to fight their way to the east, where the King and Maitland would have their apartments. They rounded the corner to the northern corridor and saw that no resistance. Hercules looked quizzically at Francis and he shrugged. Through the windows they could see Coleville was still fighting his way around the other side.

There was nothing for it. Francis sheathed his sword and drew both his pistols. Hercules followed suit with his single firearm, then they hurtled down the full length of the hallway as fast as their legs could carry them.

A musketeer appeared round the far corner, muzzle raised and Francis dove at the ground. Hercules, instead, aimed his pistol. The two black powder pieces fired, casting flames at one another. The musket ball whizzed past Hercules, while his shot connected with the soldier's steel helmet with an enormous clang. Francis rolled at the bottom of his dive and prepared to fight the man, only to watch him fall backward and slump against the wall, knocked out cold by the blow.

Francis turned to Hercules, "Nice shot Brother!" He said, with a little too much incredulity for Hercules' liking.

They kept low as they approached the corner and Francis peered around it. The middle of the eastern hallway was where the main staircase opened up to the first floor. The borderers were fighting their way up to them and he could hear they were still shouting his name. The top of the stairs was thick with guardsmen.

Francis retreated back and looked at Hercules. "How do we get through? Can ye see Coleville through the windows? How's he doing?"

Hercules popped his head up above the windowsill to look across the courtyard at Coleville. "He's still fighting but it looks like they've barricaded off his route. They're exchanging fire, probably going to be a stalemate for some time."

"Curses! We'll have to go through the guest apartments," said Francis. "No doubt the occupants will have locked and barricaded the doors by now."

Francis drew his sword and pointed it at the nearest door. "*Tulexto,*" he whispered. Despite the musket fire echoing off the walls, he heard the satisfying sound of the lock clicking open.

"Yer wand still works through your sword?" asked Hercules.

"Why do ye think I put it in the handle," said Francis with a wink. "Ready?"

Hercules nodded and leaned forward. Silently the two charged the door, crashing into it with their shoulders lowered. The door swung open and they tripped over the furniture that lay scattered on the other side, accompanied by a woman's scream. Francis ducked at the ear-piercing noise and then saw a countess with her night skirts bundled about her in the corner of the room.

"My apologies dear lady," he said touching the brim of his helmet, "we mean ye no harm. Act as though we were not here."

Hercules thrust his head out of the door they had just barged. "Seems like nobody noticed," he said pushing it back closed behind him.

Francis nodded and prepared exactly the same way for the connecting door into the next apartment. This time the door was unbarricaded but when he pushed through, Francis was stopped short by a sword point. He raised his hands slowly and looked up from the tip to see an exceedingly elderly gentleman with a steely look in his eyes.

"We're not here for ye old man," said Francis.

"Then what're ye here fer, eh!? Yer rampallion. Yer'll nit invade the King's hoose on ma watch, no sire."

"Ach! We've no time fer this!" shouted Hercules. He thrust the old man's sword away with his own and punched him the guard of his hilt. Francis widened his eyes and stared at his half-brother.

"Hercules! Yer villain!" He laughed. Hercules simply tutted and made for the next door. This time he tested it and found it was unlocked. The door opened up into a narrow service corridor. On the left was a spiral staircase leading back down to the ground floor and in front of them was a second door.

"This is the Kings apartments," said Francis, "This leads to an ante-chamber and his bedchambers lie beyond. Are ye ready? There will be guards inside."

Hercules nodded. Francis unlocked the door, then sheathed his sword, redrawing both pistols. "I'll go first," he said.

He kicked the door open as hard as could. Then ran inside.

"Justice!" He shouted, then fired his left pistol at one shocked guard and his right at another. Hercules followed behind doing the same. Francis coughed as the black smoke filled the room. Then, with no sound at all, a bullet struck his helmet.

"Down!" Hercules shouted, he grabbed a table and threw it over for cover, then pulled a dazed Francis down with him.

"Are ye alright? Did they get ye?" He said.

"Nay, I don't think so," said Francis, using a hand to feel his head under his helmet as more missiles struck the table they were hiding behind. "Their muskets, they make no noise?"

"They're not muskets," said Hercules, reloading his pistols and cranking the wheel mechanism, "They're crossbows."

Francis shook his head, then, sure enough, saw the head of bolt protruding through the wood of their table. He reloaded his own pistols, shouting taunts at his attackers. Then appearing over the top of the table fired both shots off at once.

"By Guinevere's skirts!" He cursed. "It's a trap!"

Hercules eyed him, uncertain. "Look!" Said Francis, "the boards are nailed to the wall. They wanted us in here, so we'd be sitting ducks."

137

Hercules fired his own pistol over the table, using his fire to glance at the doorway. They had nailed boards up the full length of the opening leaving only a small slit from which to fire.

"Oh no!" said Francis suddenly. "Hercules, we need to get out! Any moment they're going to come in from behind us too."

More bolts cracked into the table which was steadily being reduced to splinters. Francis looked behind him at the service entrance, but it was too late, he could already see lights coming up the spiral staircase. The only other exit was a door to their right which led back out into the hallway where more fighting was still underway.

"A pox on Maitland's lumpish arse!" cursed Francis. "I'll have to use magic," he said, "Hopefully no-one will notice, ye should too if we're to make it out."

Hercules frowned but nodded. They fired their last real shots at the barricade then Francis cast his shielding charm so the two could move towards the hallway door. They hid themselves behind a huge oak dresser facing the two entrances and their backs to the hallway exit.

"Remember the pistol mimic spell I taught you?" He said, "use that, we'll take pauses pretending to reload but it'll be quicker and we won't get caught half-cocked. We'll pin these down then go back into the hallway."

"*Gasdh!*" Francis shot at the first man to appear through the service door. He fell back and the others wisely stayed out of kill zone in the door frame, instead opting to try and fire their crossbows at an awkward angle. Hercules continued to concentrate his fire on the men barricaded inside the King's chambers.

"Now!"

Francis pushed open the door behind them and burst through it, bracing themselves to be shot at any second. No musket cough sounded. Instead, he was met by cheers.

The borderers had succeeded in fighting their way up the staircase and were now pillaging the upper floors for anything that could be carried. Francis's shoulders collapsed in relief and he quickly slid his wand back into his sword hilt.

"In here lads!! The King's in here! To me! To me!"

Some of the borderers wilfully ignored him, continuing to loot but those nearest obeyed the order. Francis commanded five of them to stay on the door and keep up a volley of fire into the antechamber, and told Hercules to lead five more back through the guest apartments and attack their rear.

It was over in minutes. Those with an escape route fled and those stuck inside the King's chambers were either too wounded or had lost their fighting spirit altogether. Most of the firing within the palace had stopped and was replaced with the clamour of men shouting.

"Hammers!" Shouted Francis, "Bring Hammers."

"Francis," said Hercules, "it's past time we left."

"I know, I know. We're so close, a few more moments Hercules."

Hammers were brought and the boards to the King's chamber were pulled down. Francis stepped inside to find all the men were dead or dying close to their doorway firing position. Apart from one, who stood near the four-poster bed, not quite knowing what to do with himself. Francis strode over and grabbed him roughly about the neck.

"Where is the King!" He shouted, slamming a fist into the man's jaw.

He stammered, trying to get his words out and Francis punched him again.

"I... The King was never here," he spluttered.

Francis rolled his eyes and pulled the man's head down, bringing his knee up into his face. He went limp and Francis let him drop to the floor.

"Francis," said Hercules, "Francis, these aren't the King's guard. Look."

He was kneeling over one of the corpses. Hercules was right. The men wore strange grey uniforms he had never seen before. Hercules plucked a pin off their chest.

"Deorum Agens Contra Malum," He read aloud.

"God's agents against witches," Francis finished for him.

Chapter 10

17th February 1592
Falkland Palace

Maitland rode to the two imposing circular towers that guarded the entrance to Falkland Palace. He looked up at them as he approached as though they would talk to him and tell him what he was entering into. He dismounted, handed the reins to a steward and stepped through the gatehouse.

James was eating his supper alone in the dining room when Maitland found him. He was reading *Malleus Maleficarum* for what must be the hundredth time. He stopped reading only when Maitland was directly next to him.

"What news have ye from the South?" He said.

"Your Grace, Francis and his men retreated from Edinburgh in the first instance. Though, now, he seems to enjoy the freedom of the town."

James stabbed the chicken on his plate with such force the juices splattered over himself, Maitland and his book. Before answering he closed his eyes and drew in a deep breath.

"I can hardly put a whole town to the gallows," he said.

"Nay sire, he is too popular for his own good," said Maitland.

"I think it not his popularity rather than your *un*popularity," said James, glowering at his meal.

"Aye sire," said Maitland. Though, there was some truth in the King's words. The Brig O'Dee rebellion had been contrived exclusively to remove him from power He'd been unable to do much since to win the powerful lords over to his side. His reports were that Francis had won over local support with speeches against him.

"Worry not Maitland. I refuse to give in to that confounded gudgeon. I have already shown weakness. Here I sit, retreated to the north while he lauds himself about Edinburgh. Damn it, man! 'Tis an insult upon my very honour! He thinks he has won a victory, yet in truth, he simply makes it so I have no choice but to make an example of him, afore any toothless apple-john thinks he might attack a King's home to get his way. It matters no longer his intentions are principally against you Maitland, my proclamation was clear that it is an action against the King!"

"I am grateful for yer protection sire," said Maitland.

"I do it not to please you or show you any favour!" he spat. "Yer trap failed did it not. Yer witless toad!"

"Only, sire, through a stroke of unreserved fortune. I still know not how he remains unscathed," said Maitland.

"Because he's a damn witch, Maitland!" James' anger had risen back to boiling point. Veins popped from his temples and his face had steadily turned as red as his wine. "He is my personal devil, sent to torment me and test my strength!

Prayer and iron are evidently not enough to destroy the man!" He stood, pacing by the hearth.

"I gave yer gold and soldiers and in return ye give me only failure!" he shouted. "He defeated your men and mine own with a handful of borderers! I have taken his lands, castles and his eldest son! What will it take to destroy this... this odious wretch!?"

"We still have our informant. They remain with him as we speak sire," said Maitland.

"And how long is it before this informant is bewitched and turned to Bothwell like the rest of them!"

Abruptly, James' anger abated and he seated himself again. He rubbed his eyes and held his head in his hands.

"How do we defeat this evil Maitland?" said James resignedly. "I fear deeply for myself and the realm if this plague is not answered for. This damned book offers no solution." He pushed *Malleus Maleficarum* away.

"Francis is predictable sire," said Maitland. "He will use his momentum and pursue us here. Mayhaps we imprison his wife?"

"It'll only gain him support Maitland, A King extorts his wroth on a defenceless countess? Bah! Besides, he has done well to keep her out of it. He knows well what he's doing." he said, looking up at the high ceiling. "Any harsh actions I take against him will only further his cause. Yet, I cannot show him kindness lest I prove myself to be weak. A puppet to be manipulated by my subjects."

"We raise an army and meet him in open battle?" suggested Maitland.

"Nay, his borderers will run circles around an army. He will avoid us and pick his battlefields. He may even be reset in England by the border wardens there. Elizabeth has been uncooperative as usual."

"Then assassination sire," said Maitland.

"I would prefer him stand trial so that I might make an example of him. Though, we're running out of options. Know you of any such men up to the task?" said James.

"We could repurpose the informant sire? They are close to him, they know him intimately. They could easily slip poison in his drink or stake a knife in his heart," said Maitland.

"Hmm, what do you think the lords will make of it?" said James.

"If 'tis done right, an unfortunate accident. Though, if 'tis done wrong, they will see it as an act of aggression against all their persons I fear. Even without Bothwell's impetus, it may cause this which he has started to become a full rebellion."

"High stakes," considered James, "too high. Unless there is some way we can ensure 'tis an accident... or someone else. He needs enemies, too numerous to count so that any one of them might have done it."

"How will you achieve that sire, the threat of punishment seems to have had no effect," said Maitland.

"Nay, you are right. We must stir up trouble for the earl." James steepled his finger and thought, he sat up in his chair when an idea came to him, then slumped again when he disproved it of his own accord. He looked like a man continually about to sneeze only to realise he no longer needed to.

"Francis relies mostly on the Stewart faction at court does he not? Lennox, Moray, Atholl, Colonel Stewart and those of that ilk?" he questioned Maitland, knowing full well the answer.

"He does, sire."

"And what will none of them abide?" said James.

"Me? Sire," said Maitland.

James smiled, "nay Maitland, none of them can abide Catholics. If we turn Francis' actions into a Catholic conspiracy, they'll have no choice but to withdraw their support."

Maitland raised his eyebrows, "And how will we achieve it?"

"You will forge letters, supposedly from Catholic lords, say, Angus and Erroll, requesting of the King of Spain funds so that they might pay Bothwell a sum he has requested to join their side," said James.

"Very good sire," said Maitland.

"The bonus is that Elizabeth will be forced to aid me and command her wardens to not reset Bothwell in England, perhaps even send me funds, lest she been seen to be soft on the Catholics," James shifted in his seat excitedly. "I will give a speech and provide concessions to the kirk if they excommunicate Francis for his devilish deeds. Thus, securing the papist connection."

"Next, we will give all of Bothwell's forfeited lands to Lennox as to inspire jealousy."

"All of them sire, I had thought I might claim rights to some of the disputed Haddington..."

"*All* of them Maitland," said James.

"Lastly, issue a proclamation offering a thousand crowns to the man who brings me Francis' head. Perhaps the rabble will react livelier to incentive rather than punishment."

"*Then*, and only then can we order the assassination of my dear cousin," said James, tossing a hunk of chicken into his mouth. "The order never came from me! You understand me."

"In the meantime, keep the channels open with our cat's paw. Let's not be caught unawares by his advances. Bring your troops here, what's left of them, and arm the castle. Get Melville or some other to furnish us with troops and disbar any ships from crossing the Forth."

"I will not suffer a witch to live in my Kingdom! Hop to it Maitland!" said James triumphantly. He pulled his book back towards him and continued with his meal.

"Of course, Your Grace." Maitland bowed and left the dining room. He placed himself, withdrawn, on a chair in the adjoining room and considered James' words. He had no qualms with the assassination of Bothwell. There were many who did not credit his chancellorship, but Bothwell frightened him the most. Not simply because he had come the closest to removing him before, but because he feared those of his powers he had not yet seen.

He had read James' literature. The pacts with the devil, the sabbats, the orgies. The horrifying illustrations of the devil's twisted face haunted his mind. He recalled descriptions of hell from his own schooling and shuddered at the thought. For, it was not Bothwell's own power he wielded, it was borrowed from the dark lord himself. To him, those powers were limitless.

Now there was this. This plot which could turn Scotland on its head. If he failed, its misgivings would surely be blamed on him. If it succeeded, there was no guarantee he would last another year in the job. Perhaps it was time for him to resign from his post. Pat himself on the back for rising to a barony and live in peace. Perhaps the King was wrong and the only thing for it was to give in to Bothwell, he thought.

No, he told himself. No, he would have no barony to go back to, he would be lucky even to retain his life. He would remain if he did the King the great service of vanquishing his enemies, what's more, further advancements. Evil prevails only when those on the side of good take no action. Whatever the motivations of others, his were at least just in the eyes of God. James was right, whatever it takes and at any cost, Bothwell needs to be destroyed.

To avoid his peril, simply, he cannot fail.

* * * * *

14th April 1592
Canongate

Francis ordered another round of ales for the table, giving the barmaid a tidy spank as she left. The tavern reeked of sweat, booze and piss. The poor candlelight only added to the filthy gloom of the place. It had been taken up by Francis' borderers whenever they were back in the town, at times booting out the previous occupants by force. Each time, he arrived back with more than he left with and the building was heaving with bodies.

"And then," said Francis, sloshing his cup, "and then I says, Nay! Yer cannot arrest me, I have no finished my pie!"

The table exploded in a round of raucous laughter and slamming of fists, spilling ale onto the table and the floor. They were the captains from the borders, the Scotts, the Grahams, and the Johnstones.

"Tell 'em Francis, aboot the Lord Maxwell's castle, just these weeks past!" said one of them, wiping a tear from his eye.

"Ah, well, James had driven Maxwell out of his home, out near Dumfries, yer know the place? Aye, and replaced him with Carmichael. We weren't to accept that lying down now, were we lads," more cheers and beating of fists were joined to the clamour. "I had with me only a score, so we could not attack with force. Nay, so, do you know what I did? I dressed as a woman, no wait!" he said, pausing their laughter and urging them closer, "I dressed as a woman and walked right in through the gate! Gave the guard a saucy wink on my way past!"

Francis couldn't help himself from joining in their laughter. "Anyway, I opened a postern gate and we took the castle within the blink of an eye."

Francis took another deep swig from his cup when he noticed someone making for their table.

"Hercules! Yer scullion! Come, make space for Hercules boys," he said.

"Francis, had I known you were back in town I'd have found ye sooner. May we walk? We have much to discuss," said Hercules.

"Ach! Can it no wait until morning Hercules?" said Francis.

"Nay, we need to talk *now,*" said Hercules, adding the last word with all the sternness he could summon.

"Alright, alright, don't get hose all in a twist," said Francis, getting to his feet. "Forgive me gentlemen, for I must bid you adieu," He took a low bow to the table and stumbled as he straightened.

The two picked their way through the tables, chairs and other inebriated guests to make it outside, where the air was only marginally better than inside. Hercules grabbed Francis roughly by the arm and led him to a horse trough where he dunked his head in the icy water and held it there.

He counted to ten and pulled Francis back up. "Better?"

"Hercules, what are..." Hercules pushed his head under the water again. Waiting before drawing him back up.

"Now?" he said.

"Yes, yes! Just stop," said Francis, panting. Hercules released him and he sat on the edge of the trough, gulping in the night air and attempting to dry his face.

"Good," said Hercules, "now walk with me. There is much we have not yet discussed."

Francis sighed and followed on behind. "What is this about Hercules?"

"The raid on Holyrood was months ago. In case you don't remember, the coven gave us only a year to rectify the situation, or we leave. That's the deal and I stand by them, Francis. With only a short time left you're gallivanting about the borders."

Francis stopped, "Hercules, the borderers need plunder, otherwise they'll leave and go home, you know this full well!"

"Aye, I do. But we have not even entertained a plan. How many more do you need? The other Stewarts will join their men to yours. We have enough already. Besides, all you do is further the King's case against you. Certainly, killing his guard wouldn't have done ye any favours."

"Further his case it may," said Francis, "but half the court are joined to me. Don't you see? I have to show strength and victories, I have to force the King's hand. All he needs do is give up Maitland."

"Holyrood wasn't even a victory!" exclaimed Hercules, before checking himself and lowering his voice again. "We didn't get to the King or Maitland. We were led into a trap, there are big problems Francis, it's time to address them. Here. Now."

The street they were walking opened up into a large square, in its centre stood the Girth Cross. Behind it, Holyrood Palace. The King's troops had reoccupied it after the raid, and, while they dared not venture out into the town, it was well garrisoned. Francis perched himself on a low stone wall.

"So, what, Maitland lay a trap, that's what's got ye all wound up? Any scout could've foretold of our coming."

"Damn it Francis," Hercules hissed, "nay, I have been racking my brain for months, they knew intimate details of our plan. They knew exactly the route we would take and how to trap us."

Francis twisted his beard with a finger, "you're right. But who could've betrayed us? There were only a handful who knew the plan in advance. Can't been Ludovic, he's the one who let us in."

"If t'was Spott," continued Hercules, "then surely he would've made his excuses and abandoned covering our retreat, or worse, turned on us and slaughtered us as we made our escape."

"And Colville and Niddrie nearly died in the fighting," said Francis, "can't see it being them. Besides, I trust them all with my life."

"Now you see the problem Francis? I had thought Lennox might've let us in only to lead us into the trap but you're right, he's still with us openly and I trust him too."

"Then who?" said Francis. He struck his forehead as he tried to clear his mind.

"I think the only thing we can say for certain, Francis, is that we don't know and must proceed with caution," said Hercules.

"Right. Indeed, you are right. A scheme then, let's put an end to this," said Francis.

"We know the King is reliant on a mole, so if we do not tell the mole, we can surely catch him unawares," said Hercules.

"Aye... Aye!" said Francis hopping back to his feet. "If we do that, then the borderers alone will be sufficient. There will be no trap and we will succeed where Holyrood failed!"

"Keep yer voice down!" said Hercules, pushing Francis back down, "see that man over there? He followed us from the tavern."

Francis peered through blurry eyes at the darkness. Then, leaning in an ally he saw the silhouette of a man. He appeared to be unmoving and facing them.

"Oh yes," said Francis, waving a limp-wristed hand, "the King's men are everywhere or mayhaps it's one of Maitland's dogs." Francis suddenly widened his eyes. "And what of the uniformed men we found in the Palace?"

"They're witch hunters Francis, funded by the King, or Maitland or maybe the kirk I don't know. Whosoever they are, we'll find out. Once we know where their money is coming from, we can disperse them or install a puppet and protect the coven."

"Ah, yes, the coven, of course," said Francis nodding.

Hercules tutted, he held Francis by the shoulders and looked into his eyes.

"I am only helping to restore ye because I believe it best for the coven, do ye understand? This was your plan and I'm helping you because I can see no other way. I'd much rather be at home with my family."

"Now, in the morning you're going to make your preparations for the ride. Tell no one. Do it slowly, unnoticed. It may take a few weeks but so be it. We'll dress someone as ye and keep them moving around with some of the borderers, maybe several. They'll not know where ye are. Understand? Even the men on the ride shouldn't know yer plan until you're across the Forth."

Francis let a sombre look drop over his face, "of course I understand. I am a man of war and strategy am I not?" His sincerity was comprised by a loud hiccup that followed.

"That's the spirit. Then let us go, back to yer drinking. We must act typical," said Hercules.

Francis stood and the two of them began their walk back to the tavern.

"And what of Florie?" said Francis.

"What of her?" said Hercules.

"How is she, she is cross with me I suppose, Agnes is still missing."

"She keeps to herself mostly," said Hercules, "I cannot tell whether she is sad or furious. She says nothing at all, just sits biting her nails. I would not see her if that's what ye were thinking?"

"No, yes, of course," said Francis, concentrating on his steps.

Hercules opened the tavern door and Francis stepped through. He turned expecting to see Hercules join him but the door slammed shut. He returned to his table and sat down smiling weakly at the others who had begun some new tale. He stared into the froth at the bottom of his cup, all the jollity drained from him. *Damn Hercules,* he thought, *he has a habit of ruining my fun.*

Chapter 11

27th June 1592
North of Falkland

Francis halted his troop close to the edge of the woodland. He dismounted and walked the remaining distance to the opening where he could see the lights of Falkland Palace. He crouched, massaging his legs from days in the saddle and gazed upon the twinkling candlelight in the high windows. The impressive circular towers of the gatehouse on the south side were visible, even from the north.

It had taken weeks to get to where they were now. James had policed any crossings of the Forth and his scouts buzzed across the lands south of the Palace like angry wasps. Instead, they had taken a ship from North Berwick, courtesy of captain Hackerston. The ships had first been loaded in secret with victuals followed by men and horse, mostly during the nights. The process had been slow, moving small quantities at a time but Francis' agents about the town heard no talk amongst its folk of the operation. When everything had been prepared, they sailed up to the most easterly part of the Fife peninsula.

From their landing point, they had been able to approach the castle from the north, where there were fewer eyes on them. Still, they had to avoid the roads and camp in deep woodland. Hiding three hundred men was no simple task. It had all proved a worthy investment though, Francis' outriders confirmed that the King seemingly had no whiff of their presence, and here they were unseen and unscathed.

He turned his gaze away from the palace and back to his men. The lords, who'd done so well in the attack on Holyrood had been replaced by the gruff border captains. Nevertheless, they knew their business and Francis was asking a lot of them this night. They gathered about him to receive their battle orders.

He and Hercules had expanded on their plan while still in the vicinity of Edinburgh. They had agreed that in killing the King's guardsmen, Francis had only entrenched his position. This time they would use non-lethal paper shot, relying on the shock of the fusillade to keep them pinned. Naturally, his soldiers would have to defend themselves and when it came to melee, some would have to die. Nonetheless, they surmised the stunt should still curry some favour, if not with the King, then at least with Parliament. Especially in Francis' inevitable defence where he must claim to have never been against the King, only Maitland.

"Understand?" he said, inspecting their expressions. He smiled when all that faced him were the cold, steely eyes of hardened men who knew their trade. "Aye," came the unanimous reply.

"Then away!" said Francis, "Let us ride."

Francis mounted his own horse and untied the rag around his wrist. The fresh, runic wound was blistered and raw, he kissed the scar and covered it. He looked behind him at the miscellaneous assortment of reivers. To them, this was just another border raid, even so, he suspected this was as far north as any of them had been.

Without a word, he kicked Valentine's flanks and rode hard towards Falkland Palace. The horsemen followed and the familiar booming applause of hooves accompanied him once more, filling his spirits.

The three hundred rode towards the eastern side of the palace, swooping around in a big arc so that they would come up on the front gates. Nobody had noticed their approach but they rounded the corner in time to see a savvy steward scurry inside and bar the doors.

That's it, thought Francis, *the alarm has been raised.*

They arrived at a low wall, thirty yards from the palace, which provided the perfect placement for his musketeers. At Francis' order half the retinue dismounted and took shelter behind it, firearms at the ready, waiting for the inevitable defensive fire from the windows. Francis stayed mounted and commanded the closest riders to him forward.

They rode at speed, skidding their horses to a stop in front of the heavy wooden doors. They retrieved conical metallic structures, roughly the size of a bucket, from their saddlebags and hastened to the gate.

It was somewhat of a relief to hear the first of the musket fire from the arrow slits above. In answer, his men behind the wall let fly their own volley. The line of muzzles belched a spectacle of fire and smoke, accompanied by the staccato clap of black powder. The smoke billowed and rose, expanding in the night air, completely obscuring either side's view. Those who'd fired stepped back and a new line of primed muskets stepped forward.

The team against the gates had succeeded in securing their devices to the doors. Keeping flat to the wall, one of them used a lit cord, touching it to the fuse and they ran back to safety. The fuse fizzed, dancing in the dark as the attackers watched on. It burned agonisingly slowly down to the housing. Then, the fire hit the compacted powder charge inside the petards.

It exploded with an almighty blast that would rival any cannonade. Men on both sides flinched behind cover as fire lit up the gatehouse. Clouds of hot iron and splintered wood fell from the sky, pinging as they hit the ground like a shower of hailstones. Francis' ears buzzed with a high-pitched ringing while he narrowed his eyes to gaze through the fumes. Eventually, the damage came into view. One of the doors had completely vanished while the other hung limp to its twisted hinges.

The musketeers let off another volley of fire with their paper shot. The King's men were running along the rooftops now, arming the battlements and raining down fire. The plan seemed to be holding though. They ducked their heads and stayed pinned to their positions when the paper volleys rattled against the walls or whizzed past their heads.

Francis raised his sword and let out an emphatic roar, before kicking his horse into the gallop through the breach. Those still mounted followed. The archway wasn't quite tall enough to allow a rider and horse through, so he lay flat to Valentine.

Francis kicked again when a guardsman raced out into the centre of the passage in a vain attempt to block the horsemen. He collided with Valentine's breast and the hulking mass of the war horse sent him flailing backward. Francis was already past before he saw him hit the ground.

He raised his head as he came out into the courtyard on the other side, slashing at a soldier's chest and spraying blood over his horse's pristine coat. The other horsemen came pouring into the courtyard whooping and firing pistols at the windows. They wasted no time in dismounting and swarmed to the entrances of the palace.

Francis jumped down from his own horse and looked around. He'd visited Falkland only a handful of times and was unsure of the nearest staircase. He dashed for one of the passageways only to be forced into hasty rearward hop by the point of a sword.

He rolled his eyes as he saw a nervous young soldier emerge from the doorway. The boy gathered all the bravery he could muster and thrust his sword point at Francis. He parried it effortlessly, stepping forward in the same move, and brought his pommel down on the boy's skull. He crumpled with a choked whimper. Francis didn't stop to see the effect of his blow, resuming his sprint.

He entered a long corridor where his bordermen were already making short work of those that had fired from the windows. *There*, he saw it, the staircase up to the apartments. He knew the king slept on the northern side of the palace, having been entertained in his chambers after a hunt.

He hopped up the stairs taking two at a time. He felt the presence of some of his men following on, flanking him. He sheathed his sword as he ran, drawing his pistols. At the top, he'd expected to find a host of soldiers firing down into the courtyard but found only a handful of men spread thin around the upper hallways. Francis, who'd loaded his pistols with real shot, fired at the nearest, sending him sprawling over the fine carpets.

He hurtled down the hallway to where it bent left towards the King's quarters. He stopped at the corner and poked his head round. He withdrew it just as shot peppered the wall and sprayed plaster dust into the air. He deposited his spent pistol and drew his sword. He had only two borderers with him now and he held up a finger for them to keep silent.

"Come on then!" Francis shouted. "Whose man enough to come kill me and collect their thousand crowns eh!?"

First, there was nothing, then came the pounding of several feet, tearing towards the corner. Francis stepped back and push kicked the first man round the bend, hitting him in the chest and sending him tumbling backward. Almost simultaneously he shot with his left, the second fool's head snapped back, showering the third with blood and brains.

Francis' kicking foot had hardly returned to the ground when his flanking bordermen charged past him, slashing and hacking at the soldiers with an unbridled battle lust. Francis rounded the corner to find they'd already slaughtered those that had stayed put and were beating the last man senseless.

Francis exhaled, calming himself. This was it, this was the King's door. He stood, pistol in one hand, sword in the other, staring at it. He motioned for his troops to open the door. They tried the handle and it was unlocked.

"Halt!" ordered Francis.

He strode to the door and began pushing it gently open with the tip of his sword. He could see no one through the gap. He unhooked the powder horn from his belt and threw it into the room. Nothing. Silently, he pointed that one man should stay outside and beckoned the other to enter with him. He tiptoed carefully into the bedchambers.

"Your grace?" he called out. No reply.

Francis violently tore up the blankets and checked all of the crevices.

"He's not bloody here!" he roared. He kicked a stool, shattering the dainty construction.

"Lord Francis! There ye are." A red faced reiver came running into the room. "I've been trying to find ye, we've got the King!"

"What!? Where!?" demanded Francis.

"We've cornered him in the towers, he's barricaded there. Though, there is some resistance."

Francis whooped. "Well damn it man! Take me to him!"

They hurried out into the hallways. They were empty now, corpses and wounded men were scattered about them. Francis took the opportunity to reload his pistols as they walked. As they got closer, he could hear the shouting, the kind you'd hear at some tavern brawl rather than a battlefield.

Francis learned why when he finally caught sight of them. The defenders must've, at some point, upended a large table as a barricade. Yet now it was raised up off the ground, supported by both sides, who were using it as some oversized shield. They pushed and heaved against each other with grunts and taunts. Sword tips from both sides probed over and under the edges. The guardsmen were greatly outnumbered by the attackers, but their backs were pressed up against a wall, leaving them nowhere to be pushed to.

"He's in there lord," said Francis' man. "Through that door. See?"

Francis did see it, obscured by the guardsmen, but there nonetheless. He allowed the corners of his lips to twist into a half-smile. He joined the back of the crowd then made his way forward through them until he was near the front. The press was so thick, he couldn't make it any further. He held his pistol as high as he could and pointed it over the table-shield.

He squeezed the trigger and the shot reverberated through his wrist. As quick as the explosion from the gun reached his ears, so did the satisfying ping of his shot hitting a helmet or a chest plate. At this range, there was no chance of surviving it.

"STOP!" Francis shouted. The taunting, grunting and shouting stopped but the men closest to the table kept up the tension.

"Now! I came here with the intention of not doing much killing. I've broken my own rule far too much already today. However! I can stand here, reloading my pistols in comfort and shoot every last one of ye clodpolls until yer all dead. OR! Yer can surrender now and leave here with yer lives. I guarantee them."

There was silence from the other side of the makeshift shield, then, slowly, outstretched hands appeared above them. The table dropped to the floor to reveal a gaggle of tired, dishevelled men. They were ferried away from the tower door to cheers and jeers of the reivers.

Francis padded confidently to the tower door and thrust it open. Inside, sure enough, was the King. He was stood confidently in the centre of the room but his white-knuckle grasp on his cane betrayed his fear. He was wearing just his long nightshirt and his hair was ruffled. Francis looked around for other guards.

"Yer would not do harm to yer King, would yer Francis? Cousin?" said James, eyeing the towering warrior caked in gore.

They were in some sort of guard captain's room. From in here, Francis could still hear the guardsmen on the roof firing down at the line of borderers defending the retreat. There was a large writing desk littered with papers, a rack of weapons and a wide circular meeting table with wine and goblets set upon it. Francis sat down and poured two cups before responding.

"No, Your Grace, I would never even dream of it. Come now, sit, drink," he said, pointing to an empty chair.

James moved slowly, keeping his eyes fixed on Francis, he proceeded towards the chair and sat down. Francis pushed one of the goblets in front of him.

"I have never born you any ill-will Your Majestie. I have tried to tell you but a thousand times, I take action against only Maitland. Where is he anyhow?" he said.

"He and his troops as in the town, along with mine," said James, "they'll be here presently."

"I estimate we still have an hour, which is plenty of time to sort this matter out my King," said Francis. "Why have you embarked on this crusade against me? On these trumped-up charges of witchcraft no less."

James steadied himself with a sip of wine. "Because, Francis, witchcraft aside you frustrate my every turn," he replied in steely tone, "I have been too kind on you for too long. I cannot be seen to look weak lest the Catholic lords decide to imitate your actions to get *their* way, or the Spanish, or even I dare say Elizabeth. The time for bending this way and that are over. I must be resolute in my fortitude against those would embarrass me and this crown."

He put both hands on the table and stared into Francis' eyes. "Then of course, there *is* the witchcraft charges. I've heard enough to satisfy my convictions Francis, ye are a witch!" He spat the last word with such venom it shook the table.

Francis laughed easily. "If I were a witch, I'd have not needed three hundred borderers at my back. Surely, I would have magicked myself here and done away wi' ye a long time ago."

James snorted, "I know not how your sorcery works devil! Nevertheless, I will not permit ye, nor any like ye, to live in my Kingdom! I will bring the hammer of Christ down on ye with all God's vengeance."

Francis sighed, "ye're determined I see." He stood and approached the guard captain's writing desk. He retrieved some paper, quill and ink and strode back to the table, placing the materials in front of James.

"We can discuss this all night," he said, "but what I want is the King's pardon, in yer own hand. I want all my lands restored, my son returned to me and Maitland removed."

"I'll not give it yer, yer roguish fiend! Ye'll get nay signature from me."

"I urge ye, my King, to consider the bonds we share through blood, the good I have done for you and this nation. I beg of you, restore me and you will find none more faithful than I to the crown."

Francis knelt, withdrawing his sword, and held it out, hilt first towards the King.

"If ye will have me, yer Grace, I would pledge my sword to you again."

He lowered his head, waiting for the response, feeling the weight of James' eyes upon him.

"Nay, Francis," he said, pushing Francis' hilt away, "ye've only yourself to blame. There are some actions I just cannot forgive."

Francis righted himself, his head still bowed with the heaviness of James' decision. He walked to stand behind the King, staring at the back of his head. For a brief moment he entertained the idea of cocking his pistol, then quickly shook the thought. He knew that would only heap on another charge of treason on top of his already less-than-perfect record.

He hesitated, then drew his wand from his sword hilt with the hiss of metal scraping against metal.

"I didn't want it to come to this," he muttered, "*kommano!*"

"Now write," he commanded. James obediently picked up the quill and dipped it in ink.

"I, his Majestie the King, in light of new evidence, do declare the charges against Sir Francis Stewart," he began.

As he spoke James wrote the words in his sprawling and elegant handwriting. His hand flicked across the paper, flourishing the feather of his quill which danced as the words formed on the page.

When James had finished the proclamation, Francis called in one of the bordermen outside.

"Bring me some of the King's guard, they must witness the signing!" He ordered.

He waited for the pair to leave then spun round to the front of James' chair. He was ghostly pale, looking straight ahead and clutching at his cane with white knuckles.

"When ye come round from this, ye'll not remember a thing. All is well in the Kingdom, peace and justice has been restored and everything is in its rightful place. Ye understand?"

James nodded vacantly. Francis watched his face, searching his heavily lidded eyes for any sign of defiance or knowing. There was none, though still, a frown spread across Francis' brow. Something didn't feel quite right, perhaps it'd all simply been too easy or maybe it was the bitter disappointment at the King not offering up his pardon willingly.

He was spared further introspection, however, by the entry of his bordermen. They dragged with them two of the King's guard. Thankfully, they had had the foresight to bring an officer of some form to bear witness. They bustled into the room as the prisoners struggled against their besiegers until they were forced to their knees.

"Have you been told why you're here?" said Francis.

They both nodded.

"James," he said, turning back to the motionless monarch. "Sign it."

He did as he was told, his quill performing its final prance. Francis pulled the paper from underneath it. He took it to the candlelight of the writing desk and read it one last time before throwing sand over the wet ink and rolling it up. He stashed it away inside his armour, taking care to keep it pristine. He walked to the door and turned around to get one last look at the docile James.

"Let us away! Sound the retreat. Our men outside must've nearly exhausted their ammunition by now," said Francis, snapping his head away from the King and marching into the corridor.

Horns blasted out the retreat, rising above the din of the duelling muskets outside. As Francis hurried down the corridors back to the courtyard, borderers lumbered out of rooms burdened with all the loot they could carry. He fought through the ambling mass to get outside. James was right, they'd spent too long. The soldiers from the town would be baring down on them at any moment.

He burst out into the courtyard where men were hastily loading their saddlebags. He did nothing to stop or hurry them, this is why they rode. To deny them of their prize was enough to dampen their future support. Some had completed their work and were already racing out of the gate. Francis spotted Valentine, the horse was truly majestic, standing a full head higher than the other wily horses of the borderers.

Francis darted toward him. He gathered up his reins and was about to pull himself up into the saddle when a loud thud took him by surprise. Valentine reared, ripping the reins from his hand. The great warhorse rose up high and beat at the air with his forelegs, his distressed whinny cutting through the noise of the courtyard.

"No!" Francis shouted.

On his way down the beast collapsed and fell heavily onto his side. Francis spotted the wound at his neck, already pooling with blood. It spread over his glistening white coat like excess red ink on blotting paper. Valentine thrashed his head, flicking his mane wildly and kicked out with all four hooves. Francis knelt beside his companion's head, trying to get close. Slowly, the thrashing stopped, replaced by a spasming of the horse's huge muscles. Francis positioned Valentine's head in his lap and stroked his muzzle. His eyes flickered but Francis was certain he was looking up at him.

Francis bent down and kissed the forehead of his equine friend, lingering while he waited for the spasming to stop. Tears rolled down his cheeks silently while he held the horse that had carried him since he was a boy. A lump gathered at the back of his throat while cradled Valentine and he felt the life force extinguish from the horse.

He stood with his eyes stinging and looked up to see where the shot had come from. A guardsman had heard the commotion and moved across the roof from the front of the castle to the inner courtyard. He was erratically reloading his musket, fully aware Francis had noticed him.

Francis' vision was blurred, yet he could still make out the silhouette of the man. He withdrew his pistol and fired. He heard the scream and saw the shape tumble from the battlements and plummet towards the ground, which he met with a powerful slap.

"Good shot, lord," Francis turned to see a borderer had already led a horse to him. "Ye can have John's horse, he died in the fighting."

Francis checked inside his armour for the proclamation and took one last glance at Valentine before leaping into the saddle and kicking the small nag into a gallop out of the castle gates.

* * * * *

28th June 1592
Falkland Palace

Maitland and Oswyn rushed into the castle's courtyard. Rain fell hard and relentlessly from the heavens, washing away much of the gore from the previous night. Soldiers were piling the corpses of both guardsmen and bordermen into a cart, while stewards were busy clearing away broken glass and doing their best to restore ransacked rooms.

The pair hurried through, weaving to avoid the men hard at work after a long night. They hopped up the staircase and made for the King's chambers. On their way Maitland glimpsed huge chunks of wall missing, where musket balls had flung into them at short range. His shoes carried the dust with him, creating footprints on the carpet.

"Wait here," he said to Oswyn. He nodded at the mass of guardsmen stationed outside the King's door and let himself in. There he saw James, sat alone at his writing desk. He still wore his nightshirt and tasselled hat, sipping at a cup of wine and staring out of the window.

"Your Grace," said Maitland, bowing despite James having his back turned.

James started, somehow caught unawares by Maitland's entry.

"Ah, Maitland, how good it is to see you," said James.

"My King... are you alright?" said Maitland, a frown spreading across his forehead. This wasn't the raging King he was expecting.

"Aye, quite alright, not a scratch on me," he said. "'Tis good yer here, there is much to attend to."

"Of course, Your Grace, I have already taken the liberty of sending most of the garrison south to pursue Bothwell back to Edinburgh. They will harry and hinder his retreat."

"What? Why on earth would you do that? The Earl Bothwell has been given a full pardon."

"Sire, you don't have to uphold the pardon, it was given under duress. It'll stand with Parliament, especially with testimony from your soldiers," said Maitland, the lines of his furrowed brow deepening.

"No, no," said James, "Bothwell meant no harm, he used paper shot, see? On my table?"

Maitland picked up the spent shot balls from the table. James was right, the balls were nothing but compressed paper.

Damn it, he thought, *a clever move on Bothwell's part, such a stunt would play well with the court.*

"And what of the bodies outside? They are the King's personal guard are they not?" He said.

"Well, ye can hardly expect Francis to walk in here, as an outlaw, without a little damage can you, eh?" said James, tittering slightly.

Maitland just gazed at James, mouth open, watching the King sat in the ruins of his ransacked bedchamber, continuing to sip at his wine and chortle to himself like all Francis had done was best him at a game of cards. He scrambled to James' chair and peered into his eyes.

"What are ye doing Maitland, yer making me rather uncomfortable," said James, recoiling from Maitland's intense stare.

"What has Francis done to you my King, are ye bewitched?" said Maitland, panicked at the sheer thought of Francis having this amount of control over the monarch.

"Nay, Maitland, no credible scholar could believe in such things. Francis has simply convinced me of his innocence. The evidence is clear and his full pardon will be easily ratified in the next Parliament."

"I was a fool to spend all this time trying to prosecute the man when I should've been bringing him closer to my court. Speaking of which, you are to be relieved of your duties immediately. Take a rest. I will decide what to do about yer future employment in due course."

"No," Maitland whimpered, "no my King, I must serve, we must rid the Kingdom of this evil lest it destroy us all."

"Maitland, yer presence discomforts me. Please, remove yerself."

Maitland didn't know what he was looking for in the King's eyes exactly, but he could see nothing. No glazed look nor defiance behind them. He racked his brain for some nugget of information that might aid him. He turned as though to leave then spun back around and slapped the King as hard as he could.

James looked up shocked, holding his cheek. "Maitland! I can see Francis was right and 'tis you who are the foul creature in my presence. Guards! Guards! Remove him!"

Two armoured men came bustling into the room and grabbed Maitland roughly by the arms, dragging him out of the chamber.

"No! Your Grace! I was trying to help you! Please, I beg of you! My King!" He screamed and kicked all the way out of the room until he was thrown roughly to the floors of the hallway.

Oswyn, who had been waiting patiently outside, picked him up and dusted off his cloak.

"I take it, Lord, that didn't go so well," he chuckled.

"No Oswyn, it didn't," said Maitland, straightening his outfit. "Come, let us get away from the King's ears."

They left swiftly, back through the chaos they had passed on their way in. The meeting had been so short their horses were still saddled outside. Maitland pulled himself onto his and kicked, riding as fast as he could away from the palace. Oswyn did his best to keep up on his small screw.

Maitland didn't feel safe until he was a good mile down the road, where he slowed and waited for Oswyn to catch up. He had unintentionally taken the southern road towards Sterling. The rain hadn't succeeded yet in washing away the rutted hoof tracks, presumably of the borderers' horses and then the pursuing soldiers. Oswyn was severely out of breath when he appeared next to him.

"Bothwell has bewitched the King Oswyn, I know it," said Maitland.

"I see," said Oswyn, uncharacteristically pensive. "What happened in there exactly?"

"Bothwell has received the King's full pardon and I am to be relieved of my duties it seems."

"Ah, yes, the King has been charmed, very common Lord, very common. So, what are we to do about it?"

"What *can* we do about it Oswyn. Without the King's funds, I fear I will have to disband you and your men. I curry no favour with men of the court nor the Kirk, so likely I will fade into irrelevance. It's over, we are at the mercy of a witch who whispers in the King's ear."

"Never Lord!" said Oswyn defiantly, "This may not be my native country, but I will not live to see a witch in control of the affairs of men! Worry not about us, I will keep the men, we will scrape our way through. We have never fought for coin, but the grace of God."

"Fine words," said Maitland, "but without the King's blessing, any action you undertake will no doubt be illegal."

"The laws of a Kingdom do not take precedence over the laws of God. Don't you fret Lord, well see the earl vanquished yet."

Maitland rode on, forcing his mind to slow down the whizzing thoughts behind his eyes. There was a slim chance Bothwell had been caught by his pursuers, though, he knew that was a faint hope.

"The only folk who know of my dismissal and the pardon are at Falkland. No doubt Bothwell will have a written pardon but mayhaps there is some action we can take before the King returns to Edinburgh. Though, if my actions are too strong, they could be seen as treason, at the very least impersonating a chancellor."

"There you have it lord, a window of opportunity. It is slim, to be sure, but it exists anyhow," said Oswyn.

"Somehow we must cast doubt on Bothwell's paper and convince others to continue carrying out their orders," said Maitland, stroking his moustache. "Lennox still holds Bothwell's lands and rents and the Catholic letters have already been issued. That should be enough for some to keep the earl at arm's length. Yet, we need more. Something to deter even his closest supporters."

"Does our mole know of the King's pardon?" said Oswyn.

"Hmm, nay, though I suspect they will turn silent upon reviewing the document. Still, it cannot harm to try them. Somehow we must get to Edinburgh first."

"If I'm not mistaken Lord, these tracks head to Sterling do they not?" said Oswyn, pointing at the hoof welts on the ground.

"Yes, what of it?"

"Well, it is unlikely Bothwell will risk getting the boat to Queensferry," said Oswyn, a grin spreading across his face. "He will take the longer route via Sterling."

"By God! Yer right!" said Maitland. "If we're quick we can ensure we act afore anyone knows of my suspension."

The pair rode side by side as they discussed their options. Maitland's gesticulations became larger as his enthusiasm for the scheme grew.

"Ye know what to do?" said Maitland.

"Yes Lord, I believe I have the gist," said Oswyn.

"Then ride damn it! Ride as fast as you can. Wait!" He shouted before Oswyn kicked his horse. He fumbled on his belt and retrieved some silver coins. "Use these to bribe your way across, perhaps this will inject some speed to your crossing. Now, away!"

Chapter 12

6th July 1592
Edinburgh

Francis rode tall on his horse as he led the procession of horsemen down the Canongate and towards the Netherbow port. He led only fifty down the pathway. Some had abandoned the ride to head straight for the borders with their loot, while a small number had lagged behind the troop and succumbed to the pursuers. Nonetheless, at the head of the ragged soldiers, Francis looked like some folklore warrior prince returning home from a long campaign.

The illusion was broken when he saw Hercules and Florie, waiting as he had asked, on the steps of his favourite tavern. He leapt from his horse, and darted to them both, nearly bowling them over as he embraced them in a hug.

"I've got it!" said Francis, "The King gave me his pardon!"

Francis pulled the rolled-up paper from within his breastplate that he'd kept safe the entire journey.

"My God!" said Hercules, inspecting the document, "so you have! Just in time too. Francis much has happened while you've been away."

"I know, I know Hercules, but let a man get a drink first!"

"No ye don't understand, it's Agnes! Her sentence has been given and her burning is to be carried out today!"

"Why didn't ye start with that man! Quick, to the Old Tolbooth! Follow on behind."

Francis stowed his papers and swung himself into the saddle. His horse was away before he'd even seated himself. He rode to the Netherbow Port, with townsfolk leaping out of the way of his horse, where he was stopped by one of the guardsmen.

"Er, Lord Bothwell," he said, surprised at Francis' boldness. "We're not supposed to permit you entry to the city."

"I have the King's pardon, here!" said Francis, thrusting the papers at the guard. "Hurry man and open the gate."

The guard took the papers and furrowed his brow, "sorry Lord, I can't read."

"For God's sake, look there!" he said, pointing at James' signature, "You recognise the King's mark surely?"

"Hmm, it does seem to be," said the guard slowly.

"Ach! Hurry will ye man, it is of national importance I get through this gate, here," he flipped the guard a groat and snatched back his papers. "Far more than my toll, now get this gate open, hurry!"

The guard looked at the groat then up at Francis' frantic expression before hurrying inside the gatehouse to wind up the portcullis. Francis tapped his fingers on the horn of his saddle as the gate rose and inch at a time, scraping with each heave.

After what felt like a full hour the gap was large enough for Francis to duck under the iron and make his way onto the high street. He raced his horse along the path towards the spire of St. Giles. Market stalls and carts blocked his progress, he weaved in and out of them while the stallholders yelled and shook their fists at him.

He finally reached the steps of the Tolbooth and jumped from the saddle while his horse was still bounding forward. He sprung up the steps and thrust open the heavy doors, looking around for the Justice Clerk. He pushed open doors to various offices and holding rooms.

The tolbooth was dank and gloomy. Francis' nostrils were fumigated with the smell of paper and ink mixed with the olfactory manifestation of angst. Self-important clerks busied themselves, hurrying along the narrow corridors. Francis pushed them aside as he attempted to find his way through the warren of rooms.

"You! There!" he shouted when he found him, letting himself into the small office. "As Sheriff of Edinburgh, I demand you release the prisoner Agnes Sampson at once!"

The Justice Clerk's face reddened, flustered by the sudden flourish of movement and shouting.

"Lord Bothwell, ye are not Sheriff, the Duke of Lennox is."

"I... what? No, never mind that now. I have the King's pardon here."

He thrust it into the man's hands, glad to be handing it to someone whose job it is to read.

After a long while inspecting the paper, even pausing to compare the signature to another royal paper at his desk, he peered up at Francis.

"This seems to be in order and in the King's hand, however, the sentence has been declared by a court my Lord. The Sheriff has no power to overturn it."

"This is my jurisdiction, why ever not!?"

"The Sheriff does have authority over the local courts, however, this case regards treason, thus it is elevated to the royal court, Lord. Only the Chancellor or the King himself has that authority."

"A pox on the Chancellor! He's been dismissed, what then?"

"Well, on the first count, this document neither confirms nor denies the chancellor's dismissal. Secondly, if that *were* the case, then it would likely fall upon the Secretary to make a decision."

"Then, what powers do I have? Might I demand the execution of the sentence be delayed, surely a Sheriff has that power?"

"Perhaps, though, today's sentencing is to be carried out on Castle Hill. Again, not within your jurisdiction, Lord. I am afraid there is nothing you can do. Now, if yer quite done with terrorising my office, I have other business to attend to."

"But the King, how can any of this be achieved without him being here?"

The clerk sighed, "Lord Bothwell, I do not believe I need to explain to you, of all people, how the courts of Scotland work."

Francis growled and seized his pardon from the desk. His cape flourished as he span to leave the room. He exited the tolbooth, grinding his teeth down the clustered hallways. He was making his way down the steps when Florie and Hercules caught up with him.

"No luck?" said Hercules, eyeing Francis' indignant expression.

"No," said Francis, kicking the bottom step. "It looks as though part of Agnes' charges include treason, as the witchcraft charges are for the storms on the King's ships. It's a royal court matter, not a local one."

Florie drew back her hand and slapped Francis as hard as she could. Tears welled in her eyes.

"It's yer fault, yer damn dog!" she wailed, beating any part of him that came within reach. "Yer took too long. Ye have everything back and Agnes has wasted away in a dungeon. Have ye no compassion ye rat? What of yer duty!? What is the point of a Warlock if a witch is left to suffer so!?"

Hercules pulled Florie off Francis while she kicked and sobbed, hushing her.

"Quiet Florie! Not here!" he said.

"No! NO!" she screamed turning on him, "yer even worse, you enabled yer brother's fantasies and adventures!"

179

Hercules held her tightly to restrict her flailing. Francis rushed in to help.

"Quiet Florie!" he hissed, "Damn it if ye don't end up burnt too. Agnes is still alive yet, maybe there's something we can do. Calm yourself and let's get up to the castle."

Florie slowed her struggling as his words sank in. She gave up on her display of defiance, wiping her eyes on her sleeves. Francis and Hercules let her go, she inhaled the noxious city air before slapping Francis again. She was calm this time, stood over him with a razor stare that cut Francis to his core.

"Let's hurry up the hill," she said, shaking, "if she burns ye have everything that's coming to ye!"

Francis massaged his cheek as the other two set off, bounding towards the Portcullis Gate of Edinburgh Castle. He hurried to catch them up.

"Any ideas?" he said when he reached them.

"None," said Hercules.

"There will be a crowd, people are already heading towards the castle."

"We could put out the fire?"

"How many times? Ye know what they're like at these things. They'll rebuild the pyre a hundred times if they must. The crowd will demand it. Same goes for a protective charm to stop the flames reaching her. Not to mention that it'd be impossible to not be seen."

"Well, what then?" implored Hercules, shooting a nervous glance at Florie.

"I don't know, maybe we'll spot something when we get up there," said Francis.

The three of them quickened their pace. As they got closer to the gate the crowd pressed in on them from all sides. They chattered excitedly about the burning, their voices raised in sheer anticipation of the day's entertainment. Francis could hear them speculating about what the witch would look like, whether she would be horned or sport a tail.

They arrived outside the gates where a huge pyre had been erected. Even the towering walls of the battery behind it failed to dwarf the structure. The stake at its centre stood empty, swaying ever so slightly in the wind, waiting for its load. At its base, logs had been stacked neatly in crisscrossing bundles that formed a flat solid platform for the accused to stand.

The trio elbowed their way to the front, trying to assess the environment. Labourers slopped pitch onto the logs, while guards formed a square around them, jostling with the crowd to keep them back.

"She's not here yet," whispered Hercules.

"They'll bring her out from the castle I expect," said Francis.

"Good, kidnap her, go get her before they take her to the pyre!" said Florie, desperation quivering in her voice.

"I can't see a way in," said Francis, peering at the Portcullis Gate. "If we'd had more time to plan perhaps, we could've brought brooms."

"If we'd had more time, we could've broken her out of jail without this crowd watching," lamented Hercules.

Suddenly the clamouring of the crowd reached a fever pitch, buzzing with excitement. Francis' head snapped to the gatehouse where sure enough, a jailor was leading a hooded prisoner at the end of a rope. Florie whimpered at the sight of her sister. Even from this distance she was visibly frail. She put up no resistance for her jailer, walking obediently, despite the cruel tugs on her rope that sent her stumbling forward.

Florie held tightly to Francis' arm. "Do something," she whispered, her voice cracking. He looked at Hercules whose eyes were wide open with anguished hopelessness.

Francis watched as the jailor pulled Agnes up a ladder onto the platform. He used the long rope he'd dragged her with to tie her to the stake. He snaked it around her, pulling it tight so that she jarred with each coil.

A herald joined them atop the platform of logs, declaration in hand. Once the jailor was satisfied the prisoner was tied sufficiently, which took a few more tugs than necessary, the herald whipped the hood from Agnes, revealing her gaunt face.

The crowd gasped, as did Florie, who's whimpering only intensified. "Wave your wand, save her, please," Florie begged, sobbing into Francis' sleeve. He glanced at Hercules who was searching frantically for any glimpse of hope, any opportunity. Francis tried to rack his brains, but his heart was already heavy with the prospect of what would come next.

"People of Edinburgh," began the herald, "before you stands Agnes Sampson, who was taken and brought before His Majestie and sundry other nobility of Scotland, where she was straightly examined for reasons of witchcraft. There she was found to bear the devil's mark, a privy mark upon the skin, evidence of the devil's foul lick before he receives them as servants."

The crowd's excitement turned to nervous chatter at the mention of the devil so easily brought into their midst. Some even looked nervously over their shoulders.

"Thereupon, she confessed her crimes of witchcraft and other sundry things which were so miraculous and strange that the Kings Majestie did say she was a liar!"

Francis felt bile burn his throat as the herald got his laugh from the townsfolk. His horning too had been laced with cheap storytelling to both appease and frighten the masses.

"Thereupon she took His Majestie a little aside and did declare unto him the very words which passed only between His Majestie and his Queen on their wedding night! Convinced of her sorcery the aforesaid Agnes Sampson was sent to trial, a right afforded every person of Scotland."

Francis watched Agnes. She did not weep or show fear. She simply looked straight ahead. He suspected she had been resigned to her fate a long time ago, having spent the best part of two years being abused and neglected by her captors. She probably wished for death. Francis felt the guilt rise up his body and knot itself in his chest. His head felt suddenly heavy, as though someone had placed lead weights on his crown, compressing his spine.

"There she did confess all her ungodly crimes, namely gathering with other witches in the North Berwick kirkyard at a Devil's sabbat, engaging with the Devil in a sexual nature and using her sorcery to bring about storms to batter His Majestie's ships with the intention of sinking them, amongst other sundry crimes. All amounting to several counts of witchcraft and treason, where she was found to be guilty and sentenced to death by burning."

Florie's body heaved silently at Francis' side as the obedient herd cheered the sentencing.

"Furthermore," said the Herald, having to shout over the noise, "furthermore, as these crimes pertain to both witchcraft and treason, the usual mercy of strangulation before burning will not be administered."

Hercules gasped and turned to Francis, his face a mask of incredulity, while the crowd cheered insensibly. Francis could only muster a weak expression of shock.

The herald climbed down from the pyre along with the jailor. There was very little pomp and ceremony as the torchbearers stepped forward on cue and touched their torches to the fuel. The pitch caught and the blood-red flames spread quickly, weaving their way through the structure.

For a time, Agnes remained statuesque, until the logs began to catch and the flames licked at her skirts. She started to scream, an unnatural ear-splitting scream that Francis had never heard before in all his years of soldiering. The fire roared and the wind coaxed them ever higher, engulfing Agnes' body.

Her shrieks echoed within his skull, colliding with all the feelings failure they induced. His head became a quagmire of desolation, precluding him from any rational thought.

Florie turned and buried her face in Francis' chest, unable to watch. Agnes continued to scream from within her fiery encasement for longer than he ever thought possible a person able survive such intense heat. Eventually, it stopped, replaced only by the deep growl of the fire, flicking up enormous flames toward the heavens.

"I hate you," Florie whispered, "I wish it were you up there. I hate you."

*****

10th July 1592
Canongate

Francis sat alone in his dingy tavern room. It had space only for a bed and table with little else room to move about in. The bed sported a straw mattress underneath a pile of moth-eaten blankets. The straw had not been changed in some time, it was completely flattened and emitted the faint smell of urine. Francis sat at the table with its solitary stool and drank.

He had stayed here the past few days, sending Florie along with Hercules back to Hailes. She had been utterly inconsolable despite attempts from both of them. Francis was worried she'd go completely mad with grief.

He had made it appear as though he'd completely left the town, then taken up residence in the inn under a false name and sporting a disguise. He told others it was so he could plan the full eradication of the witch hunters, but the truth was he was lost.

He played the events of the past few weeks over and over in his head. He still felt immense pride at his successful action against the King. The guilt, however, overshadowed everything. He tried his hardest to rationalise it all. First, he didn't know where Agnes was, and even when he did, Hercules had given the reasons himself at the coven meeting of why it'd be a bad idea to rescue her. The public would be incensed into a fever at the seemingly magical disappearance of a witch from captivity.

Still, perhaps they should've done it anyway. Had he been selfish or smart? They must've done unspeakable things, worse than burning, to break her spirit so. *It's no use reliving the past,* he told himself again and again. Yet, he could not think straight on the fate of the coven either.

He cursed under his breath as he recounted his experience at the Tolbooth. Despite all he'd done to reclaim his long list of titles and his dominance over the King, he hadn't been able to get a stupid judge to release, what must've been to him, a worthless prisoner.

He rubbed his eyes and drained his cup. He kicked down hard on the floorboards, his signal to the kitchens to bring up another drink. For the past few days he'd swung drastically from painfully recounting all the events to just wanting to forget. His usually neatly trimmed moustaches were wiry tangles amongst his unkempt beard.

He kneaded his temples. Perhaps Hercules had been right all along, it was time to stop playing the great game of politics and focus on what he had. He had his titles back and his land, he could still wield his influence at court. He had a wife who, while she was older and more content than he to live the family life, played her part to perfection. Then, he had the coven. Likely frightened out of their wits right now, in need of a leader and shepherd more than ever.

A knock rapped at the door. "Come in," said Francis in a gravelly, weary voice. He didn't look up as the person entered. "Just put them on the table and go."

"It has come time to pay your bill Lord," came the gruff response. Francis didn't recognise the speaker, the accent wasn't Scottish, it was a Welshman. Then, confirming his fears, he heard a pistol cock. He kept his head down.

"Lord? I don't know what you're talking about man, I'm a sailor," he replied. He glanced at his sword which was sheathed next to the bed.

"Come now mister Stewart, no games, how about we head outside for a nice chat eh?" said the cloaked figure, holding his pistol outstretched.

"Who are ye? Ye don't sound like ye can afford that pistol." said Francis, keeping his gaze on the floorboards.

"Oh, you'll be surprised what I can afford mister Stewart. You likely know of me, but we've never met. I'm Oswyn Fletcher, Witch Hunter General under the command of John Maitland Lord of Thirlstane, agent of God and the crown. I think you know why I'm here?"

"Didn't ye hear?" said Francis, "Maitland's done for, relieved of his position."

"And how would a simple sailor know that, eh?" said Oswyn, chuckling. "Come mister Stewart, I tire of this. Up!"

Francis rose slowly from his chair, hands by his head. Then, halfway up, he grabbed for the pistol, pointing it away. Oswyn pulled the trigger. The ball whizzed past his skull, cutting his ear as it did. The burning powder and smoke shot from the muzzle, stinging Francis's eyes and he cried out in pain as the searing hot barrel blistered his hands.

He brought up his leg swiftly, kicking Oswyn in the groin and scrambled over the bed frame to retrieve his sword. Oswyn recovered in time to tug Francis' leg, pulling him away from the weapon. He kicked out again with his free leg and caught the Welshman on the nose, breaking it with a colossal crunch and spurting blood down his front.

He scurried to the end of the bed, grabbed his sword and turned to face his attacker. Oswyn stood in his grey uniform at the end of the bed, glaring at Francis, paying no attention to his gushing nose.

"Oh, you'll pay for that mister Stewart," he said, drawing the dirk at his belt.

There was so little room in the cramped space, Francis couldn't draw his sword, so he leapt at Oswyn, smashing the guard of his hilt into his face. Oswyn dropped and Francis sprung over his bulk to the door.

He opened it, before thrusting it shut again as crossbow bolts thudded into the wood, showering him with splinters. Rough hands grabbed at him from behind, securing themselves around his neck. Francis kept one foot on the door, barring the witch hunters outside as they tried to barge their way into the room.

Oswyn tightened his forearm around Francis' neck, pulling him away from the entrance. Francis could feel blackness closing in around the edges of his eyes as he tried desperately to keep his awkward position, jostling with the gruff Oswyn.

He kicked with both feet at the door, forcing himself rearward into Oswyn and sending them both tumbling over the table. Francis sprung up first and drove his heel down onto Oswyn's skull. There was no time to inflict further damage, as the now undefended door crashed open. He dove headfirst for the small window, shattering the glass and frame just as a second volley of bolts thumped into the walls.

He fell, limbs flailing until the floor of the alley came up to meet him. He hit it with a short and unforgiving wallop, falling chest first on to the pommel of his blade. He gasped for air, emitting staggered wheezing sounds as he tried to recover himself.

He couldn't even swear when he saw more of the grey uniformed prigs come sprinting from the front of the tavern. He rolled to the edge of the alley and hobbled into the stables at its rear. None of the horses were saddled so he just picked the closest and jumped on its back.

He kicked it forward, holding onto the mane for dear life. They burst through the stable doors and galloped out into the fields behind the Canongate. He heard the twang of crossbows before the bolts came whistling past him.

He turned the horse after they fired, watching them as they hollered at him. Some were reloading while others came chasing after him on foot. There was about a score, and those from inside the tavern were spilling out to join their ranks. Their uniforms blended with the walls of Edinburgh that was silhouetted against the sky behind them.

His ragged breathing steadied as he considered his position. He wore only a thin, dirty shirt and baggy hose with no stockings or boots. He took one final glance at the city and his attackers before pulling his horse away and riding for the tree line.

Well, Francis thought, *if anyone's counting, add horse thief to my list of crimes.*

Chapter 13

1st August 1592
Holyrood Palace

James strolled down the main staircase of the palace. Much of the immediate repairs after Francis' raid had been taken care of, the carpets had been changed or cleaned, carpenters had restored much of the woodwork and the broken windows had been replaced. However, the evidence lingered, the walls bore the pockmarks of musket balls and the grass in the courtyard had yet to grow back.

As he approached, a steward opened the door that led into a private dining room, where a simple breakfast was already laid out. He sat down and tucked into a small roll of buttered bread.

"Have you sent for Maitland?" he asked an aide.

"Yes, Your Grace, a messenger was sent to find him over an hour ago."

"Excellent," he said, grinning through a mouthful of crumbs.

He sat merrily enjoying his food and sipping at a small ale until Maitland was announced at the door.

"Maitland! How good you made it, please do sit," he said.

Maitland walked nervously into the room and pulled out a chair facing the King.

"How goes the Bothwell situation, any luck?" said James, peering over his silver tankard.

"The Bothwell situation?" asked Maitland, "I... You had me dismissed Your Grace."

"I did? Well, I do not remember doing such a thing. Why in God's graces would I do that? Ah! You jest with me!?" said James, laughing.

"No, Sire, I'm afraid 'tis true, I am no longer Chancellor."

"Oh? Well who is then?" said James, his eyebrow cocked as though still expecting a joke.

"Ye haven't appointed one," said Maitland flatly.

"Well, then I appoint you, satisfied?" said James, ripping off a hunk of bread with his teeth.

"Well... I... Yes, thank you, Your Grace, I am honoured," Maitland sat forward in his chair.

James' cocked eyebrow lowered, "You're not fooling are you Maitland? I dismissed you?"

"No, Your Grace, you did dismiss me."

"Then, why don't I remember? This is why you departed in Falkland?"

Maitland considered his next words carefully before offering them, "I was under the impression, Sire, that you had been bewitched by the Lord Bothwell."

"Preposterous!" said James, slamming down his tankard.

"Sire, what exactly do you remember?"

"I know not, I had assumed my faculties intact. But now you mention it, everything seems muddled. I... the Kingdom is in good order, yet I remember that Francis did conduct a raid here. I remember him in Falkland, yet I do not know why," James frowned as he waded through his own mind. "Damn it Maitland, just tell me what is going on!"

"I know not where to start, you remember your voyage lord? The storms?"

Maitland relayed the events of Francis' plight to James as speedily as he could, choosing to embellish some details and lessening others. James gasped and raised his arms in shock at different intervals, as though he were watching a mummer's farce.

"I... I remember all of it Maitland, truly I do. It's as though I'm waking up from a dream and realising the cold reality of day," said James softly.

"Aye, sire, it has been a horrifying experience," said Maitland. James looked into his eyes and could see it was true. "I had thought to have lost you forever sire to the beguilements of the witch Bothwell."

James gritted his teeth, "That currish snake! Performing dark magicks on his own King! That man continues to heap treason upon treason. Maitland, if I know you, you did not let up on Francis did you, else he'd be here, in Edinburgh."

Maitland sighed and smiled, he had not thought his meeting with the King would achieve success so quickly when he had left his lodgings that morning. His stomach turned as though it were a pinwheel caught in the gust of his soaring spirits. Unwanted tears of relief formed in the corners of his eyes.

"No Sire, I did not. My witch hunters chased him out of town," he said, trying his best to hide his glee.

"Most excellent Maitland!" said James with gusto, "I knew I could count on you in all this chaos."

"We also moved up the burning of the witch Agnes Sampson, she provided no further use to us," said Maitland, trying to stay focused on business in the face of the praise he could've only hoped for in his wildest of dreams.

"Aye, we've had her for some time have we not? Good riddance, a witch removed from our Godly Kingdom," said James.

"My King, I have awaited your guidance for so long, what do we do now?" said Maitland.

"Right, of course," said James, "it would seem we have been given a new chance. We have Francis on the run again, we must not repeat our prior mistakes. The speeches and bluster did not work nor did our efforts to contain the borderers by force."

"Nay sire, unfortunately they did not."

"Nor did our guile in ensnaring the wastrel. It would seem to me my dear Maitland that we have always been on the back foot, relying on others to do our work for us. No more!"

"Very good Sire, what would you suggest?"

"It is clear we cannot rely on the good faith of my lords to pursue the devil spawn. Nevertheless, I will issue a speech to those who currently reside in Edinburgh removing Francis' pardon. It may, in fact, win some over to our cause to display the sheer scope of his sorcery and the extent of his treason. I should think even the Stewart faction will have a hard time refusing to aid me. That seems a logical starting point think ye not?"

"Since the burning sire, Edinburgh has not stopped discussing witches, I should think that will aid us," added Maitland.

"Very good, I will issue a pamphlet, let us stoke the fire. Let us make them fear Francis so that he dare not cross any threshold in Scotland."

James rose to his feet and gazed out of one of the windows that looked upon the gardens and the abbey at the rear of the palace. It was already a bright morning and James could see not a single cloud in the sky. He held his hands behind his back and spoke, continuing his scan of the lawn.

"I think Maitland, perhaps we plan too much. Mayhaps we have been overthinking this problem. Afterall, a hunter does not debate upon the actions of his quarry. He conducts the finding, cuts off the escape then makes the kill. We must do exactly that Maitland."

"We shall assemble the hunting party first, see which lords we have at our disposal, if the fickle bunch decide I am too harsh on their darling, so be it and I will deal with them once our work is done. Then, we remove every option one by one of the necromancer Francis until we have him at our mercy." A foul grin spread across his face as he walked back to the table. "When he has nowhere to run, nowhere to hide, we will gut the artless dog!"

At his final words he stabbed a fork into what remained of his morning loaf with such force the table leapt from the floor.

"What of the borderers Sire, what if he uses his sorcery again?" said Maitland.

"Hah! Let him try Maitland. I refuse to hide behind walls any longer, I will remain here in Edinburgh. Let him cast his devil's magick and let all those who see bear witness to what he truly is. My proclamations have been seen as fantastical, senseless even! An assault on a precious and pious lord. Let the people of Scotland look upon the real darkness of that man's soul."

"As for the borderers, I would think their chests be full of the treasures of Falkland and Holyrood. How many times will they risk life and limb for an outlaw, when they have enough silver to last ten winters already? Though, there is some truth to your words, he does command their loyalty. Have the border wardens hang some of those who rode with him. I suspect they will not be hard to identify. Offer the wardens triple their usual entitlement on recovered loot. The next time he tries to raise them he will find his yield diminished."

James' toothy grin widened, "we will destroy Francis so utterly and completely he will beg for my sword."

"And the..." began Maitland.

"Ah ah ah Maitland! The hunter does not over analyse the movements of his quarry, remember. We follow the tracks and stick the hart."

"Now, see to it whatever process to undo my pardon is followed and set a date for the lords to gather. Don't delay! Lest our prey wander too far."

"Of course, Your Grace, right away," said Maitland, jumping to his feet.

James watched him as he left the room, smiling inanely to himself.

* * * * *

13th August 1592
Hailes Castle

Francis gave his horse to the stable boy and walked slowly towards the castle. His ride from Kelso had been long and slow. He was back to avoiding the King's scouts on his every journey, taking only the small cattle trails or staying off the roads altogether. He had also been in no rush to make it to Hailes. He hadn't heard from Hercules since Agnes' burning and his mind formed disparate imaginings of how he might be received. Still, Hercules had sent a raven, so he must have a reason for summoning him.

He climbed the stone steps and lifted the huge brass knocker to beat on the doors. A haggard looking servant dragged it open halfway. Francis stepped inside the entrance hall and the servant hurriedly slammed the door shut after him, sliding heavy bolts across it.

"I shall let Mister Stewart know yer here," he said before scurrying away.

Francis waited in the dimly lit hallway for some time before Hercules showed himself at the top of the stairs. He looked grim, far beyond his usual seriousness, he wore an expression of tortured concern and the bags under his eyes sagged like half empty sacks of grain.

"Francis," he said, "I was not sure if you'd come."

"You summoned me and I'm here," said Francis plainly, "is there to be a coven meeting?"

"I thought it best, we've not had one in a full year. Somehow the last meeting feels like it were both yesterday and a lifetime ago. I suspect we may've lost some who've travelled north, or south."

"Is Florie here?"

"Aye, though, she has kept mostly to her rooms. She won't see anyone. She's stayed here since, well, since Agnes. I don't know whether she'll join the meeting."

"Aye," said Francis.

The two stood on different floors, Hercules made no move to come down the stairs. Francis looked up at him, unsure what to say. He knew Hercules wouldn't want any reassurances from him or to hear of more hair-brained schemes. Desperately he wanted his brother to take action for once, to give him some kind of impetus, a goal to strive towards, a strategy to debate but neither said anything. The truth was, there didn't seem like much left to strive for.

"What is the agenda for the meeting?" said Francis, breaking the heavy silence.

"It's good to check in once in a while, we will take a roll call to see who's still with us. Perhaps try and piece together information on whether others have left of their own accord or been captured. Though, I suspect mostly it'll be about you."

"I?"

"Yes, not only did ye let Agnes burn, ye have been outlawed again. I would not blame them for wishing punishment on ye. Ye sold them false hope and promises, and I know not what you or I can do to remedy that."

"Aye, I had not known the King would come round so quickly, if I had, I might've hung around Edinburgh for a while longer."

"Wait," said Hercules, suddenly electric with energy, bounding down the stairs, "'come round'? Please by Flamel's cauldron, don't tell me ye charmed the King to get ye pardon!?"

"I don't know what to tell ye Hercules," said Francis, sheepishly looking away.

"Ye really are an egotistical, compassionless, belligerent toad aren't ye!" he spat through his clenched jaw. "Performing magick, not only in front of, but actually on mundanes. Is it some kind of mission of yours to break every single rule ye possibly can? Is all this some great game to ye!? Eh!?" He poked Francis vigorously in the chest with every question.

"Nay matter how many people get killed along the way? If James didn't truly believe in witches before, he certainly does now doesn't he!? Did ye ever stop to think, did it ever even occur to ye, what that means for the folk of this coven!?"

Francis bit his tongue as he thought of all the other times, he'd used magic in front of non-magick folk. He hung his head, Hercules was right of course. Everything was his own fault. He wasn't sure if he'd even be able to look Florie in the eye if it came to it.

"And to think I've been debating how best to protect ye from the coven and keep ye here. Ye don't deserve it Francis! Do ye hear me? Do ye understand? I'm done with ye schemes and yer manipulations!"

"Yes, Hercules, I understand," said Francis.

"Yes, well, ye can wait in the drawing room until the meeting starts," said Hercules, lowering his tone, "my servant will bring ye food an ale."

Hercules shot a final disparaging look at Francis before pivoting on his heel and heading back up the stairs.

Francis entered the drawing room to the left of the entrance hall. It was an average sized room with an earthy feel to it. Dark wooden beams ran across the ceiling while on the walls chiselled masonry framed its features. They depicted scenes of Scotland's countryside with the peasants ploughing fields or driving cattle.

Two chairs, upholstered with flowery patterns, sat facing the unlit hearth. They looked comfortable but Francis didn't feel much like lounging in his brother's house after the tirade he'd just received. Instead, he pulled up a hard-wooden stool and sat at the end of a long table that filled the centre of the room.

The servant from the door came shuffling into the room carrying a tray with a wooden tankard and a pitcher of ale.

Francis poured himself a cup and sipped at it slowly. Hercules had not said anything he hadn't told himself already, over and over. With his lands forfeit again, all he truly had left was his wife, his brother and this coven. Although, if he needed to arrange a ship to France or Spain, even those would be left behind. He had little time before someone came to evict him from Kelso.

He paced about the room while he waited, keen to not over drink before the meeting. He examined the carvings in the stonework and at patterns on the tapestries, trying to distract his mind. Time passed quicker than he expected, even from the other side of the castle, he could hear the thumping of witches arriving on the roof above the Great Hall. He decided he would wait where he was until summoned. He didn't want to have to sit in that hall any longer than he had to.

Francis waited, biting his fingernails and finishing the ale on the table. The servant eventually came waddling in and beckoned him to the Great Hall. When they arrived at the huge doors, Francis inhaled deeply before pushing them open just wide enough for him to slip through.

The hall turned to stare at him as one as he entered. He surveyed all the faces that had once looked upon him with awe, now replaced entirely with anger, unease or fear. He strode up the centre of the aisle, where he saw Hercules standing at the podium and Florie behind him. Her eyes were glazed over with cold hatred producing an involuntary shiver as he walked.

He reached the dais and, without looking at Florie, sat in the wooden throne. He'd never considered before how absurdly large and ornate it was. He shifted his rump nervously on the seat and tried to look as serious as he could with the carved branches reaching high above him. He steepled his fingers, then undid them, placing them instead on his thighs.

Hercules cleared his throat, "as I was saying. It is self-evident through Agnes' burning that the Warlocks of this coven failed in our mission to remove Maitland, the Witch Hunters, and rescue her. I would like to put it forward to the floor to decide what we do next."

"Sister Mary of Kelso. It seems to me the Warlocks of this coven, few as they are, have not only failed in their mission but failed in their duty to protect this coven. What is the use of a coven at all if our leaders cannot protect us!"

"Thank you, sister Mary," said Hercules, "it is true we have failed. Nonetheless, we need, now more than ever, to stick together and protect each other."

"Brother Donald of North Berwick. How exactly, do you propose to protect us, the motion from last time said we were to go north or into exile?"

"I don't have all the answers for you right now, we will build our support and defence network, we'll have to adapt and change the way we conduct ourselves. I think it not acceptable we just leave."

Florie stood calmly and made her way to the podium. "I am with Sister Mary. *I* think this debacle has shown the inability of our Warlocks to defend and lead this coven. I am through suffering at their ineptitude and flagrant disregard for the lives of the members here in front of me. I think it about time we led ourselves and not suffer at the whims of the nobility. There has been no punishment for their continual failures. I propose we strip them both of their titles, banish the Warlock Francis and run this coven ourselves!"

She let her words hover over the room while the crowd murmured, turning from side to side, debating with their neighbours. Francis could see Hercules in his peripheral vision looking at him angrily, but he kept his eyes firmly fixed on his shoes.

"And," continued Florie, "I propose the council does not vote, but the members of this coven."

The hive of wittering buzzed again until one member stood up. "Brother Bruce of Fife," he said, "I agree with sister Florie! Let's do away with the lords!"

"Sister Anne of Coldingham. What of their wand magicks? How will we defend ourselves without skilled wand users? Most of us are healers and alchemists."

"There is no reason you or I, sister Anne," said Florie, "cannot learn wand magick. We will teach and defend ourselves."

Florie looked around the room, nobody else challenged her.

"So be it," said Hercules drawing his wand resignedly, "Those of you who agree the Warlocks should be abolished, a new council elected and Francis Stewart banished will gather on the right of the room, those who oppose to the left, and those who wish to abstain remain in the middle."

He flicked his wand as he gave each position, generating a lightning blue zero in the air above each of them. A small bunch were quick to cast their vote, separating themselves evenly between the ayes and nays. As they did the zero counted up in roman numerals. Most of the crowd were still in the middle, looking left and right, unsure of which option to choose. They debated and argued with each other until, eventually, they shifted themselves, beginning with a trickle and ending with a flourish of movement, causing the numbers to flicker rapidly as they counted up the new arrivals.

Francis had kept his eyes down the whole time. He waited with his heart and stomach occupying his throat. He felt sick as he waited for Hercules to announce the final count. The shuffling seemed to have stopped and it was a while before anyone spoke.

"The nays have 24 votes, the abstainers have 33 and ayes have 56. The motion passes." said Hercules. He swivelled slowly to face Francis, he paced to the throne and knelt to match his eye level.

"See what you've done Brother," he whispered. "I fear for their safety without guidance. They're not ready yet. Look what you've made them do."

Francis remained tranquil. "Damn it man! I've never seen you unable to utter a word on anything. What say you!?"

"You're right Hercules, I deserve it. I suppose I should be going now," said Francis.

He stood and pushed past Hercules, walking as fast as he could to the double doors at the end of the hall. His heavy footsteps echoed off the rafters, cutting through the dense fog of deathly silence that hung over the rest of the coven.

Chapter 14

15th August 1592
North of Kelso

Francis sat hunched over in the saddle as his nag trudged through the wild fields. He had not shaved in weeks so that his beard was a tangled mess of hair. The usually finely pointed tip of his goatee protruded from the fuzz like a tuft of weeds breaking through turf. Heavy bags sat under his eyes, a result of his fitful sleep. He had camped in the forest overnight, avoiding the roads and taking the direct route south to Kelso.

Despite the huge disappointment of being banished from the coven, he felt somehow lighter too. The burden of responsibility for those people's lives had become heavier of late and a part of him was glad to see the burden removed. Someone else was making the decisions now. They could lead themselves into peril or safety but whichever they chose, it would not be Francis' fault. Besides, he was sure with himself removed, they would more likely be safer.

Hercules had sent a raven to follow him with a message. The coven had elected a Warlock-less reformed council on which he still sat along with Florie and three new members.

Those that could had all decided to stay in the castle while they figured out the best course of action.

In truth, Francis did not know what that was anymore. He had thought being restored would've all but ensured their safety, though now he questioned his own integrity on how much that'd been about the coven. Besides, he'd been proven wrong so emphatically, the reasons almost didn't matter. Maitland's lackeys were back to their usual business of scouring Scotland in search of witches, barely more than a month after his raid of Falkland.

Moving away didn't seem like a viable option either. Hercules was right, sooner or later elsewhere will catch up and there will be nowhere left to hide. The Germanic countries were already burning witches like candles. The new world perhaps? Though, he'd heard too many stories of wildmen with powerful shamans.

Francis was stirred from his thoughts when he realised he was coming upon a wide road. He dug his heels in and drove his horse to the edge of the field where he tied the reins to a tree and went to investigate.

He recognised it as the main route north between Kelso and Edinburgh. He must've already come within less than a mile of the town. He was considering using the road for the last portion of his journey, when, as he got closer he saw the hoof prints. At least fifty horse had ridden through recently. He swore and walked back to his horse, keeping his eyes on the road, ready to drop flat at the first hint of a rider.

He made reached his horse and rode east, there was an estuary of the Tweed nearby and he could follow it all the way to Kelso. When he found it, he saw to his relief the water level was low. It was summer and the estuary had been reduced to a trickle of water winding its way through the smooth stones.

He walked his horse along the riverbed, splashing the cooling water up his legs. It twisted and took meandering detours in places, making the journey longer, but he knew it would cover his tracks, particularly if they'd brought hounds. When he thought he was close, he dismounted and made for a small ridge he was certain looked into the town and his residence.

He used the shade of a beech tree to mask his outline and crouched. As he suspected the cavalry were gathered outside his home. A few of the men tended the horses while the rest appeared to be inside.

Then, he saw Margaret emerge from the front doors, carrying bags and ushering the children towards a carriage. Men followed, appearing to be cordially carrying more luggage to load onto the rear of the carriage.

Before even the bags were loaded, soldiers from inside the border house began throwing clothes and furniture from the high windows, sending it all clattering to the ground. Someone had got into his study and began emptying his papers from his desk, sending them fluttering in the breeze like a hundred swallows crisscrossing towards the ground. The mesmerising illusion was broken by the crash of his whole desk that sliced through them onto the stone path below.

Margaret was screaming something he couldn't quite make out at the soldiers causing the destruction. She had to be forced towards the carriage while she scolded them. Francis would've smiled at her unwavering tenacity, had the soldiers man-handling her not caused a knot in his stomach.

As one of them shoved her, he noticed it wasn't the King's livery they were wearing but the Duke of Lennox's. *Ludovic*! The word clanged in Francis' head like a forceful oath. So, it had been he who'd double-crossed them at Holyrood. He'd been playing both sides! It made perfect sense! He hadn't known about the Falkland raid which is why it was successful. The snake had sold him out for his lands and titles.

Francis' mind raced as he thought what else the man knew. He had known where he was staying in Edinburgh, he knew to find him at Hailes with Hercules, he perhaps even knew about Florie. His speculations were brought to a grinding halt as he saw one of the soldiers push Margaret to the floor, laughing as he did so. The knot in his stomach tightened, she didn't deserve this, even now in all his disgrace she stood by him.

Without thinking he stood and dashed to his poor excuse for a horse. He threw himself into the saddle and kicked his heels back. The nag went hurtling over the ridge and down towards the soldiers. He unsheathed his sword and lowered himself, streamlined against his horses back. He thrust it out forward, aiming for the men guarding the horses.

The cries of alarm sounded weak in the open space when they noticed him, careering down the ridge towards them. Francis was upon them before they could untie their horses, his sword point cut through the foremost man's neck, wrenching Francis' arm and shoulder. He let the force take his sword away from his body then brought it viciously down on the next opponent, who had raised his arms as his only defence. The broadsword cut through flesh and sinew with a nauseating efficiency. Francis rode onward, past them and towards the men harassing his wife.

"That's my wife!!" he shouted, brandishing his weapon high above his head. "Unhand her you cowardly curs!"

He slashed at the back of the man who'd pushed Margaret down and heard his anguished cry as he flew through the outer courtyard of his home. Left with no enemy ahead he turned his horse in a wide arc to reverse his charge. He could see men were pouring from the house now, running to their steeds and gathering their lances.

"Go Margaret!! Take the children and go!" he yelled as he thundered past her.

Out of the corner of his eye, he saw she was quick to obey and he heard her order the carriage driver onwards. Francis, confident in her resourcefulness, turned his attentions back to the enemy who had loosened their horses and were ready to ride.

He rode in a straight line towards them, sword lowered, as though to charge the array of lance points that had been lowered in the face of his impetuous charge. Despite their limited number Lennox's horsemen still rode in a line formation, two horses deep, trotting until the very last moment of the charge.

At the last possible moment Francis feinted his charge, heaving on the reins of his nag, pulling himself abreast to the line of lance points and away. His horse, however, wasn't as responsive as the well-drilled Valentine and the lancer at the end of the line caught his unarmoured midriff. He cried out as he felt the point rip through his skin and grind against his rib cage.

He grit his teeth and urged his horse on. He glanced briefly down at as his wound and could see blood had already soaked through his shirt down the whole of his right side. He looked back at the lancers who had wheeled themselves skilfully and were bearing down in their pursuit. Their warhorses would be faster than his malnourished beast.

He winced as he kicked his horse again, willing it up the small crest he had so rashly come stampeding down a moment ago. With each collision of hooves on the ground pain shot up his side, like he was being stabbed over and over again. He chanced a look behind him and saw he had enough space to slow his horse. He turned side on to his pursers to review his skirmish. Behind the lancers he saw that no one had taken off after Margaret.

"Tell Ludovic," he shouted to the duke's men, "next time I see him, he's dead!"

He didn't wait around to hear their response, though he heard their taunts over his shoulder, as he rode over the small crest and into the riverbed. He continued to push his horse hard as they splashed upstream. The rocky channel was even worse on his gash, making him gasp for air with each agonising lungful.

He glimpsed at the pursuers behind him. The stream had slowed their heavy horses down to a trot while his own screw was making light work of the uneven ground. Though, he saw a savvy few were driving their horses up the steep banks and into the field on his right. They would ride on ahead and cut him off eventually, so Francis veered left, taking the bank in a few strides and galloping over the edge into the woodland.

He couldn't see them now, it'd take them some time to climb out of the river and continue their pursuit. Francis sheathed his sword and let his horse pick the route through the trees, keeping it at a steady canter. He did not know Lennox's men and whether they'd give up the chase or whether they'd continue to track him.

Blackness started to creep in around the edges of his eyes. He checked his wound again only to wish he hadn't, his right leg was stained crimson and he noticed the fingers on his right hand had started to turn white. He ripped off the sleeve of his shirt covering his left arm and tied it as tight as he could around the wound when he heard the renewed shouts behind him.

He managed to touch a hand to his sword hilt and utter "*Wotekwo,*" before he slipped from the saddle and the dark void behind his eyes took him before he hit the ground.

* * * * *

22nd August 1592
Hailes Castle

Oswyn positioned his men one hundred yards from the castle with care, ensuring everyone was crouched and silent in the darkness. They had blackened the metal of their crossbows with dubbin and exchanged their grey for dark cowls.

They had searched Haddingtonshire ten times over but finally, they had cornered the coven. Even now all the lights of the castle were extinguished, save for a few glimmers through the windows of the great hall. The townsfolk of the area had sworn the castle was empty and even his own scouts had reported as much. Maitland, however, had been convinced the witches would be here.

Francis' residences, as fortified as they were, weren't safe enough to hold any sort of gathering. At the King's orders, most of them were heavily watched for any signs of the earl and the Duke of Lennox had begun to move into others already. No, it made sense that he would seek refuge with his half-brother Hercules. Agnes had managed to keep the place a secret, the hag, and so had their informant but after weeks of stalking they had eventually seen the signs of life. Hercules was careful, to be sure, but no one could escape the wroth of God for long.

Oswyn had been under strict orders to remain patient, noting the comings and goings of the castle. Meetings were always at night. They had recorded people arriving down a ladder that led from the roof and entering through the front doors. Such ladders were common along the borders, it could be hiked up to prevent attackers but it was an oddity this far north, a giveaway they should've spotted sooner Oswyn thought to himself.

They'd observed them leaving in the opposite fashion too. They had thought they'd seen the folk fly from the roof directly up into the sky. However, it was hard to tell in the darkness whether they were just imagining such things or witnessing real witches on broomstaves. Either way, they clearly travelled via some form of magick.

Maitland was right to caution him. He would've attacked on first sight, but now they knew there was a meeting going on inside. They'd watched them all enter one by one, ninety in total by his count. Typically, they all left at once, and that's when he'd strike. It was the waiting that frustrated him, he wrung his hands constantly, anticipating the door would open at any moment.

Then, it did. Only a crack at first, as the old servant of the place poked his head outside, holding up a small candle lantern and peering into the night. He signalled that the coast was clear and the cloaked figures stepped into the brisk evening air. Oswyn couldn't help but let out a small squeak before silencing himself with a hand, holding his assault until they'd all left the safety of the castle.

"Loose!!" he shouted when the majority were finally in view. Thirty of his witch hunters stood up in unison from the tall grass, and the thwack of their strings broke the silence as their bolts zipped into the crowd. Some cried out and toppled while those left standing screamed and raced around the corner, towards the ladder.

"Loose!" Oswyn shouted again, a manic glee tingeing his voice. Thirty more witch hunters revealed themselves on the dexter side, firing into the panicked the mass.

"Charge!" came his next order. His men dropped their crossbows and withdrew an assortment of weapons. Some produced cudgels or knives, while others carried simple pitchforks and axes. The men roared as they raced the hundred yards to their prey, who were forcing each other up the ladder and away from the danger.

A large solitary figure, who'd realised he wasn't to make it up the ladder turned to fight the oncoming tide. He had no weapon so raised his fists. He athletically ducked the first man's attack and slammed a heavy, ploughman's fist into the next. The first attacker rounded on him, keen to exact his revenge when a musket shot cracked, dwarfing the rest of the clamour. The witch hunter dropped to reveal a gaping puncture in the back of his skull.

Oswyn swivelled his head trying to see where the shot had come from when it's familiar crack made him jump. A wisp of smoke from the upper windows gave away the shooter's position. Oswyn commanded ten of his nearest thugs to retrieve their crossbows and shoot at the window. A third shot made him duck as he felt a ball whizz past, whistling menacingly in his ears.

By the virgin Mary's chamber pot! he swore, he hadn't seen any troops enter the castle! Then, a smile crept across his lips. He'd heard tell of Francis' pistols or whatever devil's sorcery was at work. He had him trapped in the castle, surrounded. The shots continued, peppering his men. The shooter fired from different windows each time, giving the illusion there was a line of musketeers up there, but Oswyn knew better. His grin stretched to show his yellow broken teeth.

He noticed his men had slowed their advance by the ladder, wavering under the continuous fire of the shooter. He hurtled towards them, shouting.

"Onward! Onward! It's not a man, just sorcery, your faith in God will protect you!"

He reached them and began shoving the rearmost men forward into the fray. The huge figure, fighting with his fists was finally subdued by a slash at his heels, and he was being bound with rope.

The rest had reached the ladder, and were pulling the witches down, pacifying any resistance with swift reports from their cudgels. Oswyn shoved past them all and began to climb. He gnashed at the heels of the witches above him, delighting in their fearful screams and whimpers.

The sound of smashing glass made him look up and he saw his crossbowmen were finally laying down fire into the upper windows. He cackled as he finally caught up to one of the women above him. He grabbed her ankle and gave it a swift tug, sending her tumbling towards the ground.

He bounded up the last few rungs until he was able to heave himself up onto the roof. There, his wicked smirk converted to a revolted glower. The witches were showing their true indiscretions against God for all to see, like a boozed-up whore might exhibit her wares. They were mounting broomstaves, as he had suspected, rising off the roof in a neat spiral before shooting up to the heavens like human-sized cannon balls. He'd seen it all in drawings, of course, but he hadn't thought to see them so easily command and flaunt the devil's agency.

He panicked as he realised he'd brought no weapon. He contented himself with throwing loose rocks and bricks instead and screaming bible verses at the top of his lungs, as they kicked themselves off the rooftop and into the air. When they'd all gone and there was no sign of them in the sky, Oswyn resigned himself to climbing back down the ladder. As he did, he noted the shooter was still active, although his rate of fire had slowed considerably as more crossbowmen had joined the standoff.

"Should we go inside sir? Flush him out?" said one of his men as he reached the bottom.

"I am not a sir, my rank was not born to me! and no, they're too crafty for that. Worry not, I have a plan." said Oswyn.

The struggle at the bottom of the ladder was over, prisoners were being tied up while the dead and severely wounded were left where they lay. The captured were being driven towards a large solitary oak, out of range from the castle. Oswyn hurried over, chiding others as he made his way to the agreed meeting point.

"Where's Gilbert?" He demanded.

"Here!" shouted back a man scurrying towards him.

"What's the count?"

"Fer the witches, there be seven dead or dying and we captured fourteen."

"Very good, there will be ale tonight! For all of you!" said Oswyn, spreading his arms out. "Get the prisoners onto the wagon and see that fifteen, no, best make it a score, see them to North Berwick. Maitland has issued instructions ahead that they're to be trialled and burnt immediately. Those ten are to give witness mind, so don't send idiots."

"And, er, what are wi to do aboot him?" said Gilbert, pointing up at the shooter still firing from the castle.

"Get a fire going and build torches. We'll smoke the swine out," said Oswyn, clapping his hands.

* * *

The first thing Francis heard was a soft tapping noise as the world came rushing back into his consciousness. He shifted and felt pain shoot up the right side of his body, jarring him awake. He realised the tapping noise was something gently rapping on his skull. He blinked open one eye, only to snap it shut in the blinding sunlight. He tried again and realised it was a raven, softly pecking him awake. It stepped back and tilted its head, watching him as he struggled to prop himself up on an elbow.

He tried to orientate himself. He was lying on a forest floor, rays of sunshine were penetrating through the canopy above. How long had he been down here? He looked at his legs and panicked, just for a moment, before noticing they weren't missing but thickly covered in the leaves, branches and forest debris.

He winced as he sat up, brushing the vegetation from his body and inspected the large gash in his side. Blood had soaked through nearly all of his clothing, but the exceedingly tight sleeve-bandage seemed to have done its job. The bleeding had stopped, and the wound was clotted with congealed gore that oozed with every movement. It needed cleaning, fast.

He found his sword lying next to him and gingerly retrieved his wand from the hilt.

"*Glano,*" he said through his dry and chapped lips. The gash glowed with a faint blue light that felt strange against his skin, like a cold burn. There was no sign of his horse, so he stood and staggered to the river he could hear babbling close by. He stripped down and washed himself and his clothes as best he could in the shallow stream. All he had with him were the clothes he was wearing so he stepped back into his damp britches and tied the shirt around his midriff.

Suddenly, he remembered the raven. He looked up to see it had followed him and had continued to watch him with its head cocked, as though it knew he needed to wake up fully before delivering its message. It cawed only once before spreading its wings and flying north.

Danger! thought Francis. He picked up his sword and hurried as best he could back to the spot he had awoken in. He quickly discovered the fresh hoof prints he'd hoped to find, thankfully the beast must've come back recently. He whistled again, trying to figure out which direction it had wandered off to. Then, he heard it, it neighed in response to his whistling and he could hear it trotting towards him. It emerged through the trees and he laughed aloud with relief to see the trusty screw had stayed with him.

"Good boy, eh," he said patting the horse on the nose, "ye wouldn't leave me fer dead now would ye."

He groaned as he pulled himself into the saddle. He looked up at the position of the sun and rode north.

Chapter 15

23rd August 1592
Hailes Castle

It was dark when Francis finally came upon the small hamlet of Hailes. His shoulders were burnt from a day's ride with his shirt employed as a make-shift bandage, rather than covering his skin. It stung as the cool night air swirled about him, making him shiver. He rode around the outskirts of the cluster of buildings, realising he must look like some dirty vagabond.

He had not seen it because of the dim clouded horizon, but as he approached the area of the castle he saw the thick black smoke curling upwards from the site. Francis kicked back and hurtled towards the site. The outer gate was open and he passed under it to find a scene of utter destruction.

The stonework of the castle still stood, yet, in the absence of all the roofing, doors and windows, it towered like a monolithic tombstone. Teardrops of obsidian soot streaked upwards from every opening of the castle, reaching high towards the crumbling battlements at the top. The fire had stopped but smoke continued to billow from all parts of the castle, combining in the sky to form one monstrous cloud that reached up as far as the eye could see.

Francis dismounted and walked towards the destruction. He drew his sword and inspected the ground as he walked. As he approached the walls, he saw heavily dented and broken crossbow bolts that had clearly struck the stonework.

"Oswyn," he hissed to himself. He kept close to the wall as he approached the main entrance. The great wooden doors had been burnt away leaving the passage open to the elements. He stopped at the edge of the opening, scanning his surroundings before forcing his head around the corner and drawing it back again. Nothing moved.

He stepped through the vacant archway and, amongst the debris, he saw immediately the very thing he'd hoped not to find. A body, so close to the exit, flat on its back and spread eagle. The charred remains of a dozen crossbow bolts jutted from the corpse, like miniature stumps after a forest fire. Francis ran to the body and knelt beside it, even though blackened and burnt he could see who it was. Hercules.

Francis tried to cup his brothers scorched head, only to have the toasted skin come away at his touch. He felt as though he should weep for his brother, but the tears never came, only a wave of tiredness and exhaustion overtaking his body.

He dropped flat to the floor and lay next to Hercules, closing his eyes, unable to look at the disfigured remains. He felt sleep creeping in, confiscating the muscles of his arms and legs. He welcomed the embrace, unsure what he was to do with himself, where to go or how to grieve.

It took all the will he had left within him to stop it when he heard a scuffling noise. He opened his eyes and began to sit up when he felt the prick of a sword at the back of his neck.

"Who are ye?" said a woman's voice.

"Florie? Is that ye?" said Francis, hoarsely.

"Francis!?" came the startled reply.

He felt the sword ease from his neck. Francis turned to find the sword was still pointed at him, and behind it was Florie. Her hair was wild, and she was covered head to toe in soot, so much so he couldn't make out her expression. He made to get up but the sword was thrust towards him again.

"No!" Florie barked.

"Florie," said Francis, "at this point, I know not what to do and I'm likely dying already anyway," he pointed at his heavily stained shirt. "If you're going to run me through, just do it. A hard thrust if you will, it takes more than you think to stick a man."

Florie remained still, statuesque, holding out the sword with a surprising steadiness. Francis could see she was fully prepared, there was a cool glint in her eyes, visible deep within her masked expression.

"Ye know, after Agnes and *this*," she pointed a lazy hand around her, "I would do it. Ye know I would do it?"

"I do not doubt it," said Francis.

"But seeing ye here pathetic and broken, it'd be like slaughtering a sickly dog fer sport. What do yer have to say fer yerself, eh? It's ye who caused all this."

"Nothing Florie," said Francis calmly, "no words come to comfort even myself, let alone another."

Florie lowered the sword, regarding him with strained curiosity. Then she let out a hollow, emotionless laugh.

"Two years ago, I'd never have thought to see the Earl Bothwell, Lord Francis Stewart, beg for death on his knees. What happened to ye?" she flicked the sword towards his burgundy and brown stained bandage.

"Lennox came for Margaret at Kelso," he said, feeling the weight of his words sit heavy on his heart, "I think I managed to distract his horsemen long enough for her to escape, but I got caught in my retreat. I know not how I am alive."

"Ye did that for Margaret?" asked Florie, her tone softening.

"What else could I do?" said Francis.

"And ye came back here," she said, dropping down to Francis' level, "to answer the ravens? Looking as ye do?"

"Of course, though, what use I'd have been... well, none at all, I suppose. Ye were right, Warlocks are a foolish idea."

"Francis, look around by a wulvers teeth will ye! We weren't ready to defend ourselves, cutting our warrior corps down by half, in *this* world was foolish. It's my fault, all mine, not yours," she said, a tremble surfacing beneath the stalwart timbre.

"Well then, maybe we're both right," he said, "I... "

Chapter 15

Francis stopped stalking abruptly. He had become aware of voices in the distance. Florie's head snapped towards the sound once she'd heard them too.

"Quick!" she said, "in here!"

She pulled Francis by arm to the adjacent drawing room of the castle. Being next to the front gate, it had escaped some of the more devastating ruination but the ashes of roofbeams still smouldered, scattered about the floor, along with remains and chunks of everything that the flames could consume.

Florie pushed Francis into the fireplace, where the backplate was already open to reveal a tight priest hole. He stooped and passed through into the space that was no larger than a wardrobe. Florie followed and they both squashed themselves inside, pressed against each other.

"Hercules cast some charm or other that protected me in here," Florie explained.

Francis held a finger up to hush her so he could listen to the voices as they came closer. He kept the backplate of the fireplace open with his foot so he could hear.

"What happened here?" said the voice.

"The King's men most like," came the grim reply.

Francis could hear the hooves of their horses as they came closer.

"Lord, there's a horse here, do you think it's Francis?"

Damn it all! Thought Francis, even here, in the shell of his sibling's castle, they couldn't help but continue their relentless pursuit. Francis touched his hand to his hip and realised with a start that he'd left his sword next to Hercules' body.

"Nay, Francis has, well... had, a stud farm, I should expect he'd never entertain the idea of riding such a beast. Looters I expect, come to take anything left of value."

The voices were still faint outside, yet they were highly familiar. He racked his frazzled brain as he tried to clear it and remember who spoke. When it dawned on him, his eyes narrowed as a scowl deepened across his brow. Florie must've sensed the sudden change in him and she shoved him in the chest, back against the wall of the cramped space and glared at him, or at least, he assumed she was glaring. The silent rebuke checked Francis and he stayed where he was, listening.

"Best still have a look around since we're here, eh."

The two riders dismounted and made their way up the stone steps, to the now gaping entranceway. Francis held his breath, listening as they inevitably came upon Hercules body, and his sword.

"Is that Francis?"

"That is his sword... yet it looks unburnt. And look, here, in the dust, someone's been here."

Francis felt Florie's shoulders slump. He was thinking the same thing, their footsteps in the ashes would lead the pair right to where they were hiding. Francis soundlessly motioned that Florie should ready her sword. He crouched, facing the partially ajar backplate, ready to spring at anyone who opened it.

Sure enough, their investigators' footsteps came pounding into the room. Even though Francis couldn't see them he imagined the puzzled look on their faces as they saw the footsteps trailing away into the fireplace.

Fingertips curled around the backplate to pull it open and Francis chose that moment to spring through it, charging the figure with his shoulder. He cried out in pain as the impact rippled through his injury, but he carried through his momentum and sent the man clattering to the floor. Out of the corner of his eye, he saw Florie follow him out, screaming at the top of her lungs as she swung the sword up above her head.

He didn't pause to see how she fared, stumbling over the form of his opponent, he bolted back towards the front entrance and his sword. He swept it up and turned. Nobody had followed him, so he unsheathed it and, in his fighting stance, hurried back to the drawing room.

He was confronted by the sight of Florie hacking at an already defeated man with her blade, spraying gore, unnecessarily buttressing the already dilapidated scenery. And there, getting to his feet, was the owner of the all too familiar voice.

"Ludovic!" Francis screamed, "I vowed I would kill you after what you did to Margaret!"

"Francis? Is that you?" said Ludovic, drawing his rapier. "My God man, you look like something that was dredged out of the Forth. I'm nay here te kill ye," he added quickly, in response to the vicious expression contorting Francis' face. Francis only snarled in his way of response.

"Florie, take my horse and run," he said to the blood-soaked Florie behind his enemy. She stood, heaving like some blood lusted Valkyrie over her vanquished foe, an unfortunate footman of the Duke.

"I've nowhere to go, I'm staying," she replied.

"Fine, but you've had yours, this here double-crossing snake is mine," Francis growled as he lunged forward, thrusting his broadsword at Ludovic's chest. Ludovic parried and span away from the attack, twirling like a dancer, light on his feet. He riposted swiftly, his narrow needle-like blade attempting to pierce Francis' heart. Francis batted away the lighter sword with a heavy-handed backswing.

"Francis, you've got it all wrong!" said Ludovic, panting as the two swordsmen exchanged blows.

"You! Set! The damn! Trap!" said Francis, striking at Ludovic with wild swings to the head. Ludovic managed to block the last with a high guard, stopping the razor edge of Francis' sword just inches from his face.

"I swear, to God, Jesus and the Virgin Mary! It wasn't me!" said Ludovic.

"Yer words mean nothing!" Francis spat before driving his forehead into Ludovic's nose. He staggered back, bringing his free hand up to his face and wiping the blood from his nose. He bellowed and lunged with all his weight behind his weapon.

Francis stepped to the side and brought his blade up to block the thrust, but Ludovic had anticipated his move and feinted, stepping with him and swinging his own sword low and slicing it through Francis' calf.

Francis barely registered the sting of the cold steel. He was battling so much pain and weariness already the only thing he allowed to occupy his mind was defeating the traitorous wretch before him.

Ludovic, who had expected Francis to retreat after his successful blow, had left his feet out of position. Francis kicked his opponent's forward foot out from under him, sending him toppling to the floor, hitting it like a dead weight. Francis brought down his boot on Ludovic's sword arm and pressed down until he let go.

"Do ye yield?" he said, sword point nicking Ludovic's throat.

"Aye! Aye! But please, tell me, what is this madness!?"

Francis knelt over his foe and grabbed him by the scruff of his neck.

"Ye mean to tell me, to my face yer not a white-livered younker!? I know everything! Ye're not fit te grace the sole of my boot."

Ludovic recoiled at the assault on his nostrils from Francis' warm nauseating breath.

"I swear! Whatever you assume was me, it wasn't!"

"The trap at Holyrood, eh!? Your men molesting my wife and children at Kelso, my rooms in Edinburgh, this place! Only you knew those things!"

"I was bringing your wife to safety yer dolt! I had to put on a show for the King. I'd never! I found her, she's safe, away from Lothian. I still have been rallying men to yer cause, I came here to find ye fer God's sake!"

"Liar!" Francis punched down with the fist still holding Ludovic's neck, slamming him into the flagstone floor.

Suddenly, through the sound of blood rushing in his ears, he heard sobbing. He looked across to see that Florie was shielding her face in her hands.

"Florie? What is it?" said Francis, loosening his grip on Ludovic.

Florie looked up. Tear tracks streaked her face, running between the ash and grime to reveal rivulets of pale skin.

"It wasn't him Francis, it was me," said Florie, "I told ye all this was my fault."

"You? But how?" Francis' face wrinkled, he shook his head as though to dislodge the information from his mind.

"I told ye..." began Ludovic.

"Shut yer trap ye!" Francis growled, slamming him into the floor again.

"The man said, well, he said he'd give me back Agnes. Agnes is all I wanted and ye were off, gallivanting about Scotland while she suffered. I just... I couldn't bear it."

She shuddered as her weeping got the better of her.

"I didn't mean fer any of this to happen. I just thought, well, I thought if I could trade you for her, I could accept that. Besides, you could've escaped, and you did! Yet, they did not give me Agnes."

"And here? The coven, you told them!?"

"No! They must've guessed, I don't know!"

Francis abruptly remembered Ludovic was beneath him and he was talking about witches.

"Florie, stay there, I'm coming back," he said.

He lifted Ludovic up to his feet, sheathing his own sword and keeping Ludovic's as a precaution. He dusted off Ludovic's jerkin and forced a grin that exhibited itself instead, as a grimace.

"Sorry Ludovic, would you help me outside?"

Ludovic, having given his surrender, put his arm under Francis' and helped him out to the front courtyard.

"Margaret is safe?" asked Francis as they walked down the steps.

"Aye, she's with my own wife and children in the north. Francis, all that in there... The witchcraft stuff, that's real?"

"Not quite," said Francis, "but I do help the healers and herbalists avoid these dreadful witchcraft charges. There's no devil at play, they're just simple folk. A sort of charity I suppose."

He hated the lie as soon as he uttered it. It was too close to the reality of his own actions. The knot in his stomach returned, squeezing acrid fluids up his throat.

"I see," said Ludovic, though his sceptical frown betrayed him. "Will you be making an attempt to fight the charges and return to court? I must say the paper shot stunt worked splendidly with parliament. How you ever got bordermen to pull that off, I'll never know."

"I don't think so Ludovic. I would think the King has invested too much already in my destruction."

"Aye, his temper has not waned and his support does grow. He makes speeches of your sorceries and the kirk has gone positively delirious at the prospect of your devil-craft. It's becoming more and more difficult for lords to support you. What then will ye do?"

"I haven't the slightest clue," said Francis. "Now listen, apologies for yer footman. Mayhaps if Margaret has any monies left she can repay you. Given time, I'm sure she can disown me and reclaim rents from her own lands and she can repay ye. If I can I will send her money also."

"Worry not, Francis, I will claim recompense from the King for a servant dying in your pursuit. No harm in making myself look good, eh?" Ludovic tried a weak smile.

"I suppose not," said Francis wistfully, "now, get on yer horse and leave us. I release ye from yer surrender. Though, I will claim the other horse, I'll need it."

Francis presented Ludovic with his sword and watched him leap nimbly into the saddle.

"Get that wound seen to man. Yer look half-dead already," said Ludovic, circling his mount. "I fear this may be the last I see of you old friend. I will pray for good fortune in your endeavours."

"Give my love to Margaret will ye," shouted Francis as Ludovic clapped his heels to the flank of his horse and rode towards the main gate. He turned in the saddle before he passed through it, waving goodbye.

Francis exhaled, letting all the pretence leave his body, and turned back to the skeleton of the castle. He felt the adrenaline seeping out of him, trickling out along with the blood from his lacerations. The intense feebleness returned to him, it felt like he was trudging through a marsh as he climbed the stone steps and back into the smoking wreckage. Every fibre of his body was screaming at him to stop and collapse into the dirt but he willed himself onward.

He steadied himself on the door frame and saw Florie in the exact place he'd left her. Her shoulders had stopped quaking but tears continued to run down her face, she looked up at Francis, utterly despondent in her grief. Francis limped the last few steps towards her and allowed his legs to give way to join her on the floor. He pulled her in close to his body and she accepted his embrace.

With Florie in his arms the intense emotions of the past month broke free from Francis' gut, rising up in his gullet and burst out with such abruptness, it startled Florie. They sat in the wreckage, weeping and clinging to each other. Neither of them cared to recall or question the transgressions of the other, just intensely grateful for the slither of comfort. Nothing else mattered in that moment.

* * * * *

2nd September 1592
Holyrood Palace

Maitland was shown into the gardens at the rear of the palace by a steward. The early autumn sun hung low in the sky, casting long shadows across the immaculate lawns. The leaves on the trees and plants had started to turn, creating a spectrum colour that sat beneath an apricot sky, and the gentle breeze wafted the last aromas of blooms before they closed up for winter.

He found the King enjoying wine and conversing in German with two gun makers, showing him their latest innovations. Maitland stayed quiet at the edge of the section of garden as he watched one of the pistol makers reload the weapon for the King and wind the mechanism for him.

James accepted the weapon and held it at arm's length, appreciating the weight and balance before firing it into a tree ten yards away. At short range, the shot punched into the green wood and sent showers of bark and splinters in every direction. James put the weapon down and noticed Maitland standing in the shade.

"Why, Lord Maitland, please do come join us," said James jovially.

He said some final words to the Germans before sending them back towards the palace. He refilled his goblet of wine, along with a second for Maitland and sat down.

"What news do you bring?"

"Good news, Your Grace, our plan of more affirmative action seems to be working. We had reports from Lennox that his men did successfully remove the Lord and his issue from the castle there. His other castles have been successfully re-occupied, and all reports say he's on the run."

"Most excellent! You have more?"

"The witch hunters, also, did pursue claims of a coven around North Berwick. They were found to be residing in Francis' castle at Hailes, occupied by his bastard brother Hercules Stewart. There, the castle was burnt and we captured fourteen witches in their escape, three died in transit before they could be burnt. It is believed that Hercules died in the castle fire."

"And Francis?" asked James.

"He wasn't there as far as we can tell sire. The last report we have is of Lennox and his servant chasing him North from Kelso." said Maitland.

"North?" said James, "Odd he should choose to go North."

"I think the explanation be either, he goes to join the Catholic Lords or he plans to arrange a ship to France or Spain."

James' eyes flashed and he let out a snarl at the last comment. "Francis Stewart must not be allowed to leave Scotland! Do ye hear!? I want more lookouts on the borders and a careful watch on shipping. Increase the price on his head if you must."

"If he does go into exile, Sire, then surely we have done well?" asked Maitland.

"If that errant cod-piece is allowed to live!" he yelled slamming a fist on the small garden table, "who knows what trouble he might cause. Nay, he must die. Think if he were to bring an army from Spain or seek to undermine my rule from afar. I shan't countenance it! Now is not the time to relax Maitland! We must press the advantage!"

"But the lords won't go for it surely, even many turned to your side would see this pursuit of his death as too strong a policy."

"Let me worry about the lords Maitland, depending on the circumstances he will die perfectly plausibly in an escape or burnt in a tragic accident like his brother, or perhaps he will simply vanish altogether and assumed in exile. I care not the circumstances of his death, just see it done!"

"Of course, Sire," said Maitland.

"Before ye go, your work in eradicating these witches has been outstanding Lord Maitland," he sat back in his chair, "I am confident you will see them entirely removed. See those pistols? One of them is for you. They are of the finest quality."

"Thank you Sire, but I am not a fighting man," replied Maitland.

"Are ye refusing a gift from your King, Maitland?" said James, though with a tinge of jollity returning to his voice.

"No, of course Sire, I shall cherish it, merely stating perhaps it will look better on my mantle than at my side."

"Good man, though, do try to fire it from time to time. Ye never know when it might come in use. Consider it a token of my gratitude and the advancements to come."

Maitland picked up the weapon and took a bow of thanks that doubled as a bow of departure, unsure as to whether he was being dismissed by the King. He raised his eyes and James was sat, facing away, merrily swilling his wine and enjoying the last of the evening's sunlight, so he turned and left James to his own company.

The evening was pleasant so he slowed his pace as he walked back to the palace, considering James' words. He, himself, had thought it enough to send Francis to Italy or France to live out his days as a pauper or forced into service, but then, would he ever leave his nightmares? Would he ever feel safe? After Falkland, Maitland frequently woke up in a cold sweat, fearing that the murderous baron had come for him.

He looked down at the pistol in his hands and realised everything James had said, despite his increasingly unpredictable anger, was cold and calculated. Either way, the sooner Francis could be removed, the better.

Chapter 16

13th September 1592
Moss Tower

Francis' first cognisance was that of a blinding headache that numbed his head, yet shot pain through his eye sockets every time he moved his head. He dared not open his eyes in fear it would make things worse. He stretched out his hands and groped around in his self-induced blindness. He was in a bed, stuffed with feathers and more luxurious than anything he'd slept on in months. As he shifted a muskiness filled his nostrils, indicating the sheets were old.

"Francis? Francis are ye awake?" said a woman's voice from the end of the bed.

Francis opened one eye and saw Florie sat on a stool, studying him with a concerned expression. He looked about the room and recognised it as his own in Moss Tower. It was a small place and so close to the border it had to be constantly defended. Francis had installed a minor lord instead of occupying it himself, but the dust that caked bed frame suggested it had remained vacant for months.

"Yes, I'm awake," he said finally. He raised a hand to his head but felt a sharp sting in his side, a jolting reminder of his injuries.

"Oh, how disappointing, ye might live yet," she said.

Francis regarded her with a bleary eye and realised she was joking. He winced and touched his side where he felt sticky poultice held in place with cloth.

"Why are we here? What day is it? How did we get here?" said Francis, all at once.

"Slow down," said Florie. She picked up a pale and spooned him some fresh, cool water. As it touched his lips he realised how dry they were, seeming to suck the water away from him before he was able to drink it.

"Lie back," she said, "I'll tell ye everything."

"Ye collapsed at Hailes after Ludovic left. I managed to wake you long enough for ye to tell me about Moss Tower. So, I strapped you to the back of your horse, yer damn heavy mind, and we came south. It took a long time, I had to bathe ye and clean up yer wounds. I was worried about ye, ye were in such a fitful fever but we couldn't take the roads. It took a few days to get here and ye've been in that bed ever since, must be nearly a fortnight."

"A fortnight!?" said Francis.

"Aye," replied Florie, "This isn't the first time I've told ye how we got here."

"But, ye did all that fer me? I thought ye hated me, after Agnes and all."

"Do ye remember what I told ye at Hailes?" asked Florie.

"Er," Francis frowned, "about Holyrood and such, aye, I remember."

"Well, I thought ye might not like me very much either. But... yer all I've got left. I knew not what else to do."

Francis lay back and looked up at the ceiling. He was in much the same boat as Florie. There was nothing left. Part of him wondered whether it might've been better to have died, but he shooed those thoughts briskly from his mind. In truth, despite all the pain Florie had caused him, he was immensely grateful for her company. Since Agnes, he had been mostly alone, save for brief cordial moments with his wife.

"Do ye hate me so?"

"No," said Francis. "I cannot hate ye. Mayhaps we've done such great misdeeds to each other, we're both in this miserable place for a reason." He lifted his head and looked down his chest at her. "I can forgive ye, if ye can forgive me?"

"I don't know if I can, Francis," she said carefully, "but as much as I've hated yer very soul, I just want to go back to normal. I have nay energy left fer anger."

Francis nodded, "I can live with that."

"Do ye think ye can get up?" said Florie. "I think we should get ye fed and moving a little while yer awake."

Francis wiggled his toes, testing them, before heaving one leg out of the covers. His limbs felt like lead weights and his muscles were so stiff he feared they might snap with the effort. He swung his other leg over the side and threw the covers off. He snatched them back to cover his modesty when he realised he was naked and offered an apologetic look to Florie.

"Francis, fer the love of all the bogles on Dupplin Moor! I've been bathin' yer for the past few weeks. I've seen far more than I care to!"

Francis kept the covers where they were. "I don't have any clothes."

"I thought when you awoke ye'd be able to conjure something, no?"

"No, ye can't materialise substances out of thin air. I always summoned them from somewhere I knew. I suspect there's nothing left in my old haunts. The wardrobe, over there, I must've left some effects here."

Florie walked over the small wardrobe and rummaged around. She found some undergarments and tossed them over her shoulder towards him. She pulled out the only assortment of clothes she could find and Francis pulled himself gingerly into them, trying his best to keep the poultice in place.

Florie turned around to look at the ensemble she had picked out and let slip a giggle. Francis stood in brilliant white stockings, some baggy brown hose, topped with an ornate orange jerkin and no undershirt.

"That'll have to do," she said. "Maybe later we'll raid the other rooms so see if we can't find something less... unfortunate."

Francis' room was at the top of the tower so they had to traverse several staircases to make it down the four floors to the kitchen. Francis sent Florie ahead as he limped down each step, holding the walls for support. It was an agonisingly slow process, made worse by the prospect of negotiating them again to get back to the soft bed he was starting to regret ever leaving.

Eventually, he came upon the kitchen where Florie had already managed to get a fire going.

"Ye mean to tell me, ye carried me up all those stairs," said Francis.

"Aye," said Florie, "I dragged ye up with rope. Bumped ye head a few times, but I figured ye couldn't get any more dim-witted than ye already are. Besides, the other rooms had the mattresses taken."

"Couldn't ye have just moved the mattress?" said Francis.

Florie hucked a carrot top at him. He smiled, painfully breaking the brittle skin that had formed on his lips. Florie smiled back, briefly, before loathing herself for doing so, dropping the austere mask back over her face.

"Where did ye get all this food?" asked Francis.

"Some of it I stole from a farm we passed on the way here, others I bought from the small town nearby. I had to sell one of the saddles."

Francis nodded and sat in silence, watching Florie cut up the vegetables and throw them into a bubbling pot over the fire. She'd cleaned herself up since Hailes and it'd been some time since Francis had seen her without the determined look of hatred she'd worn so often lately. He reflected on all the hardships she must've gone through to get him safe. Setting up camp in the woods, sourcing food, and not least nursing a useless carcass.

She had always been strong-willed, he knew that for sure, but he realised he'd overlooked her resourcefulness and canny wit. He remembered her talking about wanting a wand and he felt a pang as he remembered Hercules' response about tradition. Suddenly, he realised Florie has stopped what she was doing and was staring back at him.

"Sorry, I was miles away," said Francis.

"Ah good, yer still in there, for a moment I thought you'd forgotten how to breathe."

"I was thinking, we should get ye a wand Florie, I'll teach ye how to use it. Next time ye won't have to carry me up the stairs," he said.

"I don't know how to get a wand," she said, continuing with her cooking.

"Any hazel bush will do," said Francis, "ye just have to draw it from the earth yerself and bond with it."

"It's that easy? And then I can do all the magic you do?" she said.

"Not quite, it takes training and it's just an extension of you of sorts. Like a sword, except it's more mental than physical, but ye have the gift, I'm sure ye will pick it up in no time."

"I would like that," she said dolefully, "but I don't think the coven will take me back after what I did, at least, not those who're left."

"Ye never told me what happened, not fully," said Francis.

"Some got caught, most got away, thanks to Hercules and yer spell. He died making sure he bought enough time for them to get away."

"How did they find you?"

"I don't know either, mayhaps they followed you or I or they just found us. They knew enough, they were waiting in the dark for us to all leave."

"So the coven are still out there," said Francis, drumming his fingers on the table. "No doubt they're as frightened as you and I. We need to help them."

"I can't think that is a good idea. The witch hunters are everywhere now, more than ever. I think it better we accept our fate and go to France."

"Somehow I can't bring myself to leave them, Florie. They may have shunned me, but I feel I owe it to Hercules and Agnes to try, so they don't have to live like this."

Florie set down her knife, "Francis it's over, they've all gone. There's no way to..."

Her eyes widened and she looked up at the ceiling, then back down at Francis.

"Quick, come outside," she said, putting an arm underneath him and helping him to the front door.

They tottered out of the tower house and walked twenty paces before Florie turned him around and pointed up to the top of the building. There, like black leaves adorning the very tip of a tree, sat scores of ravens. They cawed and stretched their wings but stayed rooted to their perch.

"Hercules' ravens, but how?" said Francis.

"They followed us here," replied Florie.

"He never taught me how he controls them."

"Ye better learn quick then, if ye want the coven back," grinned Florie.

* * * * *

21st September 1592
Moss Tower

Francis sat on a low wall at the end of the causeway that led to the tower. The causeway was the only accessible route to border fortress, its three other sides were surrounded by deep marshland. It stuck out from the landscape like some giant stony finger reaching from the swamp.

Being so close to the border it had been cast down and rebuilt many times, by both English and Scots. As a result, the building was a patchwork of stone, old and new jammed together to create the imposing tower.

He kept an eye on the skies, watching the ravens as they flew back to the keep and perched themselves on its lofty heights. It hadn't been as hard as Francis had expected to control the ravens, though he'd only seen Hercules do it a handful of times. They were already charmed and trained to listen to the whispers of their master. He only hoped the witch hunters weren't shooting them down, for he didn't know how to repeat the spell. It maddened him to think all that knowledge died with Hercules, and all the books he kept were destroyed by the fire. He'd taken his brother for granted, assuming he'd always be there and now, well, now he wasn't.

Francis' eye was drawn to something bigger than a raven approach in the sky. He cursed, even though the witch was high up, they were still visible, especially to anyone similarly keeping an eye up above. He'd tried to get the ravens to deliver the message that they should arrive on foot or by horse, but had settled for a scroll attached to their legs. Still, most seemed to have ignored the warning and arrived by broom.

They had been arriving in drabs, starting from the very first day he'd sent out the message. He had tried to avoid them as much as possible until he had enough to call the meeting. Some regarded him with edged glances, while others seemed to be fearful of him. He'd left Florie to take charge of them, since she was still a council member, and stuck to his room or outside.

The airborne witch touched down on the narrow causeway and looked around confused.

"Head on in!" shouted Francis after her. "Florie will set you up in a room."

The witch nodded and ambled over to the door. Most of them had shared the feelings he thought they would. They were scared and lost. Without the structure of the coven there was no way to support each other. The tower was already brimming with members that had hurried to find any form of sanctuary, despite the dangers of gathering in one place again.

Francis was roused from his musings when he spotted Florie strolling towards him. She looked strong. Her new responsibilities had emboldened her rather than discouraged her and given her a dignified radiance.

"How're the new arrivals?" asked Francis.

"As well as they can be," she replied. "They're just like us really, they have no place else to go."

"How many are we at now?"

"Must be nearly fifty," she said, turning her head to follow Francis' skyward gaze.

"That must be most of them after Hailes," said Francis. "I figure we should gather them soon and decide what's next."

"What is next?"

"I've sent a messenger to Elizabeth. One I can trust," he added quickly, "I've done her some service in the past and she dislikes the King. Mayhaps we can go to England, somewhere in the south ideally, it may be there's even another coven we can join ours to. Though, the members of this one will decide what we do and whether they even want me."

"I would think they have little choice," Florie jested. "What about staying? Fighting?"

"If the coven wills it, so be it, though I don't recommend it. It seems more are flocking to the witch hunter ranks, from what the new arrivals say. Maybe if I still had support, taking on the might of the King, despite past failures, might still be an option. But, it lacks the evidence that it's a worthwhile pursuit."

"*If the coven wills it,*" Florie mocked Francis scornfully. "Damn it man, my... actions... were because ye didn't take yer responsibilities seriously and now ye've given up on them altogether. These folk need ye. They need a leader. A strapping borderman to help them survive," she punched his arm. "They're here because they don't know how alone. It's time to pull yer stockings up and convince them ye can help them."

"I can't leave them, and I wish to serve them, but I cannot even be certain they will accept my help," said Francis, looking down at his toes.

"It is your duty to them. Surely, they rejected you. Yet, I think some small part of why they're here is fer you. Besides, they will have to take ye back when ye tell them what I did."

"Nay," said Francis, "not a soul need say anything. It was me you betrayed, not them. You say they need me, but 'tis you who clothes, feeds and councils them. I won't allow anything to deny them that. If they reject both of us, then they're alone again."

Florie sighed and clapped her flanks, "then, I know not what to do. Either we tell them the truth and let them decide, or we are strong for them and be the folk they need us to be."

Francis didn't answer, he just peered into the grey-green waters of the marsh. He had no response for the options on the table. Florie, once again, was right. Telling the truth so that the coven might choose its own course felt the right thing to do, though it'd undoubtedly cause a, likely fatal, turbulence.

"We are both wretched," said Francis, conjuring a wry smile.

"Aye," said Florie, "well, sleep on it if you must. However, if they do follow ye, ye need a scheme and battle orders to match. '*Mayhaps we'll go to England*' isn't good enough, ye hear? Do whatever ye need to do to awaken the ass Francis who knows how to fight and lead. That's the man they need right now. Just don't bring too much of him back, eh."

Florie patted him on the shoulder and walked back towards the tower. Francis watched her leave. In his mind, he'd already gone over the details a thousand times, to the point of numbness. He wished they didn't only have to talk about the coven, the impending danger or how they were to feed everyone. Nevertheless, he enjoyed her company whenever he was granted her presence, and now that he was left alone again, he swore he could feel heart sink.

He shifted his gaze when he realised she'd already passed through the doors and he was staring at empty space. Besides, he wasn't sure if she'd forgiven him completely. He'd found her a few times, gloomily busing herself with chores wearing a vacant expression, or crying when she thought she was alone. It only made his admiration of her resolve in front of the other witches all the more powerful.

A resolve he would need to emulate if he was to do what's right.

Chapter 17

30th September 1592
Hermitage Castle

Maitland rode at the head of his column of witch hunters. He had mustered nearly every man employed into the service to attend the borders. The only ones that weren't there, were those who continued the hunt for Francis Stewart. They numbered two hundred and they all wore their rough grey uniforms. Amassed, they resembled some long procession of monks, carving their way through the heather strewn landscape. The tips of their crossbows swung above their heads as they stepped, creating an untidy ripple of wood and iron.

There had been talk of replacing the crossbows with firearms, however, they were cheaper to produce and Maitland preferred their quieter thrum. In an open pitched battle, the musket was indeed a fearful weapon, nonetheless, his men were not traditional soldiers. They were to be silent killers, dispatching the devil's surrogates with a ruthless efficiency.

Oswyn rode his small pony to his right. Maitland noticed he'd developed a nervous habit of twitching his head skyward, as though some invisible adversary would drop from the sky at any moment. He'd heard Oswyn's accounts of the witches on broomstaves and his behaviour had infected Maitland with similar fears.

They climbed over the crest of a hill and the cubic Hermitage castle came into view. From a distance, it looked like a solitary grey brick dumped onto the landscape. It bore none of the large windows and openings of more northerly castles, just narrow slits barely visible on the exterior. The only exception was the gaping archway on the eastern side, that protruded twenty feet from a dwarfed entrance, so defenders could drop all manner of missiles on any would-be attacker. The whole thing had been built with a cruel and cold efficiency. It was rugged and uncomplicated, just like the border lords who lived here.

Maitland could see much of them must had already arrived. Their horses, men and stewards were taking their leave outside of the castle, lighting fires and preparing meals. *Praise the heavens*, he thought to himself. He didn't want to stay any longer than necessary.

He gave the order for Oswyn to halt the men and have them gather separately from the other soldiers, by the small brook. Then, the two made their way on foot to the east entrance, crossing the earthen bridge across the deep trench that surrounded the structure. Maitland felt a shiver crawl up his spine as he stepped into the shadow of the imposing archway. The door was not centred into the wall in front of them, but rather positioned to one side. It had been left ajar, presumably for servants and messengers of the lords inside. Already Maitland could hear the boisterous shouting and laughter coming from within.

He found the border chieftains sat around the main table, in the castle's equally brutal great hall. There was no grandeur here, no panelling or tapestries. The bare stone provided the only decor, save for the plain wooden ceiling. Some of the men would have been here for days already and the ale was in full flow.

Maitland glanced at Oswyn before standing at the head of the table, which had been left vacant.

"Ahem, gentlemen of the borders you have been assembled..." he began. The lords barely acknowledged his presence and continued to chatter while Maitland blushed in an indignant shade of claret.

Oswyn stepped forward and slammed a gnarled fist onto the table.

"Quiet!" he yelled, "The Lord is speaking."

The assemblage turned their heads to the foreign vulgarian with a unisoned look of umbrage, even so, they held their tongues and waited for Maitland to speak. Maitland gave a curt nod to Oswyn who retired from the table, back to his position behind him, half-hidden in his shadow.

"Before I continue, do we have everyone here?" asked Maitland.

The room stayed silent, not wishing to indict their fellows.

"Very well, Oswyn, take a note of everyone who *is* here. We shall consult the records later."

"I can't write, Lord," said Oswyn sheepishly.

"Ah, yes, well, just remember them then," he hissed over his shoulder. "As I was saying, ye are gathered here because we've had reports that the outlaw, Francis Stewart, is moving south and attempting to cross the border into England."

"What, ye expect us to keep him in? After near a thousand years our families keeping the English out and now ye want us to keep someone in? Ha!" said one of the bordermen.

The rest joined in with his hearty laughter, spilling the ale in their tankards.

"They didn't do a very good job of it against old Henry now did they, I'd hoped you might be better at keeping someone in," retorted Maitland.

The room went silent as the lords looked to one another, then burst into abrupt guffawing again. Maitland's lips twitched into a brief smile, emboldened by his ability to spar caustic wit with such gruff men.

"Aye, I'd like ye to keep him in. We've also intercepted letters we believe to be between Francis and the King of Spain. If he leaves these lands, there is a risk he comes back with an army of Catholics."

Another borderman wiped a mirthful tear from his eye before donning a more serious expression and speaking.

"In truth, my Lord, I have ridden with the Lord Francis, so have many of us. I like the man and am convinced he is nay a Catholic. If the King wants to try the man for treason, so be it, but if Francis chooses to wander into exile then I am inclined to oblige the poor man."

Several around the table nodded their heads in agreement.

"Besides, the border must be nearly a hundred miles long," said another, "how're we supposed to guard the whole thing? We can raise the alarm when armies are marching, aye, but a single man, maybe a few followers. There's not a chance."

"Do ye even know where he is?" asked a third.

"We've captured and tracked a few of his witches headed in a south easterly direction. We are informed he is to leave with them from Scotland. We were thought to assume he may have attempted to reclaim Kelso, but our searches of the area found nothing, hence he could be anywhere currently, in the East and Middle Marches."

"Therefore, I expect the respective wardens, Lord Home and Sir William Ker, for you to be the most vigilant, though we should not discount him taking the westerly route to Carlisle."

The bordermen exchanged uncomfortable glances. The mood in the room dropped from a mirthful gathering of old friends, and in its stead a nervous energy occupied the space. Maitland had known the issue would be sensitive, some of the assembly were even distantly related to Francis.

As he watched them, he could see that some were more agreeable, co-operative even, to their given mission, while others would be hard-pressed to turn on one of their own. The difficulty, he suspected, was that each side was fearful of the other and as a result, nobody was willing to speak first. After a long silence, William Ker stood.

"With all due respect, Lord Maitland, the Middle March spans much of the border. I don't have the men to picket its whole length. Even with the combined men of the borders, it'd be near impossible to stop a small group, led by a man such as Francis Stewart, getting through. Need I remind you, this was his castle for decades, he knows the land better than any."

"Do not think the magnitude of this undertaking has escaped me," said Maitland. "The King is mustering troops to gather here as we speak. For the time being, your role is to simply provide a watch and reactionary forces to deter Stewart from crossing the border. If he has witches with them, they will be slow."

"I fer one, refuse to take action against the man," said laird Spott. "The Earl Bothwell has been a loyal servant of the borders and the crown. I refuse to take any part in this action against him."

"I had not thought it necessary to remind you, nonetheless, to hinder the Crown and aid its enemies amounts to treason *and*, since Francis Stewart harbours witches in his midst it is furthermore accessory to witchcraft. Making wilful ignorance a crime against the Crown, the Kirk and God."

Maitland placed both hands on the table and stood.

"Ye are good loyal men of Scotland. Do not let this Francis Stewart obstruct that reputation. Ye shall all call wapinschaws to gather men, for now, their purpose need not be known. Those men you already possess in your service shall be deployed as soon as humanly possible along the border, every half mile. If they come upon the outlaw, they are to relay their message down the line in the direction of this castle."

Maitland made as though he was finished, adding in his own dramatic flair to the piece.

"Oh, and I should also mention the price on Francis' head has doubled to two thousand crowns. That ought to be enough incentive for your men to catch the scullion and what is the lord's tax on such rewards? One tenth? A fifth? Still, perhaps with that reward, ye can supply Sir William with the men he needs for the Middle March, your man, your reward."

Maitland gazed around the table, eyeballing each and every borderman. Some of them concealed their emotions well, though most bore the symptoms of reluctant acceptance. They knew they were trapped. Even if they allowed Francis to slip through their carefully crafted net, they would fear retribution if it were revealed he slipped through their section of the border.

"I will bid you my leave," said Maitland, "though I expect action sooner rather than later. Sir William, this castle is now in your possession is it not?"

"Well, the Duke of Lennox's, Lord, though I have been deputised to keep it, aye." replied William.

"Have one of your servants make me up a room will ye. I see Lennox has not invested well in furnishing the place, but a simple bed will do. I am to reside here until the King arrives."

Maitland noted a momentary grimace flashed across Sir William's face before he nodded. He gave it no thought, he was acclimated to the dislike he inspired, even amongst his own burgh. He was self-aware enough to know these bordermen would detest his, or indeed most outsiders', presence.

He twitched his robes and left the hall, beckoning Oswyn to walk with him. When he passed through the narrow exit, he closed the door behind him and paused, listening. Several seconds passed before the border chieftains erupted into discussion. Maitland could not hear what they were saying, though he was confident enough in both the carrot and stick he'd used.

"Do you think they'll follow you Lord?" asked Oswyn, as they saw themselves into a small drawing room off the castle's main entranceway.

"They won't follow *me*, but they'll abide the King's orders. Right now, those left with any doubt are being converted by others. If one of them fails, they shall all come under scrutiny."

"Just to ensure their loyalty, ye will send men to attach themselves with the borderers. Give them some excuse such as extra hands or what have ye, and send a messenger to the King. He'll want to hear of the progress we achieved here today."

"Of course Lord," said Oswyn, bowing.

"And have the men doing something to occupy them, send them scouting. I want this business over by mid-winter."

* * * * *

1st October 1592
Moss Tower

Moss Tower had no great hall. The largest space was a modest dining room, so all the tables had been removed and everyone sat on the few chairs available or on the floor. Francis watched them through a crack in the door frame while he waited in the kitchen. Due to his unknown status with the coven, its members had kept their distance from him still. Though, he'd still been in close enough proximity to get a sense of where their sentiments lay.

They'd received news that the captured witches from Hailes were all summarily burnt at North Berwick. Tensions were high and for many, their frayed nerves had got the better of them. A small few had sworn off witchcraft altogether and returned to their homes, but the vast majority remained, in hope that this meeting would give them something to latch onto.

He could see Florie waiting patiently at the front for everyone to settle in the room and make themselves as comfortable as possible. The sounds of chairs scraping against the floor and shuffling were the only noises. The solemnity of their plight had diffused through the room like poisonous gas, infecting everyone with a restrained anxiety.

"Welcome," began Florie, "in these our darkest of days, I would like to forgo the usual honoraries. We are here as people, not just witches, who're being hunted from our native land. Tonight, we must agree on an action that sees us all safe."

"First, however, you will have seen Francis Stewart about the castle. I would like to appeal his banishment on his behalf, so that he might help us. At the very least, he is another pair of hands."

Francis braced himself. He didn't want Florie to argue on his behalf, so he stepped through from the kitchens. The room turned in unison to face him and a near silent gasp rippled through it. He strode to the front, next to Florie and, with his chest fluttering, prepared to begin his appeal.

"Members of this coven, if you will allow me to speak. I know I have failed you greatly in the case of Agnes, and in my former duties as Warlock to protect this coven. You banished me, and you were right to do so..."

"Brother Donald of North Berwick," said Donald standing. "Brother Bruce and the Warlock Hercules gave their lives to protect this coven. We all know ye can give a fine speech Mr. Stewart, yet I find it an insult ye would stand here before us and ask us to follow ye? Ye must be mad!?"

"Sister Anne of Coldingham." another introduced themselves. I think, Brother Donald, you are too hasty in yer words. Ye are right indeed, we are a warrior down. It takes courage to come before those who have forsaken ye. The simple fact Mr. Stewart is here leads me to believe in his earnest appeal to help us. Not to mention, this is not a time to be picky over those we choose to provide that help."

"Sister Mary of Kelso. Perhaps it is Mr. Stewart who caused our coven to come under attack! It happened only shortly after his banishment! His very presence here could be a danger to us all!"

The gathering collapsed into heated debate between neighbours, pointing and gesticulating against one another. Francis flicked his head from side to side as he watched them all argue.

"Quiet!" shouted Florie, "Francis did come to the coven responding to one of Hercules' ravens. He was too late to save us and grievously wounded from protecting his family. It was there we found each other and did retreat here. I can assure you Francis is not the cause of our ills."

She gave Francis a knowing look, doing her best to convey her earlier statements regarding his leadership. She nodded signalling that he should continue his appeal. Francis bowed his head and lowered himself to his knees.

"I am not here to assert my power over you, nor am I here to waste yer time. Ye have all made a different choice to elect your council and I think it a wise one. However, in this time of peril, I beg of you, allow me to serve you the only way I know how, as a soldier and leader. I can promise nothing other than I will do my utmost in service to you and give my life to protect every single witch of this coven."

Francis stayed on his knees and heard only the shuffling of nervous feet. He risked a glance upward and sensed a critical trepidation amongst the small crowd. Mary stood up.

"I, and I'm sure others, find it hard to trust a man who pledged the very same to bring back Agnes. Ye have failed, including in yer endeavours to reset yerself with the King. I believe the sincerity of yer willingness to serve this coven, yet the stink of disaster follows ye."

Florie stepped forward to speak and Francis tugged hard on her skirts, silently beseeching her not to say what he knew was coming. She didn't look at him, simply pulled her skirts from his grasp and continued.

"Francis' failures are not his own," she began. A rumble of voices pierced the uncomfortable silence. Florie spoke over them. "It was I who hindered Francis' labours. I thought I could get my sister back by handing over Francis in her place."

The murmurs erupted into a cacophony of noise, bouncing around the small room and bombarding the eardrums of Francis and Florie. Francis' head drooped even lower, as he heard cries of "who can we trust?" and "what now?" above the din. He swallowed, gulping in the stale air before standing.

"Enough!" he bellowed, imitating his best battlefield delivery. The room settled and he softened his tone. "I had not wanted Florie to speak of her wrongdoings as they were against me and me alone. Nonetheless, ye have all heard the truth of it. I ask of all of ye, since ye arrived here, who has clothed, fed and looked after ye? If Florie or I meant this coven any harm or hadn't the conviction in ourselves to help, we'd nay be here."

"Florie has nay forgiven me for the catastrophes I still have under my charge. Yet, we have found a way to move beyond it and work together. This coven must do the same, or the reality is we all perish. We can stand here and debate every action or where to place the blame. But this is not a time for debate, 'tis a time for action."

"Mayhaps when this business is done, Florie and I are due some form of punishment and I welcome it. For now, I am a professional soldier and the best hope ye have of making it across that border. If ye still want a coven after mid-winter ye must put yer faith in me and I shan't do it without Florie. *Every* member of this coven comes with us. So, vote if you must, but I ask ye do it now."

Francis, continuing with his military officer's parody, glared about the room, daring anybody to speak up. No one moved a muscle. Francis sensed that despite his misgivings, they knew he was right. Through the sheet of falsified confidence, Francis felt a glimmer of his real self-conviction shine through. He desperately didn't want the coven to vote against him, the only purpose he had left was to help them, even so, he mustered himself for the deciding vote.

"This room is not large," he said, "but those for accepting me back into this coven and leaving Scotland under my guidance, proceed to the wall on my right. Those against, to the left."

He held his breath and waited while only a small number made their way to either wall. Most stayed resolutely in the middle, standing behind Mary with her stern expression. Clearly, those behind her saw her as a figure on whom the vote rested.

"Sister Mary of Kelso," said Francis, "you take issue. Speak it now."

"Thank you," she said graciously, "I am moved by yer words and, ye speak truth. It is beyond doubt we stand a better chance of crossing the border with ye and perhaps yer fate is better decided from a place of safety. Yet, Sister Florie's actions are worse than you presume. Ye neglected yer duty and perhaps mislead us. Florie took direct action against a man, who was at the time, a Warlock of this coven."

"She did it for Agnes," said Francis, "she did it for her sister and because she, rightly, had no faith in me."

"That is so," said Mary, "yet, it does not refute or excuse her actions. We would see her banished from this coven in yer place."

Francis was about to respond when he felt a gentle hand touch his shoulder.

"She's right Francis," said Florie, "I had no right to ever do what I did. The reason I cannot forgive ye, is because I cannot so easily forgive myself. I will go."

Florie walked down one of the channels left by the voters. They eyeballed her as she left. She did not walk with her tail between her legs, but rather with her head held high. As though she had accepted this fate a long while ago.

"No!" shouted Francis before she reached the door. "No! We are a damn coven! I vow," he dropped to one knee and placed a hand on his sword, "to do everything within my power to ensure a fellow witch, within or without this coven, does not suffer the way Agnes did. I swear this oath in front of you all." He stood, passion flaring in his eyes. "Leaving her behind is as good as a death sentence. I shan't leave a witch behind to that fate, no matter their history. She stays, for better or worse. Now, cast your vote."

Francis watched as some of those behind Mary made their choice, as the defectors moved, they inspired more to make their own choices until Mary herself moved over to the right. By the end, only ten stood against the left wall. Francis addressed them first.

"I stand by what I said about Sister Florie, I shall not leave you behind to face the witch hunters if you would only come with us. I recognise your vote, though I beseech you now to move over to the right and come with us. If you still desire to leave, so be it, I cannot stop you. Though I do beg of you, stay with us, we're stronger together."

Half crossed over the room and joined the ayes on the right.

"Then, I wish you luck," he said to those who remained. "I suggest you pack your things and leave this place quickly. If you find yourselves in peril and want to join us, I will send a raven every year to this tower. It will lead you to us, wherever we end up."

He turned to the rest of the coven and Florie, who was still by the door. He searched her face for a clue as to what she was thinking, but it resembled nothing more than a blank canvas. So, he snapped back to the coven.

"Let's resume our seats," said Francis. "There is much to plan and even more to be done."

Chapter 18

3rd October 1592
Scottish Border - Middle March

Francis rode ahead of the others with a few of his scouts. They did laps, riding out to investigate the terrain around them and looping back to give their reports and rest. They had only a few horses, the rest of the coven were either on foot or in wagons some had brought with them. They travelled as light as possible, knowing that everything rested on crossing the border. Anything that couldn't be carried or ridden had been sold. Food and necessities would have to be sought in England.

He did not know what awaited him in England, though he knew the witch hunters would never dare try to pursue them in the lands of the English Wardens. He asked his messenger to wait with the reply from Elizabeth in York. He'd not asked for much, no titles, lands or rents, just for the opportunity to disappear in the countryside. He'd even proposed to pay taxes under the guise of a false name. If that didn't work, they'd need to travel further afield to France, Spain or leave Europe altogether.

Some had proposed flying across the border. The idea had merit, even if they were spotted, they could evade musket balls and make it out. The main issue was landing. They would not know the terrain once in England and they'd have to land somewhere. If they were spotted and became outlaws in England too, it was over. Not to mention, they lacked brooms for everyone, the sheer length of the journey, the sickness that came with flying at great heights, and that there was no way to carry luggage.

Instead, Francis knew of a valley that ran from Liddesdale across the border and into English lands. It was well vegetated and would keep their march hidden, even now winter was setting in. Where it came out on the English side, the valley could be followed and avoided all the castles that were typically on higher ground. He'd used it many times to penetrate deeper into England where villagers were less accustomed to raiders.

The sun was beginning to rise, shading the clouds a deep crimson, as though the colour had bled from the fibres of an unwashed paintbrush. Francis blinked in the early light, he was tired, but the brisk, dewy air awakened his senses. They'd left as early as possible to make the most of a day's march. They would keep going through the next night to get as far into England as they could.

Francis heard the faint patter of hooves before he saw his outrider appear over the ridge. She was waving her arm above her head. He rode towards her, each jounce in the saddle pounding the hope out of him.

"What is it?" he said as he got near.

"They have placed sentries, I saw the first one, but I was spotted by another. They were only half a mile apart, they know we're here."

"What do they look like? How far?" demanded Francis.

"Like soldiers, about half a league ahead."

"Curses! The rest will never make it on foot before the first riders reach us." Francis punched the horn of his saddle, momentarily spooking the horse. He thought for a moment before giving his orders.

"All of you," he addressed the scouts still with him. "We're going back to Moss Tower. Ride back in different directions. Cover our tracks. I'll ride to the coven."

The riders with him nodded and spurred their horses. Francis did the same and hurtled as fast he could back to the coven. The wind in his hair gave the odd sensation of providing the force behind his thoughts as they whizzed through is mind. He steered his horse into the shallow river of the valley to cover his own tracks.

He came upon the coven sooner than he expected, they had been making decent progress. The two wagons formed the centre of the group while others walked beside them. The only other person on horseback was Florie, guarding the rear of the train.

"Turn the wagons around!" shouted Francis. "Turn around! We're going back!"

He could tell they couldn't hear him, so he kept barking his orders as he approached. When he arrived with them, they had only just begun the process. The valley had no trail, but the ground beside the river was flat and solid enough for the two lightweight farm wagons to traverse. However, it was not wide enough to turn them around with the mules still attached.

Francis leapt from his horse and helped with unbridling the animals. The elderly and young coven members who'd occupied the wagon were forced off while Francis and the able-bodied teamed up to heave the vehicles around on the spot. Satisfied the wagons and their teams were facing in the right direction, Francis was only just back on his horse when Mary came sidling up to him.

"Mr. Stewart," she called, "Mr. Stewart, what's going on?"

"It would seem the King has ordered the border chiefs to place sentries all along the border, one of our scouts was spotted. Could be nothing, but it's safer to head back to the tower than continue."

"And what if they follow our tracks back?" asked Mary, walking beside his horse as the train got moving again.

"I suspect they might, we may need to evacuate or form a defence. I haven't decided which yet."

"Some of the others and I, we know runes. We might be able to shield the tower."

Francis touched the runic scar on his wrist. He realised he hadn't performed his usual routine before leaving the tower. With a start, he realised he had gone charging in at Kelso without it too. He'd always thought of runic magic as an unpredictable and unreliable art. Certainly, he'd been injured while his rune was still fresh. He'd mostly developed it as a habit, a kind of superstition all soldiers had in one form or another. Still, a bit of luck never seemed to hurt. He halted and climbed down from the saddle.

"Do you know what you're doing?" asked Francis.

"I've managed to keep the witch hunters from my house," she said. "With more, who knows what's possible?"

"Take my horse," he said, "ride ahead, gather the materials you need and get started. The others can join you when they arrive."

"Will you be alright?" she said. "You're still broken."

"I'll be fine," he said, "the healers have done a fair job on me. Now go! Hurry!"

He placed his hands on top of his thigh and helped Mary up onto the horse.

"You know how to ride?"

"Some," she said.

"Take it easy, this is one of Lennox's men's war horses. Keep him at a trot. You'll still get there quicker."

Before he'd even finished speaking, he gave the horse a heavy slap on the rump and it went shooting forward with Mary clinging to its back.

Francis jogged past the wagons to Florie, who, after the turn, was now at the front of the small caravan.

"How goes it?" she asked.

"It's going to be harder to get across than I thought," said Francis. "And if we have to defend the tower, who knows how long we can hold out?"

"So, good then," said Florie dryly.

"Ye have your wand?" asked Francis.

"Aye but I'm nay good, I cannae even do the simple spell ye taught me."

"Magick can come easier in a crisis. Fewer distractions. Keep it on ye, even if it's for my sake, eh."

Francis gave up on his jog once his breathing became short, laboured pants. He rubbed at the tightly wound bandages at his side and settled for a hurried walk. Florie returned to the rear of the column, so he kept ahead of them, striding towards Moss Tower at the quickest pace his body allowed him.

When the solitary tower came into view, he saw that Mary was busying herself at the walls of the structure. She had repurposed a horseshoe clinch into a chisel and was carving intricate runic shapes into the wall. They were nothing like Francis had ever seen before.

The characters themselves looked more like swirling shapes than an alphabet, and the strings they formed twisted and turned in knots. Together they created a striking image that, despite being crudely carved were still beautiful to behold.

"Those don't look like runes?" said Francis.

"Ye mean they don't look like *Norse Runes*," retorted Mary in an overly sweet tone, clearly enjoying her lecturing. "I thought ye were educated. These are older, from our druidic ancestors. Of course, the highlanders have something different altogether. These are just what my maw taught me."

"Aye, well done I suppose, I hope they work."

"They will," said Mary confidently, "the others can help when they get here. I'll need more tools by the way."

"Of course, I believe there's some tools in the vaults and I'll see what I can fashion from what's left in the kitchens."

Francis hurried off to find more tools. He gathered anything metallic that could be used as a chisel or hammer. When he returned, he found ten or so of the witches hard at work on the floors and the walls. He went around them all, gazing at their designs and distributing his make-shift equipment before returning to Mary.

"What will all the runes do?" asked Francis.

"They're all different," she said, "some will make intruders forget why they're here. Some will disguise the tower, making it appear as a tree or a crag in the eyes of those who behold it. Others do... other things. It is not so much a book science as it is an art, Mr. Stewart. All the girls here were taught differently, and they all express themselves differently. Individually, some mundanes can see through the illusions, or they are determined enough to ignore them. But my hope is with so many, we shall be able to trick an army into never knowing we're here."

"Ye know, Hercules read his books and I went to the continent and then we, or just he rather, tried to teach ye all. It should've been us learning from you. It might've saved him at Hailes."

"Aye, there's more to magic than that wand ye wave. In truth, it hadn't occurred to me either. For so many years we've been safe enough meeting behind the walls of a castle and the runes above our doorways have been but simple charms. It is only today I thought to use them all together." said Mary.

"It's a good job ye did," said Francis, "Good work Mary."

He smiled and patted her shoulder.

"And to you Mr. Stewart, yer the one who brought us all together."

"And Florie, she did a lot of the heavy lifting and I'd not be alive if it weren't for her."

Mary's face soured at the mention of Florie and Francis decided not to push the issue. Instead, fearful of appearing useless, he decided to busy himself and hastily prepared a barricade inside the tower. He used his wand to levitate anything that was large and heavy to the entrance hall. By the time he was finished, it looked like an entire village's possessions had been dumped there.

After surveying his work, he returned to the amateur masons. Most had stopped and stood back from their creations, while the last few kept up their frantic hammering. The high-pitched clang of metal on stone seeming to echo, despite their barren surroundings.

When they were done, Mary gathered them all next to their runic circles and handed a kitchen knife to those that didn't already carry one. She then proceeded to lead them all in an ethereal chant in an ancient language. Everyone seemed to know the words and their voices carried on the gentle wind, which seemed to pick up as the transcendental chorus flung their words up to the heavens.

As their chanting sped up, reaching a seraphic crescendo, they used their blades to slice their palms and allowed their vitality to drip into the crevices of their carvings. Francis half expected some otherworldly glow to emanate from them but no such thing materialised. The witches finished their incantation in an abrupt silence. Their shoulders dropped, spent with the effort of suffusing their life force with their carvings and they used fresh linens to cover their cuts.

Francis remained motionless, stunned by the profound ritual he'd just witnessed. He was rattled from his spiritual paralysis by the shouting of someone behind him. He turned to see one of his outriders galloping towards them, Francis didn't need to hear the message to know what it was.

"Hurry!" He shouted. "Everyone inside! Now!"

He ushered the sorceresses through the entrance to the tower, helping them collect their belongings and make it to the safety of the stone structure. They bustled inside, pushing and shoving despite Francis' calls for order. He sent them to the very top of the tower.

When there was enough space in the entrance hall, he began the process of moving the assembled furniture in front of the small wooden door. By the time he was finished, even if they blew the doors the articles behind it would create a treacherous obstacle course.

He bounded up the stairs, even before reaching the summit, he was hit by wafts of the warm stale air generated by scores of nervous bodies. He elbowed his way through the throng to the south-facing windows, where Florie and Mary were already waiting.

"Everyone," he hissed, "back from the windows!"

He peered out and saw, steadily coming more into focus, two outriders dressed in the manner of the bordermen approach. He could see they were riding slowly and chatting idly as they rocked up and down in their saddles. He knew this meant there will have been other scouts dispatched, branching out across the landscape. They were following the tracks the wagons had left, up towards the tower.

Florie gripped his arm as they watched on, and Francis could see Mary's knuckles whiten on the windowsill, betraying her earlier confidence. The two men continued to chat while the tracks brought them ever closer to their ridiculous hiding place, a gargantuan structure that imposed on the landscape around it. They reached the edge of the marsh and Francis could see their gaze follow the tracks around its edge and towards the causeway, then, Francis could see their eyes flick towards the tower. He could've sworn the foremost rider was looking directly at him.

He had no idea what was going through their minds, but instead of making toward the causeway, they continued their path along the edge of the marsh and away from the tracks. They patrolled out of sight from the southern windows, so Francis stepped over the mishmash of bodies sat down to cross the room.

He managed to identify them again, traversing the edge of the marsh on their nimble horses. When they reached the northernmost point on the circumference of their protective swamp they simply rode away in that direction. Francis kept his gaze on them until they were completely out of sight before turning back to the room and sliding down the wall.

He smiled with relief and, without saying a word, the tension in the room broke in a collective sigh. Francis lifted his head to see a patchwork of faces was grinning back at him. He couldn't help feeling though, this had been a little like his 'victory' at Holyrood, it was shallow. They hadn't made it across the borders.

"I don't know what yer all smiling at me for," said Francis, "it's Mary ye need thank for her quick work on the runes!"

Mary blushed as the heads turned to look at her. They gave her a quiet round of applause, to which Francis joined in. She sat down when she could tolerate the admiration no longer. Francis turned and saw Florie's face was the only other that wore the anxiety he felt.

"What now?" she asked.

"This won't last," said Francis, "they'll find us eventually or figure something odd is happening here. The bordermen should know of this tower. Their reports won't match up. We need a distraction to pull the sentries away from the border. I think I have an idea."

* * * * *

7th October 1592
Liddesdale

Francis padded along the border, using the marker of a man every half mile. He'd chanced that whoever was organising the force would not have stationed themselves in the East March, so he'd headed west. He figured they'd be centralised, using Hermitage Castle or any number of border strongholds in Liddesdale.

It'd been a much slower march on four legs, but even when he'd been spotted, as a fox, he aroused little suspicion. It enabled him to hear snippets of conversation with the sentries as he passed. Some of them were not bordermen, but part of the witch hunters, which seemed to be growing into more of a legion than a small personal force.

He'd learned that his suspicions were correct, and headquarters was at Hermitage, more than that, both the King and Maitland were there. The King seemed to have gathered a sizeable force and was on high alert ready to dispatch them at any moment. Francis could only think what great luck it had been that their charms on Moss Tower had worked so well, otherwise they'd have had an army bearing down on them.

All was quiet along the front and many of the men seemed disgruntled at their duty. Francis knew the men better than to station them as pickets, they needed reward, loot or sometimes just good company. None came from standing around in a field. It bodes well though, that they might be neglectful enough for the witches to slip through.

He stopped when he reached the edge of the forest he was crossing. There it was, the blockish structure of Hermitage castle consuming the peaceful landscape around it. It was barely visible through the smoke of campfires around it. Clusters of tents, varying greatly in opulence and design, spread out from the defensive walls. Francis estimated there must be some one thousand soldiers, plus those currently stationed along the border.

He could see in the distance a smaller ring of pickets, circling round to the forest he was currently standing in, and he realised he must've already passed the picket line without noticing. Still, how to make it to the castle was another matter entirely, let alone make it inside. The windows were all too high and too narrow for anyone to climb through, so the only entrances were two small doors on the east and western sides.

The river would be bustling with activity, nonetheless, he decided it was more usual for a fox to be slinking between the reeds than crossing the open fields towards the castle.

Fortunately, the night was already setting in and he found few men along the river. Those that did whiff his presence simply dismissed him as some animal rustling through the bushes. Finally, he came up the section of river that was closest to the castle. It was a mere hundred yards away but between he and it, the camp was thick, and he'd still need to make it around to the east-west faces.

There was nothing for it, so he climbed up the riverbank and used the edges of the tents to curl his way through the maze.

"Oi! Stop that rodent, it'll be after the food!"

Francis cursed, and from his vulpine mouth it sounded as a low growl. It'd taken all of five seconds for him to be spotted. He decided to use the opportunity to sprint headlong towards the castle. As he ran, soldiers sprung out from gaps between the tents to grab at him. In this form he only came up to their knees, giving the sensation of towering giants swinging their meaty hands towards him.

He raced between their legs, jumping and ducking the guy ropes as he tried to make it across the treacherous ground.

Abruptly, the end of the tent line went rushing past him and he tumbled down into the ditch surrounding the castle. The soldiers gave up their chase, content the fox was no longer in their section of the camp. It'd also conveniently put Francis behind the sentries at the end of the turf bridges that led to the castle's entrances.

He made his way along the base of the ditch to the eastern side and prowled up the steep bank. At the top, he made his way under the towering archway to the tiny entrance door. To his luck, he found it open, likely so messengers and aides could pass through it with ease. Francis flicked around the edge of the door to find the hallways blissfully empty.

He knew the castle well and that most areas would be occupied with this many soldiers about. The kitchens and servants' quarters would be bustling all hours, carrying out orders and preparing meals. Equally the great hall, drawing rooms and apartments would all be being made use of.

He slid into a small storage room and caught his breath. Thinking about his next course of action. The King, no doubt would be at the very top of the castle in the largest room, his room, but that wasn't his objective. He closed his eyes and let the world shrink around him as he returned to his human shape.

He was already wearing heavily soiled rags and his beard was now fully grown out. He decided his best chance was to act as a servant and brush his hair over his face as much as he could and keep his head lowered. Hopefully, no one would be expecting danger within the walls. He practiced before leaving, hunching his shoulders and diminishing his frame as much as he could. He stuffed his sword down the leg of his britches, disguising it as best he could.

When he was ready, he stepped from the closet and shuffled his way towards the staircase. Busy servitors breezed past him and through the corridors and no-one gave him a second look.

Despite its simple exterior, the castle's interior was a maze, designed to confuse attackers as they navigated it. No staircase led more than one floor, and in some cases came out on a split level or directly into a room. Francis weaved about the castle, taking extra precaution to change his route when others appeared, doubling back if necessary after they passed.

Finally, he reached the uppermost floor. He took a gamble and decided to head to the rooms on the opposite side to the King.

He opened one door to find a border lord, hands crossed above his chest lying on the bed. Francis stopped brusquely, keeping his head down, waiting for a reaction. When none came, he lifted his eyes to see he was sleeping heavily with an empty tankard on the table.

Francis closed the door gently and hurried from the room and quickly into the next. He couldn't see into it with his gaze fixed firmly on the floor, so waited again for any reaction. His spirit soared when he saw everything he was hoping to find.

It was a treasure trove of barrels, neatly stacked with rope instead of iron bindings. The whole army's gunpowder was in here. The magazine was typically stored at a high point to avoid an explosion causing a total collapse of the building, as well as keeping it dry from the typically damp vaults. All iron and fittings had to be removed and usually, the handlers wore felt shoes to deal with the volatile substance.

Francis didn't need to collapse the whole building though. Just make a big enough splash that the sentries and soldiers along the border would be called back once the alarm was sounded.

He strode to the tiny window at the end of the room which had been covered over with linen. He yanked it back and whistled, then while he waited, he shifted the barrels up against the corner wall.

Before he was finished a raven perched itself on the windowsill, regarding him merrily as though nothing were amiss. Francis whispered in the raven's ear, an odd practice he'd only recently become accustomed to, and the bird took off, flying eastward back towards the coven.

With everything in place, he closed his eyes and drew in a breath, pausing, just for a moment to dwell on his aspirations that the coven would make it out. He pulled down the linen that remained over the window, and ripped off a single thin strip, placing it carefully in the cork hole of one of the barrels. He positioned himself by the door and drew his sword pointing the tip at the rag. If his aim was off by half an inch, he would be blown off the face of the earth along with the powder.

"*Bousdo,*" he muttered, then, seeing the linen fuse catch fire, raced from the room.

Chapter 19

7th October 1592
Hermitage Castle

The explosion shook the entire castle, to Francis it felt like the surface of the world was opening up to swallow the castle whole and drag it to the depths of hell. There was no ringing in his ears like after a musket shot fired too close, the only sound was that of his own pulse throbbing through his head. Dust and masonry were shaken from the walls, producing thick grey clouds that made it impossible to see beyond a foot. The force of the eruption had knocked him off his feet and now he had no sense of where he was, stumbling through the hallways trying desperately to blink the grit from his eyes.

A lord came running from his apartment and grabbed Francis by the scruff, demanding something he could not comprehend. The man threw him roughly back to the ground when he provided no answer. Slowly, the ringing started to materialise in his ears, along with a shooting pain through his whole skull, pinpointing itself behind his eyes. He sat and kneaded his temples, trying desperately to clear his head and orientate himself. When he opened his eyes again the clouds were already starting to dissipate and he realised where he was, half a minute too late.

Oswyn came charging out from the King's bedchambers, closely followed by Maitland.

"I knew it! Witch!" he screamed as he leapt towards Francis.

Oswyn had no weapon to hand so he contented himself with a shoulder charge into Francis' gut, knocking the wind out of him and returning him crashing to the hard floor. Oswyn kneeled over him and pummelled at his head and chest, while all Francis could do was bring up his arms to protect himself. Between the heavy blows, he looked up to see Oswyn's toothy sadistic smile.

For a time, it felt as though he were not within his own body, he could still feel the pain, but it was far away, like being between fully asleep and awake. It was a ham-fisted crack to his jaw that brought him spiralling back down to earth. With a rush, all his senses came flooding back to him.

He managed to catch one of Oswyn's fists with his left hand and threw his own wily counter. Unlike Oswyn's wild frantic blows, Francis knew how to fight, and he'd gone straight for the chin, following through with his fist and snapping back Oswyn's head. He was hit with such force it drove him up to his feet and he stumbled backward in a daze.

Francis regained his footing and drew his sword from his trouser leg. Oswyn saw what was happening just in time to bundle Maitland back into the King's chambers and bar the door behind them. Francis roared and kicked at the door, but its iron bolts kept it sturdy in its frame.

"*Tulexto,*" he roared pointing his sword at where he imagined the bolts would be on the other side of the door. He gave it another hard kick and door was flung open, almost bouncing back shut after colliding off the wall.

Francis stepped through into the antechamber to find Maitland stood next to Oswyn wielding a finely crafted pistol.

"Stay back Stewart! Or I'll shoot! What is your business here?" he demanded.

"I have no business," said Francis, spitting blood onto the luxurious rug. "But ye two have caused some good friends of mine a great deal of pain."

He raised his sword and pointed it at Maitland, daring him to pull the trigger.

"*Skeito!*" shouted Francis as soon as Maitland's finger twitched on the trigger. Though he needn't have. Maitland had pulled the trigger on the gaudy wheellock mechanism, but the wheel, instead of spinning rapidly, let out a low scraping noise as it failed to complete even a quarter turn.

"Hah!" said Francis, "you kept it wound didn't you Maitland you clodpole! Looking now at ye pair of white livered imbeciles, it truly is a wonder ye were able to thwart my every move."

Francis laughed and shook his head. The weaponless duo just stayed put, rooted to the spot. Where Maitland showed fear, Oswyn's expression emanated pure hatred.

"I am prepared to die," snapped Oswyn, though Maitland's reaction indicated he had other intentions. "You'll still have to face the wrath of God for your crimes against him Mr. Stewart."

"And what will God have to say of yer murders? Yer slaughtering of innocent women? My brother? Yer conscience should be far from clean Oswyn."

"All heathen devil worshipers!"

"Lucky for you, ye may meet him soon enough."

Francis lunged forward with his blade. Oswyn, in a surprising display of agility, dove out of the way of the sword's pointed tip and it instead sliced through Maitland's robes, opening up a large gash at his side.

He cried out in pain and crumpled to the floor. Francis spun and kept his attention on Oswyn. He tried a repetition of his previous charge, but Francis simply stepped to one side, like a Spanish bull fighter, and sliced at Oswyn's legs, ripping through his thigh.

Oswyn's stride faltered and he clattered to the floor. He raised his head and let out a strained howl before launching himself back to his feet. He regarded Francis with a crazed glint in his eye, a glint which said this man was not only prepared to die, but could endure through the most unthinkable pains to see his goal through.

He picked up some crockery from the table he'd found himself next to and flung it at Francis, hurling every item within reach until he exhausted his options. He looked frantically for his next weapon, his gift from God to slay his enemy but found nothing.

Francis approached slowly this time, his sword pointed at Oswyn's throat. He retreated and tried to bat the sword away, but only succeeded in cutting his hands and forearm as Francis kept the sword steady, along with his controlled gaze on the Welshman. It was not fear, but panic that set on his face as he found himself backed up against the wall with nowhere to go.

Francis was tired of games and was preparing to run him through when a voice shot out from behind him.

"*Swivajie!*"

* * * * *

7th October 1592
Hermitage Castle

Oswyn was pulled violently forward onto Francis' broadsword, jerking his arm, and almost sent him toppling over backward as the weight of the man bore down on him. He looked, horrified, into Oswyn's wide-eyed vacant stare as blood foamed at his lips. Oswyn fell limp to the floor and Francis had to use his boot to pull his sword from the gurgling, twitching body.

"Didn't yer mother ever teach yer not to play with yer food," said the voice behind him, "he was a useless beef-witted bastard anyway."

Francis turned to see the King standing in the door frame between the antechamber and the bedroom. He was fully dressed, wearing bright jewelled armour that was more ceremonial than functional. His gaze was drawn to James' hand, which was holding out a long dark wood wand and in the other, he held his cane, missing its ostentatious pearl knob.

Francis, his mouth agape with shock, snapped his jaw shut and returned his eyes to match the King's, which were alight amidst his sardonic glare. James' face twisted into a mocking smile.

"Ye...? What? Yer a witch!?" Francis managed to stammer.

"Nay, ye are a witch. I am a King."

"I fail to see the difference."

"*Gutsu!*" shouted James, firing an orb of azure light that hit Francis in the chest and sent him reeling into the wall behind him. He collapsed on top of Oswyn's lifeless body.

"That is your error Francis," said James, his wand still astutely trained on him. "These... *gifts*, come directly from God, just like a King's authority. Man cannot command God's will and heavenly powers, but a King is chosen. When I learned ye were a witch, truly a witch, I must confess my dear Francis, I was shocked. Ha!" he barked with laughter. "Ye really thought yer poxy memory charm worked. Ye truly are a simple border fool. Though, ye did force me to act my way out of that one, that's to be sure!"

"Though, it stood to reason. Ye were just some bastard offshoot of my grandfather's shortcomings. An unlikely blight on the divine lineage."

"There are others," said Francis, "Hercules was a witch, before your dog murdered him!"

"Bastards! The lot of them and unworthy to wield the forces of God!" he bellowed. "*That* is self-evident in all the trouble ye've all caused, only a King who speaks directly to the

Lord above has the grace and authority to command such power!"

"*Gustu!*" he shouted again.

"*Skeito!*" Francis was ready this time, he'd been loosening his wand as James spoke and drew it in time to block the oncoming ball of energy. The orb collided with his conjured shield, discharging the light around him, exposing the shape of his invisible defence. The whole room shook with the collision, like an aftershock of the earlier explosion.

"Ye will die Francis, it is my duty to send you to the devil!"

Francis hopped to his feet, ignoring the agony coursing through his body.

"If ye've been given these powers by God," he posited, "then why have ye not used them to help yer people? Defeat Scotland's enemies? Is that not also the duty of a King?"

"Have I not been shielding them from your malevolence!?"

"And what of the witches of the coven, surely you know of them, are they not subjects too?"

"Their cheap tricks are an affront to my person, a rank impersonation and mockery of God!" Spittle flew from James' lips as his passions flared. "Either they will cease their practices and fade into obscurity, or they will die. The choice lies with them! *Tawqnos!*"

A jet of flame erupted from the tip of James' wand. Francis shielded himself again, but it didn't take him long to feel himself cooking in the oven of his own creation. He held his spell for as long as he could bear, then, with a flourish of his wand, he broke his shield charm and rolled, landing clumsily on his injured side.

"*Winto!*" he yelled before James could readjust his aim.

A directed gale of wind burst forth and, while it fanned the flames, sending them swirling around the room, it knocked James off his feet and clattering to the ground. Francis stole his moment and sprinted to the King, swinging his leg to kick the wand from James' hand.

The wand bounced off the wall and landed next to the quivering and scorched Maitland. Francis shot a brief scowl in his direction, a silent order to stay put then turned his attention to James, keeping him pinned to the floor with a heavy boot.

"Stop!" James yelled, shielding his face with his one free arm. "Let us talk!"

Francis' scowl deepened before he nodded, indulging James' defence.

"Perhaps I have been too hasty," he wheezed, "you are of my blood after all. Mayhaps it is not such a bad idea to have someone who shares my ancestry as chancellor..."

Francis' glower relented as he considered James' abrupt about-face. James, seizing his opportunity, hurried on.

"Of course, you will be reinstated and there will be further advancements," he waved his hand casually, as though he were having a reasonable conversation while lying on his back. "There are still those who support ye in court, I shouldn't think the process to difficult. It'll be as though none of this happened, back to normality."

"And what will happen to Maitland?" said Francis, inclining his head to the man in the corner.

"Hmm, yes Maitland. Well, he knows of our pact. He'll have to die, some accident or other" said James, his eyes widening as an idea formed. "Show me your faith, spare me and kill him so that ye might take his place."

Francis turned his expressionless face from James to Maitland, who was still cowering under his hapless furniture barricade.

"That," said Francis, "Is exactly why I will never join with ye. Ye promise immaterial promotions with one hand, and with the other, a loyal servant such as Maitland is cast aside on a whim. I was loyal to ye once, but ye tyranny knows no bounds. One cannot serve under you with a mutual faith. Mayhaps ye do have the divine right to rule over these folk, but so far ye have shirked yer duty to them."

"That, Your Majestie, will be yer undoing."

The failure of his gambit slowly took shape on James' face, morphing haphazardly between gut-loosening fear and maddening exasperation.

"Ye would not kill yer King!?" he squawked. "Francis! Lord Bothwell! Be reasonable!"

Francis calmly removed his boot from James' chest.

"Nay," said Francis, "Though I have dreamt of it near every night, I would not kill ye."

He gave the King a sharp kick to the ribs before striding across the room and retrieving his abandoned sword. He regarded the timid Maitland, clutching at his wound, so clearly panicked by the sight of his own blood. Francis made towards him and the wretch winced as he came near. Francis knelt and held out the sword hilt first towards the man.

"I believe ye have heard enough from ye King," he said, "do with it what you will."

Maitland stretched out a shaky hand and retrieved the sword.

"Do it Maitland! Kill him! Run him through! Now!" came James' screeches.

Maitland, swung his head between the King and Francis, studying them both with a hopeless bewilderment.

Francis bowed his head and stood, leaving Maitland frozen with his ludicrous expression. He picked up James' wand and snapped it in two, scattering the pieces on the stone floor.

When he reached the doorway, he took one last look at the farcical scene of Maitland, sword tip resting on the floor, assessing James as he cursed intermittently at both of them, purple in the face and eyes popping from his skull.

Without a word he slipped through the door and was gone.

Chapter 20

9th October 1592
South of Liddesdale

Francis was woke slowly to the rumbling of the cart over uneven ground. He roused himself, prizing his eyelids open to a dazzling whitewashed sky. He shivered and took in his surroundings.

He was piled into the cart nestled under some rough spun blankets, along with crates and barrels of supplies. Everything, including himself, was covered in a thin layer of snow. It was still falling, each snowflake slowly descending and gently nestling itself on top of the others.

He blinked and was surprised to see Florie riding behind the cart. At first, he had not recognised her. She wore armour, and from the look of her, it was likely pillaged from a borderer who got in her way. A patchwork of different coloured stains marked her from head to toe, sweat and blood amongst other indistinguishable blots of colour, each one undoubtedly with its own story of hardship and bravery.

"Ah! Our mighty prince awakens!" she said, a warm smile crossing her lips.

"Aye," said Francis sitting up, "and who, pray I ask, is this hardened borderer before me, where is Florie the housemaid?"

Florie's arm twitched in a knee-jerk response, wanting to thump him or throw something at him.

"Well, someone had to defend the coven while you went fer dinner with the King."

"What happened?"

"The plan worked, whatever distraction you made it turned the picket's guts to liquid. Though, they were savvy enough, they still left some of their number to guard the borders. We were slowed by bands of them, riding down the line towards ye. A few caught up with us, but we dealt with them. What did ye do to stir them into such a panic?"

"I blew up half the castle," said Francis sheepishly.

Florie burst into raucous laughter, slapping her thigh.

"Ye always did have a flair fer style, yer rogue! How'd you do that then? I hope not with magick?"

"Nay, I blew up the army's powder store, depending on what day this is, they're probably still clearing up the mess," said Francis, joining his own chortling to hers.

"Ye've been out fer a day and a half. We found you at the rendezvous, horseless and collapsed in the dirt," she said returning to a more serious tone, "yer in a bad way Francis. Yer old wounds are still nay healed, not te mention the new ones. And the cold hasnae done ye much good either. The healers have done their best, but you need rest."

"I'm cold, I need to ride," said Francis.

"What ye need is to rest and eat!"

Francis thought about rebutting the order, but instead decided it was wiser to nod his head and obey. She was probably right anyway, every single bone, muscle, organ and sinew in his body ached like they had all been stretched on the rack and released. His body was utterly broken, and he was clothed in tatters that wouldn't suffice against the bitter cold.

"What of Mary? Did ye have any trouble?" asked Francis.

"For a time," said Florie, "but they all shut their mouths when I slew the sentries and got us across the border safe."

"Good," said Francis, he meant it too. He had hoped adversity would bond her back with the coven, not that they were a coven anymore. Just a ragtag band of outlaws making their way through Northumberland.

"Does anyone know where we are? Do ye know where we're going?" said Francis.

"We re-joined the road this morning," said Florie, "it's quicker and there's no one looking for us this side. The further we are from that poxed border the better."

"Agreed," said Francis, chancing a glance over her shoulder to the north.

"We've passed a sign already for Carlisle, and if yer map, which is cow fodder by the way, is anything to go by we just have to keep them hills up ahead on the right and we should find our way to York. So far this trail has taken us in that direction."

Francis popped his head up over the edges of the cart and looked around.

"I'm not sure where we are, but if you're right this road should take us to Durham and from there it's a simple matter to get to York."

"And what after?"

"Well, hopefully my messenger from Elizabeth hasn't assumed us dead and is still there when we arrive. Either way, if 'tis bad news we will have to find somewhere to stay for the winter. Harvest is over so we can't become farm hands, we'll have to make the best of a good cave or something nearby to a town."

"So, what ye mean to say is, ye don't know," said Florie, half sarcastically, half despairingly.

"Aye Florie, I don't know. Though, hopefully we are given time to breathe."

Francis looked at himself, peeking beneath the furs and covers at his frail and oddly wizened body. It was wrapped tightly in bandages or plastered with poultices of herbs in the worst places.

Then he looked up, past Florie in the direction of the borders. A voice in his head told him he should be relieved to turn his back on the chaotic world of politics and even more so the disillusionment of the King. Yet, a louder side to him had still not grieved the death of his life as a proud statesman, a Baron, Lord High Admiral, Sheriff and even husband to Margaret Douglas.

Here he was, a man who had rallied men behind his anti-English rhetoric and beguiled the virgin Queen so that he might get away with more slaughters and plundering, now slowly listing away in the back of a ramshackle cart into the very country he'd vilified, hoping that the Queen would somehow grant him a mercy.

He was sure Scotland was no longer visible, and he was honoured beyond words to be with the people of his coven. Even still, he gazed upon the horizon and wept openly for everything he'd left behind.

* * * * *

2nd February 1593
Sussex

"It appears the east wing, both floors, were previously the living quarters. There's still some furniture, but it'll need work. We should make it habitable for now. The rest can wait until I have taught you well enough to place stones and beams with sorcery, it'll be easier then and we'll make a better job of it," said Francis, striding past a work party near the castle's great gatehouse.

"Yes Francis," replied a bright young woman, grinning from ear to ear. "We'll get on it right away."

The trail south had been hard on everyone, but Francis prided himself that he'd got every single witch safe to this new haven. At York he'd found his messenger. Elizabeth had granted them a disused castle on the south coast. After the Spanish Armada, it became apparent that the heavily fortified channel coast was no longer a deterrent, wherever possible the enemy would simply sail around it. As such, many lords had given up their upkeep of several of the numerous fortifications.

It came with no titles, though it still came with the rents of titled land. Fortunately, Elizabeth had been savvy enough to follow his advice and have them be paid under a false name. Francis couldn't have cared less, he, along with everyone else, were just pleased to have somewhere to lay their heads and call home.

He walked out through the vast double doors and into the sunlight. He went slowly, crossing the stone bridge over the moat, admiring the countryside and the dragonflies that zipped over the clear waters.

At the other end, another work party of witches was already carving the same runic protections they had at Moss Tower. Sat watching them, still in her armour was Florie. She had cleaned it all up as best she could once they'd had more breathing room, stitching repairs and sharpening the long sword she wore at her side. Francis had seen women in armour before, though it was usually some mistress of the court primped up for show. Florie, on the other hand, looked rugged as any man, ready for battle.

"No sign of the witch hunters then?" said Francis, startling her.

"Phwar, I stand not a chance if they are as sneaky as you. How goes it inside?"

"Most of the castle is crumbled, but nothing we can't handle. We're lucky it's brick, simpler to repair than stone. Plenty of space for everyone and more, we'll soon have this place lively."

"And what then?"

"We settle I suppose," said Francis, "It's all we can do in this world for now. These witches deserve a safe place to live."

"Do you think their wards will work?" asked Florie, nodding at the labouring masons.

"They'll work for now, as far as we can tell nobody is looking for us here. Given time we'll ward the whole grounds. We'll find new ways to protect ourselves. I have no doubt we can have this place stacked to the hilt with defensive charms and traps and all manner of things. We'll make it into our own fortress."

"Ye'll need a warning system should someone break through, protocol and defenders."

"Aye, that too. Mayhaps, ye can command the watch?"

"Me? I know nothing."

"I'll teach you, I promised didn't I? I'll teach everyone. I've found a good spot for a library and we can gather books to rival Hercules' collection. I'll go to the continent, get copies. The runic and ritual magic of these here witches we'll write down too and make new ones. Mayhaps we can find other witches and covens, we'll protect them, and they'll teach us their skills."

"Day upon day we will grow stronger as a community. I dare any mundane army to attack a fortress of learned witches!" Francis chuckled at the thought, his thoughts a disorganised mesh of all the opportunity that lay ahead. "We will build a safe place, a sanctuary for any witch to come and live with us. There are more out there no doubt, as scared and frightened as we were only a few months ago."

"A fine vision," said Florie, placing a light kiss on Francis' cheek. "I so hope it comes true."

"You sound doubtful," said Francis, turning to her.

"Hope is good," she squeezed his hand, "Just... don't lose the fear Francis, carry it with you."

"I carry the pain of Agnes and Hercules with me every day. This place," he said, looking about the overgrown grounds, "and the coven, they're the only things that give me purpose. It gives me hope. That's why it's so important we don't let it happen again. Not just to our own but the rest of them out there."

Florie nodded, "Have ye thought of a name fer it yet?"

"Hah! I hadn't thought on it. Though I always found it odd, despite my Earldom, I never had Bothwell Castle. Perhaps we should call it: Bothwell Sanctuary. What do ye think?"

Epilogue

1st April 1603

Francis paced in front of the frustrated witches as he gave his lesson.

"Okay good, some of you are getting there," he said, "but remember the magick doesn't come from the wand. A mundane can't just pick up a wand and expect it to work. It comes from within you, the wand just helps you concentrate and focus that thought. Retreat within yourselves, and push that energy out from your very core, and through the wand."

There was a pause, as though the whole room were drawing breath before it filled with emphatic cries of "*Swivajie!*" Each student had a goblet placed in front of them and they cast their spells upon it, trying to move it. Some of them twitched promisingly but no-one had yet moved their own.

Francis had already helped the class craft their wands. He'd found a hazel grove and taught them how to extract their wand from nature, keeping the properties intact before imbuing it with their own energy.

He'd felt a pang of guilt when one student had asked him why use hazel and he realised he had no answer. His own wand was forged by his hand, using metal from a stone that had fallen from the sky. He'd also seen a variety of others in his time, staves even, and he remembered James' crafted with some form of dark wood.

297

He was brought back from his thoughts when he was forced to duck suddenly, as a goblet came careering towards his head. He whipped round to see one student looking horrified and the distinct absence of a goblet in front of them.

"Gloria! Spectacular!! Ye see everyone! Ye can do it! Gloria, tell them all what ye did."

"Well... I just did what you said, I cleared my mind and just did it."

"I promise all of ye, this bit is the hardest. The first spell will take ye a long time, but once ye've done it ye'll be able to cast more and more until ye have an arsenal of spells. Ye'll even create yer own in time."

"The words even. They're are from our ancestors, yet I've seen Highlanders use Gaelic words for the same spell. It's all from within ye, it's all inside. Keep going, ye -"

Francis was interrupted by a rap at the door.

"Come in!" he yelled.

The door opened and on its other side stood Florie, a pained expression on her face.

"I think ye best come out here," she said.

"Of course, keep practicing everyone!" he said as he hurried from the room. "What is it Florie?"

"I was scouting as ye asked, but, well, there's a problem."

"What is it? What's wrong Florie?"

"Elizabeth is dead. James is to be crowned King of England."

Honour Roll

Below is a list of some of the most generous backers that helped make this book happen. The Kickstarter funding project for this book reached over 400% of its target, and it is in large part due to the momentum and enthusiasm of the people listed here.

Charlie Pearson

Dawn Ladd

Diana Whittaker

Eileen Marcionetti

Emily Ellis

Gina Hooper

Neil Wilcox

Sean Smith

Sina Koppel

Thank you all for making this crazy dream come true.